W9-CFI-971

PRAISE FOR MARTI GREEN

"Marti Green's look at the potential for abuse and corruption in the privatized, for-profit juvenile-justice systems across America is taut, edifying, and, at times, terrifying. The thought that some of the terrible things described in this book really happen to youngsters charged with minor offenses made my skin crawl. This is an important novel as well as a top-notch thriller. I'd recommend it to anyone."

—Scott Pratt, bestselling author of *Justice Redeemed*, on *First Offense*

"*Unintended Consequences* is an engrossing, well-conceived legal thriller. Most enjoyable."

—Scott Turow, *New York Times* bestselling author of *Presumed Innocent*

"This one will grab you by the neck from the very first page!"

—Steve Hamilton, Edgar Award–winning author of *Die a Stranger*, on *Unintended Consequences*

JUSTICE
DELAYED

OTHER TITLES BY MARTI GREEN

Help Innocent Prisoners Project Series

Unintended Consequences
Presumption of Guilt
The Price of Justice
First Offense

JUSTICE DELAYED

MARTI GREEN

THOMAS & MERCER

This is a work of fiction. Names, characters, organizations, places, events, and incidents are either products of the author's imagination or are used fictitiously. Any resemblance to actual persons, living or dead, or actual events is purely coincidental.

Text copyright © 2017 The Green Family Trust
All rights reserved.

No part of this book may be reproduced, or stored in a retrieval system, or transmitted in any form or by any means, electronic, mechanical, photocopying, recording, or otherwise, without express written permission of the publisher.

Published by Thomas & Mercer, Seattle

www.apub.com

Amazon, the Amazon logo, and Thomas & Mercer are trademarks of Amazon.com, Inc., or its affiliates.

ISBN-13: 9781477819876
ISBN-10: 1477819878

Cover design by Cyanotype Book Architects

Printed in the United States of America

GARY PUBLIC LIBRARY

3 9222 03151 0444

*To my sister, Judith, who put up with me long
enough for us to become good friends.*

GARY PUBLIC LIBRARY

To delay Justice is Injustice.

—*William Penn*

All truths are easy to understand once they are discovered;
the point is to discover them.

—*Galileo Galilei*

1994

The night Kelly Braden disappeared, she had been babysitting her cousin Lisa. Jenny Hicks usually drove her niece home after she and her husband, Todd, returned at the end of the evening, but this time they'd attended a wedding, and since they wouldn't get back until close to 2:00 a.m., they'd asked Kelly to sleep over. When they finally arrived home, Jenny peeked into her daughter's bedroom and saw that both Lisa and Kelly were sound asleep in the twin beds. She tiptoed inside, kissed Lisa's forehead, damp from the unusually warm March evening air despite the open window, then quickly undressed and flopped down on her own bed.

Jenny awoke with a start the next morning. The bedside clock read 9:18, well past the hour when five-year-old Lisa usually awoke. Todd lay next to Jenny, snoring softly. She smiled at the thought that Kelly had gotten up with Lisa and given her breakfast so her aunt and uncle could sleep in. *She's such a good kid,* Jenny thought.

She roused herself from the bed, then quietly stepped outside the master bedroom so as not to disturb Todd. She expected to hear the TV, and see Lisa quietly curled up on the couch watching her favorite cartoon show. Instead, she heard only silence. As Jenny walked down the hallway, she saw that Lisa's door was still closed. She opened it, found her daughter fast asleep, and the other bed empty. She continued down the stairs into the living room. Empty. She knocked on the door to the half bathroom in the hall. No sound. She opened it. It, too, was empty.

Could Kelly have gone home? Had her parents picked her up? Jenny reached for the phone and dialed her sister.

"Hi," Susan Braden said when she answered the phone. "How was the wedding?"

"Fun. Is Kelly there?"

"What do you mean? She's at your house."

Jenny had a sick feeling in her gut. "She's not. She was asleep last night when we got back, but she's gone now. Could a friend have picked her up?"

There was silence on the phone. "I'd think she'd leave a note if she took off. Did you look around for one?"

"No. I'll do that now. I'll call you back when I'm finished."

Jenny hung up and began a search. There was nothing on the counter or table in the kitchen, nothing on the living-room cocktail table, nothing tacked to the inside of the front door. She went back upstairs and entered Lisa's bedroom. No note there. She looked over at her daughter, still sleeping soundly. Too soundly. Lisa always awoke at 7:00 a.m. overflowing with energy. Jenny leaned over her daughter and felt her forehead. It was cool to the touch. She gently shook her daughter to wake her, then shook harder when she got no response. She fell down on her knees, her face close to Lisa's. That's when she saw the bump under her silky blonde hair. Big and red and ugly.

Her chest tightened with fear. She jumped up, ran into her own bedroom, and screamed at Todd to wake up. His eyes shot open.

"What's wrong?"

Jenny tried to tamp down her rising hysteria. "Lisa won't wake up, and she has a big bump on her head, and Kelly's gone."

Todd jumped out of bed and ran to Lisa's room. After his unsuccessful attempt to rouse her, he turned to Jenny. His face was pale, and his hands shook. "Call 911. We have to get her to the hospital."

———

Two hours later, Jenny and Todd paced back and forth in the hospital waiting room as their daughter underwent a craniotomy to remove an epidural hematoma and reduce the pressure on her brain. Jenny was simply unable to sit down.

"Mr. and Mrs. Hicks?"

Jenny spun around and saw two policemen.

Her lower lip trembled as she asked, "Have you found Kelly?"

"No, ma'am," said the older of the two. "I'm Detective John Thompson, and this is my partner, Detective Ed Cannon. Other officers are searching for your niece. We just had a few questions to ask you, if you don't mind?"

The man talking had a kind face. His soft features seemed to match his protruding stomach and the patches of gray sprinkled throughout his wavy hair. Not so the other one. He was tall, slim, and young, with chiseled features and spiked hair that combined to give him a harder look.

"Sure," Todd said. "Anything you want."

"Mrs. Hicks, you told the ER doctors that your niece had been with your daughter last night," Thompson said.

"That's right. We were at a wedding, and Kelly babysat."

"When did you get home?"

"A little after two a.m. I checked on the girls, and they were both sleeping. Everything seemed all right."

"When did you notice something was wrong with your daughter?"

"This morning, a little after nine, when she didn't wake up. That's when I saw the bump on her head."

"And you noticed Kelly was missing then?"

"No, just before that. I thought she was downstairs, but she wasn't. That's when I went into Lisa's bedroom." Her hands were held in front of her, squeezed tight. She tried to concentrate on the officer's questions, but her mind kept wandering to Lisa, picturing her small body lying on the operating table, doctors drilling into her skull. Jenny ached to be with her, holding her hand.

"Did you hear any unusual noise during the night?"

Jenny shook her head slightly, to clear it of the worry that gnawed at her. "No. But we keep a sound machine on at night."

"Excuse me?"

"It's white noise," Todd cut in. "Our bedroom faces the front, and it drowns out street sounds."

"Oh. Okay."

"Have you ever seen Kelly act aggressively toward your daughter?" Cannon broke in.

"What?" Todd said, baffled. "Kelly?"

Jenny was taken aback by the accusatory tone in the man's voice. "God, no," she said. "They adore each other. Kelly would never hurt Lisa, not in a million years."

"Sometimes teenagers hide things from adults," Cannon pressed. "Have you ever seen her high on drugs?"

"No! She's a good kid. Straight-A student." Why was he asking these questions? They should be *looking* for Kelly, not treating her like a suspect. She looked up at Todd, silently beseeching him to put a stop to this. Her heart hadn't stopped racing since they'd taken Lisa to the operating room.

Todd took a deep, audible breath and said, "Listen. We're both pretty rattled now."

"I understand," Thompson said. "Just a couple more questions, then we'll leave you alone. The doctors said Lisa had been hit with something hard, like perhaps a baseball bat. Is there anyone else you can think of who might have hurt Lisa? Maybe someone who has a grudge against either of you?"

Jenny stared at the detective. Her body was numb, but her mind swirled with horrific pictures of some stranger standing over her precious daughter, beating her senseless. It seemed unreal to her. "No one we know would do this to our daughter." Her voice was hoarse, her vocal cords stretched tight by the dread that had filled her ever since the doctor had taken their daughter away from them.

"Can you think of anyone, sir?"

"No," Todd mumbled.

"Is there a baseball bat in your house?"

Todd shook his head.

"Okay, we won't bother you any longer." Thompson held out a card and handed it to Todd. "If you think of something, give us a call."

With the detectives gone, Todd sank into a chair, and Jenny returned to her pacing, her arms wrapped tightly around her body. The minutes dragged on and seemed like hours. She kept glancing at her watch, trying to will time to pass, for the surgery to be over, for her daughter to be all right. Finally, a doctor dressed in scrubs entered the room and walked toward them. Jenny ran up to him. "How is she?"

"The surgery went well," Dr. Burton said. "We've removed the hematoma and drained the fluid. She's still sedated now, but I think she should recover completely."

Jenny fell into Todd's arms and sobbed as relief flooded through her. Lisa was okay, Kelly would be found, and their life would return to normal.

~

Jenny's sister called every one of her daughter's friends, and then called Kelly's boyfriend. No one knew where she was. No one had heard from her. It made no sense to Susan. Kelly was always so responsible. She would never have hurt Lisa, would never have disappeared without a word. Was it possible that she didn't know her daughter? That Kelly had been keeping secrets from her? She shook her head. No, it simply wasn't possible. They'd been close from the moment Kelly had been born. Just a few years ago, Kelly had told her mother that she was her best friend. That's how close they were.

The alternative terrified Susan. If Kelly hadn't run away, that meant someone had taken her. Someone who was cruel enough to hurt a five-year-old child. Her hands started shaking first, then her whole body. Her husband, Carl, came over to her and pulled her into his arms. "It'll be okay," he said. "She'll come home."

Susan wished she could believe him, but she knew, in the deepest part of her, that her world had just tilted and would never be the same.

Jenny hadn't left Lisa's bed since she'd come out of surgery. Her daughter, normally so robust and pink-cheeked, still had a ghostly pallor the day after her surgery. Her hair had been shaved in spots, and her head was wrapped in bandages. Tubes ran from her thin arm to the metal pole next to her bed, and an assortment of beeps periodically sounded from the monitor on the wall. She still hadn't awoken since being rushed to the hospital, but the doctors reassured Jenny that was to be expected. "It's still early," Dr. Burton had told her just an hour earlier.

A knock sounded on the door. Jenny looked up and saw the two detectives from the day before standing in the doorway.

"Ma'am, how's your daughter doing?" Detective Thompson asked.

"She hasn't awakened yet."

"We just spoke to the doctor. He thinks she'll be fine."

"That's what he told me, too."

"Do you have time for a few more questions?"

She wanted to say no. She wanted to be back home, baking cookies with Lisa, chasing her around the house in a mock race, reading her favorite books to her. She wanted normal, not a hospital with a detective looking pityingly at her. She glanced over his shoulder at the other detective, his face set in a rigid mask. Whoever had done this to Lisa needed to be caught. And Kelly was still missing.

She stood up and said, "Let's go into the hallway." Even though the other bed in the semiprivate room was empty, Jenny didn't want to have this conversation by her daughter's bedside.

Once outside the room, Detective Cannon asked, "Is Mr. Hicks here?"

"He's on his way. He went home to shower and change, and then had to stop in his office briefly. He should be here any minute. Do you want to wait for him?"

Cannon glanced at Thompson, who gave a quick nod. "No, we can go ahead. Do you recall if the window in your daughter's bedroom was left open the night she was attacked?"

Jenny nodded. "It was warm. Not enough for air-conditioning, but we left it open for the breeze."

"Was there a screen on the window?"

"Of course."

"We've had some of the technicians out at your house. There are marks outside Lisa's bedroom that suggest a ladder had been propped up against the house. And the screen over the window appears to have been tossed into the shrubs. We think that's how someone entered your daughter's bedroom."

Instantly, Jenny knew what that meant. Although she couldn't imagine Kelly harming Lisa, a small part of her had hoped that was the case. Maybe she'd taken drugs, had a bad reaction. If her niece had done this to Lisa and then run away, then maybe Kelly hadn't been harmed. But a ladder up to the second floor? The screen gone? That meant some monster had struck Lisa and taken Kelly.

"I wonder if you've had any more time to think about who might want to hurt your daughter?" Thompson asked.

"No one we know would do this."

"What can you tell us about your neighbor Jack Osgood?"

"Jackie? He's slow—you know, brain-wise—but he's harmless."

"Some of your neighbors say he frightens the kids on the block."

Jenny felt a flare of annoyance. "Only because of his size. And because he's different."

"Mrs. Hicks, did Kelly ever tell you she was afraid of him?"

"She never mentioned him at all."

"Has he ever been inside your house? Would he know which bedroom is your daughter's?"

Jenny nodded. "A few months ago, we bought new furniture for Lisa's room. He helped my husband carry it inside."

"Ever see him with a baseball bat?"

Jenny froze. She had seen him with a bat many times, hitting tennis balls against the side of his garage. And once, she suddenly remembered, he'd told her he thought Kelly was pretty.

"Oh, God," she moaned, then looked up at the detective. "Could it be Jackie? Could he have done this?"

"He's a person of interest. That's all we can say."

—

Susan Braden jumped when she heard the doorbell, then ran to the door. Her nerves had been frayed to tatters since her daughter had disappeared two days ago, and with each ring of the telephone or knock on the door, she was flooded with the hope that it was someone with news—good news—about Kelly.

She pulled open the door and saw two men dressed in suits, one holding up a badge for her to see. They were different from the policemen who'd been to her house the morning Kelly disappeared. Those men had been wearing uniforms. They had asked for a picture of Kelly, then asked her and Carl questions—about Kelly's friends, her boyfriend, whether she had any enemies, whether *they* had any enemies. They'd asked where she and Carl had been the night before, as though they were suspects, but Susan didn't care. They could ask her questions all day if it would bring Kelly back.

"Ma'am, I'm Detective John Thompson, and this is my partner, Detective Ed Cannon. May we come in?"

Susan nodded. Then, with trembling hands, she held the door open wide for them.

The two men entered the living room, and Thompson asked, "Is your husband home?"

"He went in to work. He didn't want to; he wanted to wait with me. But I made him go. We were making each other more nervous together. Have you found Kelly? Do you know where she is?"

Thompson's voice lowered. "I'm sorry to tell you, Mrs. Braden. Kelly is dead. Her body was found at Wilson's Creek."

The walls of the room crept closer and closer; the air felt heavier and heavier. Susan couldn't breathe, couldn't see, as darkness descended over her. And then there was nothing. No light, no sound, just emptiness.

Moments later—or was it longer?—the light crept back in. A dark mass huddled over her body, now lying supine on her living-room carpet. "Mrs. Braden, can you hear me?"

It was the detective. She remembered his voice. She remembered him saying the unthinkable. Kelly, her beautiful Kelly, was dead.

"Mommy, what's wrong?" Lisa asked Jenny. The little girl had finally awakened that morning. Her speech was still fuzzy, her voice soft, but again, Dr. Burton had reassured Jenny that was to be expected. "Why are you crying?"

Jenny had just hung up from her sister's call, the call she'd dreaded receiving. Through her sobs, Susan had told her Kelly was dead. Murdered. Susan was meeting Carl at the morgue, she said, where they would have to identify her body. Jenny wished she could be by her sister's side, hold her close, and try to console her, even though she knew if it had been Lisa, she would be inconsolable. But she wouldn't leave Lisa. Not until she was home safely. If she would ever feel their house was safe anymore. Todd had already arranged to have a security system installed. No window in the house would ever be left open at night again, no matter how clammy the evening.

Jenny hadn't wanted to question Lisa yet. Better to wait until she was stronger, she'd thought. But now that she was awake, now that Kelly's body had been found, the police were certain to be back at the hospital, asking her daughter the inevitable questions. She wiped her eyes dry with a tissue, then picked up Lisa's hand and asked, "Did you see who did this to you? Who hit you in the head?"

Lisa's spoke something so softly, Jenny couldn't make it out. She leaned in closer to her daughter.

"Who was it, sweetie?"

Lisa whispered into her mother's ear, "I think it was Jackie."

2016

A s she'd promised Bruce Kantor, the director of the Help Innocent Prisoners Project, Dani Trumball had returned to work three months after Ruth Emma was born. She'd handled only appeals, though, and usually only where DNA was available to prove her client's innocence. It was the kind of work a junior associate would normally handle, not someone with Dani's experience or impressive win record. But Bruce had been willing to accommodate her in exchange for her promise that she'd return to handling cases from their outset once Ruth turned one. And that happened two days ago.

Dani began reviewing letters from inmates seeking help from the project—or HIPP, as the staff called it. All, of course, were assertions of innocence. Dani knew that convicted felons rarely admitted their guilt, and those who did often tried to justify the crime. She'd become expert at recognizing the pleas of those who truly seemed innocent, but whether or not they were could be determined only after HIPP began an investigation.

There were dozens of letters on her desk from inmates throughout the country. Although HIPP's office was in Manhattan's East Village, there were no geographical boundaries for their services. Their mission was to help overturn convictions of men and women they believed were wrongfully convicted, imprisoned anywhere in the United States. She was stopped cold by the third letter. It wasn't from a convict or his family member. It came from a guard at a prison where the inmate was incarcerated on death row. Dani leaned back in her chair as she read his letter.

> I'm a guard at Georgia Diagnostic and Classification Prison, and I've been assigned to death row for the past eighteen years. Jack Osgood is one of the inmates here. Whenever I've asked him about what he did, he's always answered that he doesn't know why he's behind bars. When I say to him, "You killed a girl," he's always answered that he'd never do such a thing. Of course, a lot of guys say that, but Jack is different than most. Mentally retarded is what we'd call him back when I was in school. Now, they don't use that term so much. But it fits Jack to a tee.
>
> Now, he's just been sitting here in prison all these years, with a death sentence hanging over him. At first, his mother came to visit, but I heard she died, and nobody's visited him in at least eight years. It seemed like the state had forgotten about him, but a death warrant's now been signed, so his execution will happen real soon. That's why I'm writing. In Georgia, we're not supposed to execute a prisoner who's retarded, and I believe Jack is. But there's nobody around anymore to speak up for him. I'm hoping you will, but you have to do it quickly.
>
> Yours truly, Paul Dingell

Dani couldn't help but think of her son, Jonah, as she read the letter. He, too, was intellectually disabled, although at the high end of functioning, as a result of a condition known as Williams syndrome.

What if he were falsely convicted of a crime and she and her husband, Doug, were no longer around to help him? Could he fight for himself? She thought not. He was always too eager to please, and that would hurt him.

She pushed aside the other letters on her desk. She'd found her next client—Jack Osgood.

Dani did what she always did first—she turned to LexisNexis to read about Osgood's case. Although the trial transcript was rarely online, the appellate decisions usually were, and those provided her with a good synopsis of the case. Jack had been convicted of the strangulation murder of a sixteen-year-old girl named Kelly Braden. According to the prosecution, on a night Kelly had been sleeping in her cousin's room, Osgood climbed up a ladder to the second-story bedroom, struck Kelly's five-year-old cousin, Lisa Hicks, with a baseball bat, and carried Kelly out of the house. The prosecution postulated that he'd choked Kelly enough to cause unconsciousness first but didn't kill her until hours later. There was no evidence of sexual abuse.

The prosecution had relied on three primary pieces of evidence. The first, and most damaging, was an identification by Lisa Hicks of Osgood as the one who'd struck her. The next was a bite mark found on Kelly's arm that an expert testified matched Osgood's teeth. And finally, although many neighbors testified they'd often seen Osgood with a bat, when the police arrived with a search warrant, the bat was missing. Three weeks later, two teenagers found a bat with Osgood's initials carved on its handle and traces of blood on the shaft hidden in shrubbery near a marsh. Forensics identified the blood as matching Lisa Hicks. The police had enough to arrest twenty-three-year-old Jack Osgood, and the jury had enough to convict him and impose the death penalty.

When she finished reading the appellate decisions, Dani sat back in her chair. The testimony of a five-year-old, awakened in the middle of the night and struck with a bat, didn't seem especially reliable to her, but she'd have to wait to read the transcript to learn more about the identification. And the scientific reliability of bite marks was the subject of considerable and increasing controversy. Osgood had claimed that he'd misplaced his bat, that he thought he'd left it behind after watching a pickup softball game, but when he went back to the field, it wasn't there. Clearly, the jury didn't believe him.

But what was most evident to her from the rulings was the absence of any discussion of Jack's intellectual capabilities. That seemed strange. Even before the Supreme Court's 2002 ruling that barred executions of those with an intellectual disability, Georgia had banned such executions, four years before Jack's conviction. So why hadn't Jack's lawyer raised that issue? Was the prison guard's assessment of Jack's intellectual ability faulty? If she had more time, she'd put the guard's letter aside until she heard back from Jack's trial lawyer. But there wasn't time. Tomorrow, she'd head out to Georgia.

———

Dani lay on the living-room couch in her Bronxville home, entwined in her husband's arms. It was 9:00 p.m., what they called "honeymoon hour," the sacrosanct time set aside every evening for each other. Both Jonah and Ruth were fast asleep. After almost nineteen years of marriage, she still loved her husband as strongly as she had during the first heady days of their courtship. She knew how lucky she was. Too many of her friends' marriages had fallen apart or had been relegated to business partnerships, maintained for the sake of children or financial considerations.

"So soon?" Doug asked, after Dani told him of her next day's trip. "I guess I thought it would be a while before you began traveling again."

"Me, too. But this one's time sensitive." If Dani were being honest, she'd admit that she missed being on the road, meeting a potential client for the first time and trying to assess whether she believed his claim of innocence. She missed the adrenaline rush she got when she uncovered that crucial piece of evidence that convinced a court her client had been wrongfully convicted. But she also knew she wasn't really shielding Doug. She was protecting herself. Because admitting that meant she was pulled toward something that took her away from her children. And acknowledging that was something that made her uncomfortable.

"You taking Tommy with you?" Doug asked.

"Of course."

"I guess if I were a different kind of man, I'd be jealous of him. Sometimes it feels like you spend more time with Tommy than me."

"Well, maybe if Tommy weren't so devoted to Patty, you'd have cause," Dani said with a smile.

"Seriously, can't someone else in the office take this case? There must be someone in the tristate area begging for your services."

Dani knew very well there was. There were far more inmates seeking HIPP's assistance than there were staff attorneys available to represent them. Each week she'd go through the new letters that had arrived and sift through the pile to choose the lucky few who'd get the golden ticket—a HIPP attorney in their corner. Each week she'd send back letters to those whose pleas seemed genuine but were turned down nevertheless because there simply weren't enough hours in the day to help everyone.

"This man—I think I'm meant to represent him." Dani hung her head down. She knew it sounded foolish. Yet, as soon as she'd read the guard's letter, she'd known this would be her next client. She just hoped that when she met him tomorrow, she walked away with the belief that he was innocent.

3

It had been a crisp late-September morning when Dani left her home, the type of perfect day that made New Yorkers forget the area's steamy summers and snowy winters. Tommy Noorland had met her at LaGuardia airport. He was the investigator at HIPP whom Dani worked with exclusively. He was older than she was by almost ten years, but with his fit body, his wavy, dark hair, and the handlebar mustache that gave him a rakish look, he seemed years younger. When she'd started there almost eight years ago, she'd only worked on appeals, so by the time the case came to her, the investigation was complete. There were a number of investigators who worked for HIPP, but since she'd started handling cases from the outset, Tommy had always been her go-to guy for ferreting out the facts. During his ten years as an FBI agent, he'd developed instincts and skills that were always spot-on. And if he couldn't dig up the evidence on his own, he had a network of former colleagues he could call upon.

After they landed in Atlanta, she and Tommy exited the airplane terminal, and she was hit by a mugginess that she'd thought should be finished by now. It's still the South, she had to keep reminding herself. They retrieved their rental car and headed to Jackson, Georgia.

An hour later, they pulled behind the state prison gates to the parking lot. She'd been at the same prison only a year and a half ago, to watch a man put to death. The man wasn't her client. Instead, he'd confessed to a crime for which her client had been awaiting the needle. She and Tommy showed their IDs to the guard at reception, then were led to an attorney interview room. As they walked down the prison hallways, their walls painted a drab gray, she heard distant shouts and smelled pine-scented disinfectant—both of which her senses were accustomed to from visiting prisons throughout the country. They got settled in the sparse room, empty but for four chairs—one side with three, the other only one—and a beat-up metal table, bolted to the floor.

Just five minutes later, a large man, at least six four, with hands cuffed and feet shackled, shuffled into the room. Before the guard who escorted him left, he locked the shackles and handcuffs to a ring on the floor.

Osgood stared at Dani with large green eyes that seemed to sag into his fleshy cheeks, just as his whole body seemed to sag when he sat down. He clasped his hands tightly together. His brown hair had started to thin, and his pasty-white complexion was typical of men who'd been imprisoned for decades.

"Jack, my name is Dani Trumball. I'm an attorney with the Help Innocent Prisoners Project in New York City. And this is Tom Noorland. He's an investigator in our office."

Osgood had a confused look on his face but remained silent.

"One of the guards here, Mr. Dingell, asked us to come meet with you. Do you know why you're in prison?"

Osgood cast his gaze on the table, then mumbled, "They said I hurt Kelly. But I wouldn't do that. She was always nice to me."

"Do you remember your trial?"

Osgood raised his chin. "It was a long time ago. I remember some of it. Not everything. I remember when the jury said I was guilty."

"Well, at that trial, Kelly's cousin said she saw you in her bedroom, standing over Kelly's bed. Maybe you just wanted to get closer to Kelly, and you didn't realize you hurt her. Is that possible?"

Now Osgood shook his head vehemently. "I would never hurt Kelly. I would never hurt anyone. That would be wrong!"

"Your bat had Lisa's blood on it."

Osgood scratched his head, and his eyebrows knitted together, as he seemed lost in thought. "I remember," he finally said. "When the policeman came to our house, I couldn't find my bat. Mama thought maybe I left it at the ball field, after the game, but I went back there, and I couldn't find it."

Had this giant of a man accidentally killed Kelly Braden and blocked it from his memory? Or, had he knowingly knocked out a five-year-old girl, carried Kelly away, then coldheartedly murdered her? Or, was he actually innocent? Dani's assessment would have to wait until she completed her investigation into the crime. Part of that investigation would include having a psychologist give Jack a battery of tests to determine his intellectual functioning and personality profile. But first, she'd probe a little herself.

"How much school did you have?" she asked him.

"I went to high school."

"Did you graduate?"

Once again, Jack looked down at the table. "I didn't do so good on tests," he answered, his voice low.

"When did you leave school?"

Jack looked up in the air, as though he could pull down the answer from the ceiling. After a while, he said, "Maybe sixteen? My mama said it was enough for me, and it would be better for me to work."

"And did you find a job?"

Now Jack smiled. "I worked for Mr. Bennett, at the A and P."

"What did you do there?"

"I swept the floors and cleaned up spills. Sometimes he'd let me stock the shelves, if he told me first where to put the things."

"Did you work there until they sent you here?"

"Uh-huh. Mr. Bennett liked me."

Jack spoke his responses in a slow, deliberate manner. Whether he met the state's definition of *intellectually disabled* would have to wait until the testing was completed. But Dani had seen enough students in Jonah's school, which specialized in treating children with various disorders that led to cognitive difficulties, to appreciate that Jack was, at the least, "slow."

"I'm going to look into your case, if that's okay with you. And if I think you're innocent, I'm going to try to get you out of here. Would you like that?"

Jack smiled, the first one Dani had seen since he'd sat down. "I want to go home."

Dani patted his hand.

"Would you ask my mama to visit me? She hasn't been here in a really long time."

Dani's mouth dropped open. Hadn't Jack been notified that his mother had passed away? Surely, he would have been told. Perhaps he had, and over the years had forgotten. In any case, it wasn't her place to tell him. At least not yet. Not until after their investigation confirmed his assertions that he was innocent. Then he'd be officially taken on as a client. Then, she'd tell him the truth—that the one person who'd loved him unconditionally was gone. That if Dani was successful in obtaining his freedom, he would be on his own, all alone.

—

"What do you think?" she asked Tommy as they drove to the airport.

"Are you asking whether I think he did it, or whether we should take the case even if he did because he's disabled?"

Dani knew how Tommy felt about the death penalty. He was all for it—as long as the inmate was guilty. It was one of the things they differed on. She'd seen too many mistakes to be comfortable with the irreversibility of putting someone to death. Sometimes the truth came out early, sometimes not until decades later.

"If you think he did it."

"Don't know whether he did or not, but he sure seems slow," Tommy answered as he pointed to his head.

"Not so slow, though, that he wouldn't remember killing a girl. And he didn't strike me as cagey enough to lie about it."

"Maybe. For once, I'm inclined to agree with you. His body language didn't say to me he was hiding something. Still—I've been wrong before. So have you. If we decide he's guilty, you'll drop his case, right?"

Dani hesitated long enough for Tommy to jump in.

"We're HIPP," he reminded her. "We represent *innocent* convicts, remember?"

"Even if he's guilty, he may be innocent of the death penalty."

"What the hell does that mean?"

"It means he may have been wrongly sentenced to death because of an intellectual disability."

Tommy swung his head around for a quick, incredulous glance at Dani. "Are you kidding me? Sounds like mumbo jumbo to get around taking on the case of a guilty man."

Dani knew Tommy wouldn't be happy working on Osgood's case if the facts came back against him. Still, she also knew he was a team player and would do what she asked of him. "When we get back, I'll track down his former attorney and get his records. After I go through them, I'll have a better sense of where you should start your investigation. At this point, like with all our investigations, let's consider him innocent."

"So, I should figure sometime next week?"

"Yeah. Assuming I can track down his lawyer. Jeez—twenty-two years. Who knows who'll be around anymore?"

Back in HIPP's office, Dani began her search for Nick Bennington. He wasn't listed in Martindale-Hubbell, the directory of lawyers practicing anywhere in the United States. When Bennington represented Osgood, he'd headed his own firm. Dani suspected he was a solo practitioner then, probably handling a wide gamut of matters, from drafting wills to personal injuries to a smattering of criminal cases. Still, that didn't mean he wasn't good. Dani wouldn't know whether he'd mishandled Osgood's trial and appeals until she got her hands on his records and spoke to him about his trial strategy. But she couldn't find him. Not even in the online telephone directories.

There were three other lawyers named Bennington practicing law in Georgia, according to Martindale-Hubbell. Maybe one of them was related to Nick. She got lucky with her second call. Or unlucky, as it turned out. Lucy Bennington was Nick's daughter. She'd graduated law school ten years earlier and entered her father's practice. Dani was right—it had been a one-man show until Lucy joined him. Then, the two practiced together until two years ago, when a diagnosis of Alzheimer's forced his retirement.

"Did your father ever talk to you about Jack Osgood's case?" Dani asked Lucy.

"Not really. I was just a child when he was tried. Even when his appeals were filed."

"Do you still have your father's old files?"

"Probably. Most are in storage, but they should be easy to locate. Dad kept a superefficient filing system. I'll have someone do a search and then FedEx them to you."

It would certainly help to have the files, but Dani always learned so much more by speaking to the original attorney. Especially here, where he'd clearly made a decision not to raise Osgood's intellectual functioning. She wished she knew why. "Do you think your father would meet with me?"

There was a hesitation on the phone before Lucy spoke again. "Dad's in an Alzheimer's care facility. He has moments of lucidity, but most of the time he's out of it. He still recognizes me, and I'm grateful for that. But—I don't know that he'd be able to help you."

"Still—I'd like to give it a try, if that's okay with you. After I go through the files."

"I suppose it wouldn't be harmful for him. Sometimes it's the old days he remembers best."

Dani thanked her, then hung up. Unless the file answered all her questions, it seemed likely she'd be heading back to Georgia very soon.

Her next call was to a forensic psychologist. She'd located one in Georgia who had a reputation as a smart, thorough, no-nonsense expert utilized by both defense and prosecuting attorneys. Dani hoped she'd be able to shed light on Osgood's limitations.

Three days later, Dani had finished reviewing Osgood's trial transcript as well as the appeal briefs and decisions. Lucy had found the files quickly, and Dani spotted them piled up on the floor as soon as she'd entered her office the next day. After her first read, she flipped through the documents quickly a second time, concerned that she'd missed something, but she hadn't. Throughout all the pages, there was no mention of Osgood's intellectual disability. Although the Supreme Court's ruling that barred execution of such prisoners didn't occur until 2002, well after Osgood's trial, the state of Georgia had barred such executions beginning in 1991—three years before his trial. Did Bennington not raise the issue because he didn't think Osgood met the legal requirement for such a disability? Or, was Bennington incompetent? He didn't seem to be, based on Dani's review of the records. So, why hadn't he? Dani realized only Nick Bennington could answer that question. And, according to his daughter, his mind might be too far gone to be of any help. Still, Dani had to try. She booked a flight back to Georgia the next day.

Dani walked into her Bronxville home shortly before 5:00 p.m. When she wasn't traveling, she usually left for work at nine and began heading back home at three. That had been her deal when she'd accepted the job at HIPP eight years earlier. Bankers' hours, with time made up by working from home as long as needed to represent her clients effectively. It had always been important to her to see Jonah off to school and to be waiting for him when he got off the school bus. Except, the latter part didn't always occur. Once she was at work, she'd often get caught up in a task, making it hard to leave when she wanted. Luckily, she'd found Katie, her sitter, who was always there for Jonah. Katie was a godsend—especially since Ruth had been born. The few afternoon hours that Katie used to work had expanded to a full day.

As soon as she walked into the house, Jonah bombarded her, and Ruth began crying. Ruth usually cried when Dani walked in—her way of telling her mother she'd missed her. Dani picked up Ruth, who'd just started to walk, and motioned for Jonah to follow her into the kitchen. She loved the smells that always greeted her when she returned home, because Katie usually had some treat she'd baked for Jonah fresh out of the oven. This time, it smelled like brownies.

"How was school, Jonah?"

"It was okay. But I have animating news. Ruthie can say my name now. Sort of. She called me *Nah*."

"That is exciting news." Dani was used to Jonah's unusual choice of words, common among those with Williams syndrome. She chatted with Jonah some more, calmed Ruth down enough so that she could put her down, then began to prepare dinner. She tuned the radio over the sink to WQXR and immediately recognized a Beethoven symphony. Growing up, she'd always cringed when her parents played classical music, but now, Jonah's proficiency in music had sparked her interest in listening to it. She'd worried so much about Jonah's future, but despite his disabilities in some areas, he was a talented composer. Last year, the Westchester Philharmonic had performed his symphony, to rousing cheers from the audience. Now, she'd become convinced that his talent would help him survive in a world without his parents' protection. How had he grown so fast? It was just yesterday he was Ruth's age. He was already three inches taller than Dani and had begun to get peach fuzz on his chin. Soon, he'd need to start shaving. Before she knew it, he'd be leaving for college. That was three years away, but Dani had been assured he would undoubtedly be accepted at a music college, one that made allowances for his deficits.

She looked over at Ruth, who was playing with toys on the kitchen floor, and smiled. At least she would have *her* when Jonah went away. Her happy, chubby, wonderful surprise.

Stone Ridge, Georgia, reminded Dani of the picture-perfect small towns she'd read about in the books she'd devoured as a child. She'd been a voracious reader when she was young. As an only child, she didn't have siblings to help her pass the hours before her parents returned from their jobs, so she'd turned to books instead.

She and Tommy had flown in to Atlanta that morning, rented a car, and driven an hour north to this small hamlet once rocked by the murder of Kelly Braden. Lucy Bennington had agreed to meet with Dani and take her over to the nursing home that housed her father. Later, they would stay in town and try to track down people who'd known Jack Osgood back then.

As they neared the town, they passed alternating acres of forest and pastureland dotted with drowsing cows packed under any available shade. Bennington and Associates was housed in a cottage directly on Stone Ridge's main street. When Dani and Tommy were led by Lucy's assistant into her office, Dani was immediately struck by how young she looked. Lucy's straight chestnut-brown hair, with a row of bangs that framed her face, made her look more like a college coed than an attorney practicing on her own. Dani knew that since Nick Bennington's retirement, Lucy had been the sole lawyer in the firm.

"I hope this isn't your only reason for coming here," Lucy said after the introductions were finished. "I don't know how lucid Dad will be today. He was pretty out of it yesterday."

"We're here for the day. But I'm keeping my fingers crossed that your father will remember something about Jack's defense."

Lucy retrieved her purse from the desk drawer, and they headed out to Meadowbrook Senior Living, a continuing-care facility located in the next town. "Dad moved in here after Mom died," Lucy said on the drive over. "Within six months, he was in the assisted-living section, and a year later in the Alzheimer's care unit. I think he just gave up after Mom was gone. They'd been married forty-four years."

Fifteen minutes later, they walked into Nick Bennington's room. The frail-looking man was slumped down in the chair, staring at the TV, his face pallid. Thin, gray hair hung over his forehead in stringy wisps.

"Dad? It's Lucy."

Bennington looked up. His pale eyes stared at his daughter as though she were a stranger.

"Dad. This is Dani Trumball. She's a lawyer, just like you and me."

His eyes turned toward Dani, and a smile crossed his face. "Millie? Where've you been? I've missed you."

"Millie was my mom," Lucy explained.

Dani realized this visit was hopeless. This man was too far gone to help her. Nevertheless, she took a step closer to him. "Mr. Bennington, I represent Jack Osgood. Do you remember him?"

"Millie?" he asked again.

Dani reached over and touched his hand. "I'm sorry. I'm not your wife. My name is Dani Trumball."

Bennington stared at her, his eyes watering. "Not Millie?"

"No. I'm sorry." Dani waited a moment, then asked him again, "Do you remember Jack Osgood? You represented him after he was charged with murdering a teenage girl."

Bennington hung his head down, murmured quietly, "Not Millie," a few times, then looked up and stared at Dani once more. After a few moments, he asked, "He the retarded man?"

Dani winced at the word, a relic of the past. "Yes. Do you remember him?

Bennington's body straightened, then he grimaced. "I'll never forget him." He stared once more at Dani. "He's still alive?"

"Yes, and I'm trying to help him."

"You got to stop his execution," Bennington said, his voice croaky. "He never should have gotten the needle. I don't know whether the boy killed her or not, but if he did, he didn't know what he was doing. Being retarded, I mean."

"But you never raised that at his trial, or even the appeals you filed. Why was that?" Like every death-penalty case that Dani took on, numerous appeals had been filed. With Osgood, the first was a mandatory appeal to the Supreme Court of Georgia, required by Georgia law, to review the sentence of death, as well as any purported errors of law during the trial. After the conviction and sentence were upheld, Bennington followed with both state and federal habeas corpus appeals. None of those appeals claimed that Osgood couldn't be executed because of an intellectual disability.

"You practice much in Georgia?"

Dani shook her head.

"I hired a psychologist. Had Osgood tested. He told me it was borderline whether Osgood was mentally retarded. That job he had, it worked against him. Made him look like he was capable. And in Georgia, even when it's clearer, it's almost impossible to get a finding of mental retardation. I had a better chance of proving he was innocent and decided that was the way to go."

"But after that failed, after he was sentenced to death? What was there to lose?"

Now, Bennington's eyes were steely clear as they locked onto Dani's face. He was silent for a time, then just shook his head. "I'd have had to admit he was guilty. And he kept swearing he wasn't. Know how many capital defendants have avoided the death penalty in Georgia because they were retarded? Barely more than ten percent. Only state with lower percentage is Florida. Know why?"

Dani did, but he didn't give her a chance to answer.

"Have to prove it beyond a reasonable doubt. Now, you ever meet a psychologist or psychiatrist who said something was absolutely certain? I sure haven't. My own expert wasn't even certain. I didn't like the odds, especially where it was a close case, like with Jack. And back then, it was even harder than now."

Dani wasn't sure she agreed with him, but at least now she understood Bennington's reasoning. She had one last question. "Did you think he was innocent?"

"I have to tell you, I knew that boy well, not just as his lawyer, and I always thought—"

"Time for your meds," chirped a voice in the doorway.

Dani turned around and saw a nurse walking toward the bed. She handed Bennington a glass of water and a small paper cup with three pills. He dropped them into his hand, then one by one swallowed each with a gulp of water. When he finished, the nurse smiled at him, then left the room.

"You were saying?" Dani prompted him.

"Millie?" he asked, a cloud back over his eyes.

───

Dani had scheduled two other appointments. She'd gotten all she could from Nick Bennington. Despite his daughter's efforts, he remained in a fog after the nurse left his room. As they walked out of the facility, Dani thanked Lucy, then she and Tommy slid into the seats of their rental car. She told him, "Let's go to the school next." Dani took out her phone, opened her notes app where she'd written its address, then plugged it into the car's GPS. Tommy was behind the wheel, as usual. She wondered if there was a bit of gender stereotyping on her part—always having the man drive. When she and Doug went anywhere together, he automatically got behind the wheel, even though she was as good a driver as he.

"Lost in thought, dollface?"

She laughed. It was sexist and offensive, and she'd come to accept it from Tommy. Maybe that's why she'd just worried about engaging in reverse sexism herself—her acceptance of Tommy's banter had perhaps made her hypersensitive. She hadn't always brushed off Tommy's sexist repartee, and still didn't from anyone else. At first, she'd tried to break him of the habit, but it was too ingrained in him. She knew how much he respected her, both personally and professionally, and so, over time, she'd decided to just ignore it. He was too important to her to do otherwise.

They arrived at the high school ten minutes later and made their way to the principal's office. Although Ms. Halstein had agreed to meet with them, Dani hadn't made an appointment for a specific time, since she hadn't known how long they'd be with Nick Bennington.

They waited outside her office for ten minutes before the door opened and a short, heavyset woman escorted out a pimple-faced boy with a scowl on his face. "This is your last warning, Eddie. Remember that," she said as the boy walked away, his shoulders hunched over.

When the boy was gone, she approached Dani and Tommy. "You must be the people from New York." Despite her small stature, she spoke with a strong voice and an authoritative manner.

Dani stood up and made introductions. They followed the principal into her office and sat down on the hard wooden chairs opposite her desk. Dani handed her a release signed by Osgood.

"Jack gave me the names of a few teachers he had," Dani said. "I'm hoping they still work here and I can speak to them."

"Some are; a few have retired," Halstein said without hearing the names. "I'm just a few years away from retirement myself."

"Did you know Jack?"

Halstein nodded. "Of course. After what happened, everyone in the school knew about him. But I remembered him. I'd always felt sad for boys like Jack. Sad because we really didn't have the right resources for him."

"So, you knew he had special needs?"

"Yes. But we're a small town. The kind of classes Jack needed, he'd have to travel more than an hour each way. His mother didn't want that. We did the best we could. Gave him special attention as much as possible. He left school as soon as the state allowed."

"Had the school ever had him tested?"

"I believe so. We have a school psychologist that's shared among several towns in the county. It's someone different now, but I'm sure Jack must have been given an IQ test back then, and we should have the records. Let me check." She turned to her computer and typed something in, then frowned. "I see he was first tested in the sixth grade, then again in the ninth. But we don't seem to have the results here." She picked up the phone on her desk and punched in two numbers. When someone answered, she said, "Betty, how hard would it be for you to find Dr. Quentin's test records from back in the eighties?" Halstein listened to the answer, then said, "I'm looking for the test protocols of Jack Osgood. From the sixth and ninth grades, first in 1983, then '86. Could you get on that right away?"

Halstein hung up. "All of the school system's paper records are stored off-site. The clerk is going to do a search for them now. I'm afraid it may take a few hours."

Dani looked over at Tommy. "Want to get some lunch?"

He nodded. Dani gave Halstein her cell-phone number, then they left to find a restaurant. When they returned ninety minutes later, Halstein said, "Betty found them quickly. Here's a set for you."

Dani glanced at the top page of the Wechsler Intelligence Scale for Children, given when Jack was eleven years old. Total IQ-68. She then looked at the next one, given when he was fourteen. Total IQ-70.

Both scores were right at the border, just as Bennington's psychologist had said. Still, the results of a full forensic examination should have been brought to the jury's attention before they sentenced Jack to die. She hoped it wasn't too late for that now.

———

Their next stop was the office of Meghan Milgram, the forensic psychologist Dani had chosen to evaluate Osgood. A relatively new specialization, those practicing it were trained to apply clinical-psychology principles to assess individuals involved in the legal system. They might be called upon to assess competency to stand trial, or whether a defendant had the requisite state of mind to be found guilty of the offense charged. Or, as here, whether a defendant met the legal definition of "intellectually impaired." Dani didn't know, but she suspected, because it was so long ago, that the psychologist hired by Bennington hadn't received the kind of special training undertaken by Milgram.

Milgram's office was just down the block from the county courthouse, thirty minutes north of Stone Ridge, in Lawrenceville, Georgia. The brick building contained a number of offices, mostly law firms, plus a few accounting firms and one architect. Sitting in the reception area was a young woman with pink streaks going through her black hair and a nose ring. She wore a sleeveless blouse, and tattoos covered both arms from her shoulders to her wrists. *Not what I expected to see in a psychologist's office,* Dani thought.

Dani introduced herself and Tommy, and the receptionist buzzed Milgram's office to announce their arrival. Moments later, a striking woman, at least five ten, emerged and, with a warm smile, shook their hands. She appeared to be in her midforties, like Dani, with wavy, dark-brown hair that fell to the middle of her back, high cheekbones, and perfect features. Dani wondered if she'd once been a model.

"Come on in." Milgram motioned to them.

Dani and Tommy took seats in front of Milgram's desk. Dani glanced at the diplomas on the wall and saw they were all from New York schools—a bachelor's degree from New York University and a PhD in clinical psychology from Columbia University.

"Are you originally from New York?" Dani asked.

"Nope. Born and raised in Hartford, about fifteen minutes north of here. All through high school, I had only two goals. I wanted to be a model, and I wanted to get away from Hartford."

"So, you applied to colleges in New York?"

Milgram shook her head. "I wasn't even thinking about college. I headed to New York after graduation to pursue modeling."

"That's a tough career to break into."

"I got signed to an agency pretty quickly. I thought my future was set. I expected excitement and glamour and instead found it excruciatingly dull."

Tommy chuckled. "I never heard anyone describe New York as dull."

"Oh, no. Not New York. Modeling. Standing around for hours while being photographed. Never being able to indulge in the incredible restaurants in Manhattan because one extra pound would show up in the pictures. You're both from New York, right?"

"We are," Dani answered.

"Then you can appreciate how frustrating it was to be in the glamour capital and always be worrying about calories."

Dani certainly could appreciate that. She'd battled with losing weight ever since Jonah had been born, getting back to her desired weight only this past year. "So, you gave it up for college?"

"I worked at modeling for two years, then applied to colleges in New York and stayed until I finished my education. When I was done, I realized I missed living in a small town, in *my* small town. So, I came back."

"And is there enough excitement for you here?"

Milgram chuckled. "More than enough. It's funny how things look different when you're older."

Dani handed her the copies of tests she'd gotten from the school. "What do you think?" she asked after Milgram had skimmed them.

"It certainly suggests that the issue should have been raised before the sentencing phase. There's enough here to indicate intellectual impairment. Whether it rises to the level of the legal standard, I won't know until after I complete my examination of him."

"These test scores aren't enough?"

"No. There are three prongs that need to be satisfied. And the timing of the past intelligence tests is significant as well. I'll go into all of that with you when I present my results."

"How long will that take?"

"I understand the need for speed. I'll get on it right away."

Dani left, satisfied that she'd know soon, one way or the other, whether she'd have an argument that Osgood was innocent of the death penalty. She'd need much more to know whether he was innocent of the crime.

Dani left Tommy behind in Stone Ridge and returned to the office. He would stay another few days and speak to as many people as he could find who knew Jack Osgood before his arrest. At this stage of the case, Milgram had said Dani would need to show the court that, back when the crime was committed, Osgood lacked the adaptive skills most people found routine—the second prong of the legal test to establish an intellectual disability. Those skills included communication ability; understanding of money, time and number concepts; self-direction and self-care; social skills; and problem solving. They needed to find evidence that Osgood was deficient in at least two of those areas. Dani knew she had to first stop Osgood's execution—later, she could focus on proving him innocent, if indeed he was.

Before Ruth was born, Dani might have stayed back with Tommy to interview potential witnesses. Now, she loathed being away from home. It was different from the past, when she'd felt consumed with guilt for leaving her son with a nanny. Now, she knew Ruth was in good hands with Katie. It was no longer guilt that tugged at her heart. She simply missed her daughter, with her infectious laugh and chubby legs that begged to be pinched. She had missed being home when Ruth took her first steps on her own. She had missed being home when Ruth said her first word, *Dada*. She'd been grateful that the first time she said "Mama," it had been on a weekend, when she was snuggled in Dani's arms.

Dani shook her head to brush away thoughts of Ruth. She'd been a stay-at-home mom for Jonah's first nine years. Now, she knew she was meant to work. She spent the rest of the day researching the law on intellectual disabilities and the death penalty, not just in Georgia but in other states as well. When she finished, she gathered up her belongings. Just as she was heading out of the office, a call came in from Tommy.

"Learn anything helpful?" she asked him.

"Maybe. Ted Bennett, the manager of the A and P when Osgood worked there, retired a few years back, but he still lives in Stone Ridge. He told me he hired him as a favor to Osgood's mother. They'd been friends since high school, and he knew she'd struggled since her husband had left."

"Did he say anything about how Osgood handled the job?"

"Yeah. Said he was always polite, showed up on time every day, but each morning had to be told what to do, even if it was the same as the day before."

That's good, Dani thought. One of the characterizations of adaptive skills was the ability to self-direct. It sounded like Osgood couldn't do that. "Will Bennett sign an affidavit?"

"I'm sure he would. He seemed to have a soft spot for the guy. Definitely doesn't believe he had it in him to kill anyone."

"Between his statement and the principal's, we should be able to show that his disability presented before he was eighteen."

"There's more."

"Go ahead."

"I know you're not focusing on innocence yet, but I nosed around a bit anyway. I got the names of some of Kelly's friends back then. A couple of them are still living nearby. Mind if I talk to them before I return?"

"I suppose that's fine."

"And I thought I might poke around the police station that handled the murder, since I'm here anyway."

Dani sighed. Once Tommy got the scent, there was no holding him back. She'd wanted to handle Osgood's case step-by-step. First, stop the execution. Then, investigate the crime. But she knew if she stopped Tommy, it would churn him up, with him constantly wondering whether or not Osgood was guilty.

"Go ahead. Talk to anyone you want. Just not Kelly's or Lisa's parents. Or Lisa herself. I want to be there for that."

———

Dani left the office and walked to the parking lot down the block to retrieve her car. She'd gotten into the habit of driving to Manhattan when she'd first returned to work. Because of the medical problems that often accompanied Williams syndrome, she was afraid to be at the mercy of the Metro North train schedule. Having her car a block away gave her the comforting assurance that she could get back to Jonah quickly, if needed. Now that he was older, she no longer felt the same urgency to have her car with her. But it had become habitual to drive to work, and habits were hard to break.

It had been a long day, starting with the flights to and from Atlanta, then into the office to start her research. By the time she reached home, she was beat. Doug had returned before her and was in the kitchen preparing dinner. Jonah was up in his room doing homework, and Ruth sat in her high chair at the kitchen table, busily scooping up the Cheerios on her tray and stuffing them into her mouth. As soon as she saw Dani, Ruth's arms shot up, and her legs began kicking.

Doug turned from the stove to kiss Dani hello. "She has strong legs. Maybe she'll run track, like you did."

Dani picked Ruth up from the high chair. "I'd like that." As soon as she said the words, she wondered if all parents wanted their children to imitate their own lives. To follow into their professions, or enjoy the same things they did growing up, or achieve the dreams their parents dreamed. Had Doug been disappointed when it became clear his son wouldn't do any of those things? She hoped not. Jonah had brought them both so much joy just by being who he was.

"Take a look at the mail," Doug said, pointing to a stack of letters on the kitchen counter.

Dani put Ruth back in the high chair, then picked up the letters and leafed through them. She stopped when she saw one from the Westchester Philharmonic orchestra that had already been opened. She pulled the letter from the envelope and began reading.

> Dear Mr. and Mrs. Trumball,
> The Westchester Philharmonic has decided to institute an honorary position of Youth Musician. The position will be awarded each year to a high school (or equivalent) student who lives in Westchester County and has demonstrated excellence in performance of a musical instrument, or as a composer. The chosen student will be honored at the annual banquet of the Westchester Philharmonic held in December and will receive a $10,000 scholarship to his or her chosen college. At the Board's most recent meeting, your son, Jonah, was unanimously chosen to receive its first honorarium.
>
> On behalf of the entire Board, I wish to extend congratulations to Jonah. We are indeed fortunate to have such a worthy musician as our honoree.

As Dani placed the letter down on the table, she felt awash with pride. Her son! Jonah! "Does Jonah know?"

"I think he's called every single one of his friends to tell them."

Dani ran upstairs to Jonah's room, the letter in her hand. "Congratulations, maestro," she said as she gave him a kiss on his cheek, then a big hug.

"I'm very jubilant," he said.

Dani tousled his hair. "As well you should be. I'm happy, too."

She walked back down to the kitchen. Jonah had phoned all his friends—now she wanted to call hers. As she picked up the phone, the words *How about that?* kept popping into Dani's head, and a smile never left her face.

———

Tommy headed over to the Stone Ridge police station. It had been more than twenty-two years since Kelly Braden had been murdered, so it was unlikely that the detectives who'd investigated the case were still on the force, but he needed to check it out nevertheless. The building was a small, redbrick one-story. He went inside and showed his ID to the officer sitting at the reception desk.

"I'm looking into an old case, the murder of Kelly Braden, probably before your time," he said to the twentysomething man. "I'm hoping I can get a look at the records, if no one's around who remembers it."

"Are you kidding? Everyone here knows about that case. It was probably the worst thing that's ever happened in Stone Ridge. I mean, she was taken from a goddamn bedroom, for Christ's sake."

Tommy wasn't surprised. This was a small town, after all. "Anyone still here who worked on it?"

"You're in luck. My uncle is the captain now, but he was still a rookie detective back then. He and his partner were the lead investigators." The young man picked up the phone and pressed some buttons. "Hey, Ed, I got someone here who wants to talk to you about the Braden case." When he hung up, he said, "You can go on back. He's the last office on the right."

Tommy found the office and stepped inside. A slim, sharp-featured man with spiked hair sprinkled with gray and finely etched lines around his eyes stood up from his chair and held out a hand. "I'm Captain Cannon. How can I help you?"

"Okay if I take a seat?"

The captain nodded.

Tommy slid into the wooden chair. "I'm with the Help Innocent Prisoners Project, in New York City. We're representing Jack Osgood in connection with his conviction for the murder of Kelly Braden."

"No question he did it. We had a solid case."

"Well, at this point, we're looking into whether he should have gotten the death penalty for it. Because of his impairment." Tommy pointed to his head as he said the last words.

"He was slow, all right. But this murder took planning. He got the ladder to climb up to the second story; he took a bat with him, which showed he expected to hurt her. And then he got rid of the bat afterward, which in my mind showed he knew what he'd done. So, maybe he's slow, but not so much so that he can't be executed."

"That may be the case. I don't know yet. We've got a psychologist who's going to give him some tests. But while I'm here in Stone Ridge, I thought I'd poke around a bit. I spent ten years with the FBI, so it's kind of hard to keep my nose out of things."

"Which office?"

"New York. First criminal investigations, then counterterrorism."

"Know Mark Knickerbocker?"

"Sure. I worked a lot of cases with Mark. He's still going strong there."

"I went to college with him. Roomed with him my second year."

"Georgia Tech, right?"

Cannon smiled. "Yeah, that's it. I guess if you worked with Mark, I can cut you some slack. Normally, we don't let private folks see files without a subpoena. Go grab an empty desk, and I'll have them brought to you."

"Thanks, Captain. Appreciate your help."

Twenty minutes later, Tommy was buried in a sea of papers. Methodically, he went through each one, making notes as he went along. After Kelly's body was found, the police had put together a list of people to question based on interviews with family. The first on the list was Jack Osgood. He lived next door, his mother owned a ladder, and his bat was missing. Osgood told the detective the same thing he'd told Tommy and Dani a few days ago—he didn't know what happened to the bat. The notes in the file said Osgood had been questioned for five hours, but no transcript had been made. *Par for the course back then,* Tommy thought. Recording the interrogation of suspects on tape or video didn't become routine until much later.

The detectives had also questioned Kelly's boyfriend, Greg Johnson. Back then, he was a freshman at the University of Georgia, in Athens. His claim that he was asleep in his dorm was backed up by his roommate, Derek Whitman. None of Kelly's friends could point to anyone who had a grudge against her, or who might have harbored a secret crush on her, or who she'd complained was stalking her. The one open strand was a man named Tony Falcone, an itinerant laborer who'd been going door-to-door in Stone Ridge, soliciting for odd jobs. Kelly's father, Carl, had hired Falcone to clean out his gutters, a job he'd let slide since the fall but knew had to be taken care of before the spring rains. Once up there, Falcone had spotted some loose roof shingles and fixed those as well. He'd used his own ladder, Braden had reported. Kelly had been in and out of the house while Falcone was working outside, and once, Braden said he'd caught the worker staring at his daughter. He hadn't thought much of it at the time—Kelly was beautiful, and most men stared at her.

Tommy couldn't find any interview of Falcone in the file. Surely, the man had to have been a suspect, or at least a person of interest. He stood up from the desk, stretched, then walked over to Cannon's office. Before he asked about Falcone, he needed to clear up something that had bothered him as he looked through the records.

"All finished?" Cannon said when Tommy filled his doorway.

"Just about. Couple of questions first."

"Fire away."

"Everyone we speak to says Osgood was slow, like, intellectually disabled. I was wondering, do you know if he had a driver's license?"

Cannon chuckled. "You're thinking he couldn't have driven the body away, right?"

"Yeah."

"We checked that out. It took him four times to pass the written test, but he did. Two times to pass the driving test. He was allowed to drive his mother's car to work and back, maybe a few other places nearby, but that was it. So, yeah, he had the ability to drive Kelly Braden to where we found her."

"Okay. Just one other thing. Did you ever question Tony Falcone?"

"Who?"

"He did some work at the Bradens' home a few weeks before Kelly was abducted."

Cannon nodded. "I remember. He worked at a few homes, including others with teenage daughters. Everyone said he did his job, collected his money, and left. No problems with any of them."

"Still—"

"I know. We would have liked to sit him down, but by the time we found her body, he was long gone. He'd only worked in Stone Ridge for one week. We checked some of the surrounding towns, but he hadn't been to any of them."

"Wasn't that suspicious?"

"Nah. That's how these itinerant workers are. They move around a lot, get some money together, then go on a drunken binge. When the money runs out, they do some more jobs."

"Didn't he have a car? A driver's license? How else did he get around?"

"Sure. Everyone said he drove a red pickup truck, but no one noticed the plates. Not even what state issued them. We did track down his driver's license, though. From Nashville. Address was a boardinghouse, and he'd moved out of it years before. Didn't leave any forwarding address. We spoke to the owner of the boardinghouse. She said he was quiet, kept to himself mostly, but was always polite."

"Had he done any work at the Hickses' house, too?"

"Tommy, I know where you're going with this, but you'll just be chasing rainbows. Osgood killed her. Everything fits."

"Did he do work at their house?" Tommy asked again.

Cannon sighed. "Yeah. Carl knew his brother-in-law needed some odd jobs done. He sent him over there."

Tommy felt a sense of rising anger. "What the hell! Why wasn't this guy pursued? He was an obvious suspect."

Cannon's eyes narrowed. "Look. I've been very accommodating to you, and I don't appreciate you accusing me of sloppy police work. The forensics pointed to Osgood, not this Falcone. We don't waste time chasing dead ends."

Despite Cannon's protests, it seemed too handy to Tommy that the man had just disappeared. Falcone knew Kelly. He knew the Hickses' home. Maybe he'd even been inside. It didn't stretch the imagination to think maybe he'd followed Kelly there that night. He had a ladder. Maybe he found Osgood's bat. Maybe their new client was not just disabled. Maybe he was innocent.

———

Tommy had found a few of Kelly's friends who still lived in or near Stone Ridge. He waited until the evening, when he was more likely to find someone at home. At 7:00 p.m., he pulled up to the first house. Stacy Carmichael had been Kelly's best friend, according to the police notes. He rang the bell, and a burly man with a closely shaved head and a goatee answered the door.

"Can I help you?"

"Is Stacy here?"

"And who are you?"

Tommy handed him his business card.

"Help Innocent Prisoners Project? What's this about?"

"We're looking into Jack Osgood's conviction for the murder of Kelly Braden. Stacy was her best friend back then. I just wanted to ask her a few questions."

The man stared at him for a bit, then opened the door wider. "I suppose it's all right. Come on in." Once Tommy stepped inside, the man shouted out, "Stacy! Someone for you." He turned back to Tommy and held out his hand. "I'm her boyfriend, Pete Antinoff."

Moments later, a woman walked down the steps holding a toddler in her arms. She looked like she had once been pretty, but now her mousy brown hair hung limply to just above her shoulders, and her skin had the leathery look of someone who'd spent too much time soaking up the sun. Stacy handed the little girl to Antinoff. "Read her a story, okay?"

Antinoff nodded, then took the child back upstairs.

Tommy gave another business card to Stacy and told her why he was there. She motioned him to follow her into the living room. After they were seated, he asked, "Did Kelly ever tell you Osgood frightened her?"

"She never mentioned him at all."

"Was there anyone else she was scared of?"

Stacy shook her head.

"Anyone you know of who had a crush on her?"

"No. They all knew she had a boyfriend. Although it wouldn't have been for long."

"What do you mean?"

"Well, she was cooling it with Greg. It was too hard keeping it going with him at college."

Tommy hadn't seen that in the police reports. "Had she told Greg?"

"Not yet. But she was going to soon."

"Did you know him?"

"Sure. We all hung around together."

"What was he like?"

"Handsome, charming. He was captain of the football team. Not good enough to play college level, but still—you know the type. Used to getting whatever he wanted."

"Sounds like you didn't like him."

Stacy frowned. "I didn't. He was too full of himself. Thought Kelly should consider herself lucky that she'd caught him. I never thought he treated her well enough."

"In what way? Did he ever hit her?"

"Nothing like that. He'd just—you know how it was in high school. Silly stuff. He'd flirt with other girls in front of her. When we'd all go out together, he'd spend the night talking just to the guys, and ignore her. He'd forget her birthday. It just didn't seem to me like he put her first."

Tommy knew his type. The kind people flocked around, but who thought only of himself. The kind, Tommy suspected, who wouldn't handle rejection very well. Maybe Kelly had told him that night it was over. Maybe he decided to pay her a visit. Tommy flipped through his notepad. The police had questioned him. He'd claimed to have been asleep in his dorm room all night. Greg's roommate vouched for him—said he'd come back from a party around 3:00 a.m., and Greg was fast asleep. When he woke up at 6:30 the next morning to use the john, Greg was still asleep. Maybe Whitman was lying. It wouldn't be the first time one friend covered for another.

Tommy finished up with Stacy, then left. It was time to head back to New York. As he got into his car, he smiled. It seemed he had two potential suspects in the murder of Kelly Braden.

1994

He drove up to the house and sat for a moment, enveloped by the darkness. The closest street lamp was four houses away. *I just want to talk to her, that's all.* She was so beautiful, with a smile that drew you to her, that said, "You're special." He got out of the car and walked to the back of the house. When he saw the bat lying in the nearby yard, he picked it up. He wouldn't use it. He just thought, *Well, maybe she'll need persuasion to leave the house in the middle of the night.* He didn't want to talk to her in the bedroom. He wanted to take her for a drive and tell her what he felt, that he couldn't stop thinking about her, that he wanted to take care of her, to cherish her. He'd taken a ladder with him and placed it against the side of the house leading up to the bedroom he knew she was in, then climbed up to her room. The window was open. He removed the screen and dropped it to the ground, then pushed the window up enough for him to slide through. Her cousin was sleeping soundly, a teddy bear clutched in her arms.

He bent down beside Kelly and just watched her breathe for a while. She was so impossibly beautiful. Knowing she would be startled when she saw him, he placed his hand over her mouth before he whispered, "Wake up."

Her eyes shot open.

"Don't be afraid. I just want to talk to you," he said. But he could see in her eyes that she was afraid. She tried to shove his hand away, but he was strong. He clamped his other hand around her neck, just to frighten her enough to stop resisting. Maybe he'd pressed too hard, because slowly her eyes closed, and he couldn't wake her anymore. He picked her up from the bed—it was easy for him—and began to carry her away when her cousin woke up and started to cry. He placed Kelly back on the bed, then picked up the bat and hit the little girl, just enough to make her stop crying. Though maybe that was too much, also.

He picked Kelly up again, this time putting her over his shoulder so he could grab the bat, and quietly walked through her bedroom door and down the stairs, then out the back door. After laying Kelly down in the backseat of his car, he went back to retrieve his ladder, then got in and drove her to the creek.

It was pretty at the creek. He thought she'd like it there. He waited next to her on a patch of grass by the water until she woke again. When she did, she immediately screamed and scrambled to her feet.

He had to stop her. She was easy to catch, but she wouldn't stop screaming, so he pressed his hands around her neck once again—just to quiet her, that's all. But this time it was too much. When her body dropped to the ground and her big blue eyes stayed open, fixed in an accusing stare, he knew she was dead even before he felt for her pulse, and found none.

He didn't expect the thrill that shot through his body when he realized what he'd done—the feeling of power that overwhelmed him. He didn't mean to kill Kelly Braden, but he had to admit, as he stared at her dead body, that he felt good. No, not good. He felt godly.

M eghan Milgram is on line one," Dani's assistant announced. Dani quickly picked up the phone. A week had gone by since she'd met with the psychologist, and Dani was anxious to hear her evaluation of Osgood. "Hi, Meghan. Have something for me?"

"I do. I'll e-mail a copy of my report later this afternoon. I'm just writing it up now. I thought I'd call, though, and tell you what I determined."

"And?"

"He definitely fits the Supreme Court's definition of intellectually disabled. My report will go into the test results and the reasoning for my conclusion."

Dani breathed a sigh of relief. Her work was cut out for her now. She needed to prepare a motion to stop Osgood's execution.

"His full-scale IQ on the Wechsler Adult Intelligence Scale was seventy-one," Milgram continued. "But in real numbers, it's sixty-eight."

"What do you mean, *real numbers*?"

"It has to do with when the test is standardized. It's explained in my report."

"And the other factors?"

"You've already given me two people who can testify about his actual behavior in the community. The tests I've performed and my interview of him confirms a deficiency in adaptive skills. And the last prong—age of onset—is shown by his school records."

"That's great, Meghan."

"Don't get too excited. This is Georgia. They're going to fight hard."

"I know. But I'm going to fight harder."

Two hours later, Milgram's e-mail arrived with her report attached. There was plenty in the report for Dani to use, and she hunkered down to prepare the brief—the legal argument—that would accompany her motion to the court. The hours went by quickly, and when she glanced at her watch, she saw it was after four, past the time she normally left for home. Leaving this late would put her smack in rush-hour traffic, extending the half-hour drive home to double that time. She was heading out the door when her assistant, who was on the phone, motioned for her to stop.

"Hold on one moment," Carol said to whomever she was speaking with, then looked up at Dani. "It's Mr. Dingell, from the prison. Calling about Jack Osgood."

Dani nodded, then went back to her office and picked up the phone. "Is everything okay with Jack?"

"You'll probably get the notice tomorrow, maybe the day after. I don't know how long they take to tell the attorney, but I thought you should know right away."

"What is it? Is Jack hurt?"

"No, it's not that. It's just—you need to move fast. The warden just got the notice. His execution's been scheduled. Ten days from today."

Damn. Dani thanked him and hung up, then took off her jacket and placed it on the back of her chair. She wouldn't be leaving for home now, after all. She'd stay as long as needed to finish up her brief, so that first thing tomorrow morning, it would be filed with the court.

—

Four days later, Dani was at the prisoner lockup at the Gwinnett County Superior Court in Lawrenceville, Georgia, sitting in a cell with Jack Osgood. He was clothed in his prison garb—there was no jury for the hearing scheduled to start in twenty minutes, and therefore no need for him to dress in a suit and tie. She suspected he would wonder why his mother wasn't in the courtroom. It was time for Dani to tell him. When she'd asked Dingell, the one guard who seemed to care about Osgood, why he hadn't been told she'd died, he'd said that since prisoners on death row weren't permitted to attend a funeral, they'd thought it kinder to keep him in the dark. Dani thought otherwise. Sometimes it was hard to hear the truth, but knowing it allowed the healing process to begin.

"Jack, I want to tell you something."

He looked at her expectantly.

"Your mother passed away many years ago. That's why she hasn't been to see you."

Osgood looked up at the ceiling, then back at Dani. Just that quickly, tears were streaming down his cheeks. "My being in jail killed her, I think."

"No, Jack. It's not your fault."

"Now there's nobody who believes I didn't hurt that girl."

"I believe you."

When the bailiff called *State v. Osgood*, Dani stood before Judge Edith Beiles. The hearing was in one of the smaller courtrooms in the building, with just four rows, separated by an aisle, behind the counsel tables. The gallery was empty. Gary Luckman, the assistant district attorney, was by Dani's side. He looked young and eager, Dani thought, with his clean-shaven face, wide blue eyes, and ears that stuck out just enough to look almost comical. But there was nothing amusing about him, or about anything else in this courtroom that stood in the way of her intention to convince this judge to spare Jack Osgood's life.

"Your client is five days away from execution, Ms. Trumball," Judge Beiles said. "Why is this claim first being raised now?" The woman looked like she should have retired ten years earlier. She was well into her seventies, and her hair was a silvery white. Still, her eyes shone brightly, and her voice was strong.

"I first became aware of Mr. Osgood's plight, and his alleged condition, less than two weeks ago. Unfortunately, the attorney who handled Mr. Osgood's trial and appeals is now confined to an Alzheimer's care facility and has few periods of lucidity." This was true. Dani thought it wasn't necessary to add that during one of those periods of lucidity, he'd lambasted the harshness of Georgia law in requiring proof of a disability beyond a reasonable doubt.

The judge stared hard at Dani. "I'm familiar with this case. Hasn't Mr. Osgood always maintained his innocence? Is he now ready to acknowledge his culpability?"

Dani glanced back at Osgood, sitting at the defendant's table, his hands clasped tightly together. His hangdog expression told her he was still distraught over the news she'd given him thirty minutes earlier. Although his hands weren't cuffed, nor his legs shackled, two guards, with their holstered guns in plain view, stood nearby. She turned back to the judge. "Whether or not he committed this crime, we wish to show that the law doesn't permit his execution."

"You haven't answered my question."

"No, Your Honor, the defendant does not admit that he murdered Kelly Braden. In fact, he continues to maintain that he is innocent, and I reserve the right to bring a future motion should new evidence come to light which proves that. But in the meantime, we have brought the current motion to address the defendant's intellectual capabilities." Despite Judge Beiles's age, Dani knew she had a reputation as a tough jurist. Dani hoped she hadn't just gotten off on the wrong foot with her.

"Are your witnesses ready?" the judge asked.

"Yes, Your Honor."

Beiles turned to the prosecutor. "Are you ready to proceed?"

"I am."

"Let's get started, then."

It was Dani's motion, so she went first. Whether or not Jack Osgood was intellectually disabled, and therefore couldn't be executed, would be decided by this judge. At least, at this first stage. If Dani lost, her appeal was ready to be filed.

Dani called Meghan Milgram to the stand. She strode into the courtroom dressed in a navy-blue jacket and matching straight skirt, with an air of confidence. After Milgram was sworn in, Dani ran through her credentials. When finished, she asked, "Have you had the opportunity to examine the defendant?"

"I have. I met with him over three days. During that period, I did a clinical interview and administered several psychological tests, designed to evaluate intellectual, personality, and behavioral functioning. In addition, I reviewed his school records, including psychological testing performed by the school's psychologist."

"Did you reach any conclusion when you finished?"

"Yes. I've determined that Jack Osgood suffers from an intellectual disability that presented before the age of eighteen."

"On what did you base that conclusion?"

"I administered the Wechsler Adult Intelligence Scale, or WAIS, in which he scored a full-scale IQ of seventy-one. But in real numbers it was sixty-eight."

"Would you explain what you mean by that?"

"Yes. The IQ of the general population rises each year. Since the norms for IQ scores are set when the test is standardized, then the farther away from the year of standardization, the higher the score will be. In the current case, the WAIS was last standardized eleven years ago, so one would expect a test-taker to score three and a half points higher than if he took the test when it was normed."

"Did you administer any other tests?"

"Yes. The Wide Range Achievement Test, or WRAT4, also used to test intellectual functioning, and the Rorschach and the Minnesota Multiphasic Personality Inventory-2 Restructured Form, or MMPI-2-RF, both of which, among other things, help evaluate a person's social adjustment."

"And what did those tests show?"

"There was no evidence of any psychological dysfunction. His lowest measure was in social introversion, which is not uncommon in those with lower IQs."

"Were you able to measure adaptive behavior skills?"

"That was more difficult. The most common tests which measure adaptive skills usually rely on people close to the subject providing information about his behavior. In this case, Mr. Osgood's only known relative, his mother, is deceased. However, I was able to review his school records, and I spoke to a few of his former teachers, the guards in his cell block, as well as his employer before he was incarcerated. From that, I was able to determine that, beginning at an early age, he was deficient in adaptive behavior. Based on all of those factors, I concluded that he is, and has been from childhood, intellectually disabled."

"Can you elaborate on which specific areas of adaptive behavior he was deficient?"

"Yes. Adaptive behavior generally falls into three different areas: conceptual skills, social skills, and practical skills. From an early age, it was clear to his teachers that his language and literacy ability was deficient, as well as his ability to understand money concepts. With respect to social skills, he had no friends in school. He seemed very gullible and naive. In the practical-skills domain, his employer said he wasn't capable of self-direction, nor did he seem able to manage money. There's also some indication he wasn't able to pick out his own clothes, because on occasion he showed up at work inappropriately dressed."

"Thank you. I have no further questions."

Luckman stood up and walked to the witness box. "Dr. Milgram, you say you spoke to the guards that oversaw the defendant's cell. Did you speak to all of them, from every shift?"

"No. I spoke to two. Paul Dingell and Harvey Bundt."

"Do you know how many guards come in contact with the defendant?"

"Not exactly."

"Would it surprise you if I said there were twelve during the course of a week?"

"No."

"So, isn't it possible that if you spoke to the other guards, they would have a different perception of the defendant's capabilities?"

Milgram paused before answering, "It's possible." She looked over at Dani, then quickly added, "But not probable."

"But you can't know for certain without speaking to them, right?"

Dani called out, "Asked and answered."

"Move on, counselor," the judge said.

"Now, you said you looked at his school records."

"Yes."

"How long ago were those records made?"

"The earliest ones go back forty years, the most recent about twenty-eight years."

"And his employer? How long has it been since he's seen the defendant?"

"He hasn't seen him since his incarceration. So that would be twenty-two years."

"So just to be clear. You spoke to only two of twelve people who have current contact with the defendant, and the other people hadn't seen him in decades, right?"

"It's unlikely that his adaptive skills would have improved while incarcerated."

"But you can't be one hundred percent certain of that, can you?"

"Of course not."

"I didn't think so. I have no further questions."

Dani called Emily Halstein, the principal at Osgood's high school, and Ted Bennett, the owner of the A&P that employed him, and each testified about his limitations. On cross-examination, Luckman had Halstein admit that Osgood was never held back to repeat a grade. He had Bennett admit that Osgood showed up for work every day and performed his chores satisfactorily. And, once again, he brought out that none of them had been in contact with him for more than two decades.

When Dani rested, Luckman called, one after another, six guards that worked on death row at the Georgia Diagnostic and Classification Prison, or GDCP. One after another, they testified that Osgood had no problem following orders, dressing himself, feeding himself, or keeping his cell neat. One after another, they testified that during the limited hours death-row inmates were permitted in the prison yard, Osgood related to the other prisoners as well as anyone else. On cross-examination, Dani was able to elicit that Osgood had no choices to make when getting dressed—he wore only prison clothes provided to him by the institution. He had no choices to make at mealtime—eating only those foods brought to him on a tray, and eating them in his cell. As a death-row inmate, he had no jobs to perform at the prison, and therefore none of the guards could say whether he was capable of performing those jobs.

After the last of the guards had testified, Luckman called his own expert—Dr. Phillip Melnick. He, too, was a forensic psychologist. He agreed with Milgram that Osgood's intellectual functioning was significantly limited, and this had been present before the age of eighteen. However, in his professional opinion, Osgood did not have deficits in adaptive skills.

When it was Dani's turn to question him, she rose from her seat and slowly walked to the witness box. "Dr. Melnick, on what did you base your conclusion that Osgood was not deficient in adaptive behavior skills?"

"First of all, the crime itself demonstrated that his adaptive skills were not limited. He planned the crime sufficiently to bring a ladder as well as a bat. In addition, he wiped the bat clean so it wouldn't have his fingerprints on it. Someone who can think ahead like that has adaptive skills."

"Is that all?"

"No. I interviewed several of the guards in the defendant's cell block, and based upon their observations, I determined that he demonstrated social skills through his interactions with other inmates; he demonstrated personal-care skills through his dressing and eating and keeping his cell tidy; and, although he wasn't afforded a work opportunity, he was able to follow the guards' directions. To me, that showed he had enough skills that he cannot be labeled as deficient."

"Did you review his school records and the affidavit of his employer?"

"I did, but I didn't give those much weight. It was too long ago."

"Dr. Melnick, how many times have you testified for the prosecution?"

"Oh, I don't know. Quite a few times."

"More than a hundred?"

"Possibly."

"And of those times, in how many did you find that the defendant was intellectually disabled?"

"I couldn't say."

Once again, Dani was grateful that she'd hired Meghan Milgram. Her knowledge of the region's forensic psychologists was exhaustive, and she'd shared a wealth of information. Dani walked back to her desk, riffled through some papers, and picked up a packet. She handed one copy to Luckman, another to the judge, then returned to the witness. "In an article in the May 2015 issue of *Forensic Psychology*, it says you've never found in favor of the defendant in a Georgia criminal proceeding. Is that correct?"

"You have to understand. Georgia has a very high standard for such a finding. Beyond a reasonable doubt."

"You haven't answered my question. Have you ever testified that a defendant you examined in connection with a criminal case in Georgia was intellectually disabled?"

Melnick cleared his throat. "No."

"I didn't think so. I have no more questions."

There were no more witnesses. Each side summed up, and with that, the hearing was finished.

"What's going to happen now?" Osgood asked after they all stood while the judge exited the courtroom.

"The judge will decide whether the state can execute you. She'll probably let us know tomorrow or the next day."

Osgood's lower lip trembled as he said, "But I didn't hurt Kelly."

Dani heard a deep voice behind her say, "Time to go."

She looked around and saw one of the guards standing there, holding a set of handcuffs. She turned back to Osgood and gave him a quick hug. "I'll let you know as soon as I hear something."

As the guard led Osgood back to the courthouse's holding cells, Dani walked out with a sinking feeling. In her gut, she knew there hadn't been enough evidence to withstand the heavy burden of proof. Once the state's expert found no intellectual disability, the outcome was predictable. Of course, she would appeal a ruling against Osgood, all the way up to the US Supreme Court. That would be necessary to slow down the clock, and hopefully stop his execution until they could find proof of his innocence. That is, if he *were* actually innocent.

At five past nine the next morning, Dani got a call on her cell phone letting her know that the decision was ready for her to pick up. She'd stayed overnight at a local hotel in Lawrenceville and had already showered and dressed when the call came in. Ten minutes later, she entered the court clerk's office and was handed her copy of the ruling. Quickly, she scanned it for the bottom line. *The defendant has a high burden to overcome in proving that he has an intellectual disability and is therefore ineligible for the death penalty,* Judge Beiles wrote. *In this instance, he has failed to prove that disability beyond a reasonable doubt.*

Dani wasn't surprised. She'd known when she'd left the court-house the day before that it would be a close call, and in Georgia, close calls went against the defendant. She returned to her hotel and made a beeline for its business office, which had computers available for use by the guests. She took a flash drive from her purse, inserted it into the computer, and opened up the draft appeal that she'd prepared before she'd left New York. She plugged in the decision of the Superior Court, printed out several copies, then got in her car and drove to the Supreme Court of Georgia, in Atlanta. With just four days until Osgood's scheduled execution, her moving papers sought an emergency stay of the execution pending a hearing and ruling by the court on the appeal.

Once that task was done, she drove back north to Stone Ridge. Normally, Tommy would be with her for witness interviews, or he'd handle them on his own, but she was already in Georgia, and time was short. Before she left, she wanted to speak to the parents of the two girls, Kelly and Lisa. Tommy had tracked down Lisa's parents—still in the same house they'd lived in when the murder took place—but hadn't had any success locating Kelly's. Dani hoped Jenny Hicks, Susan Braden's sister, would tell her where they were.

She arrived at the home of Mrs. Hicks an hour later. A middle-aged woman dressed in jeans and a loose-fitting blouse answered the door. Her blonde hair was pulled back in a ponytail, and she held a rag in one hand.

"Yes?"

Dani had her business card ready and handed it to the woman. "I'm representing Jack Osgood. I wonder if I could speak to you for a few minutes?"

Jenny's eyes narrowed into a glare. "We've been waiting twenty-two years to watch him die. Why would I help someone who's trying to stop that?"

"Because I believe Jack is intellectually disabled. If he murdered your niece, he should stay in jail for the rest of his life. But the Supreme Court has recognized that someone who's 'slow' may not have fully understood what he was doing, and so shouldn't be put to death. Just like a child who kills shouldn't be put to death, because his brain hasn't developed enough to appreciate right from wrong."

Jenny just stood in the doorway, her arms folded.

"Jack was your neighbor. Didn't you notice he was different from others? Slower than children his age?"

"Of course. But that doesn't excuse murder."

"No, it doesn't. Look—can't I just come inside?"

"I'm cleaning now. The house is a mess."

A man's life hung in the balance, and this woman didn't want another woman to see a messy house. Dani would have laughed at the absurdity, only nothing was funny about an execution. "Please."

Slowly, Jenny nodded, then opened the door wider. Dani stepped inside and followed Jenny into the kitchen. They both sat down at the round wooden table. Although the house had to be more than twenty-three years old, the kitchen looked like it had recently been redone. The countertops were all granite, and the wood cabinets showed no wear. Ceramic tile covered the floor of the large room.

Dani dove right in. "How well did you know Jack and his mother?"

"Pretty well. They lived next door. We didn't socialize, but we'd chat when we'd see each other."

"Had you ever seen Jack do something violent?"

Jenny shook her head.

"Mean-spirited?"

"Not really."

"How *did* he seem to you, then?"

Jenny frowned. "Look, I really don't want to talk about him."

"Please. I really need your help. Before this happened to Kelly and Lisa, did you think Jack was an aggressive person?"

Jenny sighed, then looked away. When she turned back, she said, "Just the opposite. He was always very gentle with the kids on the block, even when they were bullying toward him."

"How so?"

"You know how kids are. They'd call him a retard. Some even threw rocks at him at times. He'd just walk away when they did that."

"I want to ask you a hypothetical. If Lisa hadn't identified Jack, would you have thought he was capable of murder?"

"But Lisa did identify him. And they found his bat with Lisa's blood on it."

"Assume that the bat can be explained. The bite on her hand, also."

Jenny wiped back a strand of hair that fell over her eyes. "What's the point? I believe Jack killed my niece. I believe he knocked my daughter unconscious. And I believe he should die for that."

———

One hour later, Dani was back in her hotel room. She'd gotten nowhere with Jenny Hicks. Well, almost nowhere. She'd learned that Kelly's parents had retired to some place in Florida, and Lisa had married and moved out of state. That was all Jenny would impart. Not their addresses, not their phone numbers, not even Lisa's married name. If she wasn't waiting to hear from the Supreme Court of Georgia on her petition for a stay of execution, she'd be back on a plane home. But it didn't make sense to leave yet, when it was possible that, instead of a stay, the court would hear arguments in the next day or two.

She made herself comfortable at the room's desk, then took out her cell phone and called Tommy.

"Any word from the court?" he asked when he got on the phone.

"Nothing, but it's still early. Hopefully by the end of the day, or at worst, tomorrow."

"Did you sit down with Mrs. Hicks yet?"

"Just got back."

"Anything good from her?"

"She believes Osgood is guilty, but only because of her daughter's ID, not from what she knew of him."

"I suppose that's good."

"We need to track down Kelly's parents. They're living somewhere in Florida. Maybe a retirement village. And it's essential we find Lisa—see how strong her ID really was. If she even remembers now. She was only five when it happened."

"Okay. Did Mrs. Hicks tell you where she was living?"

"No. And she's married now. I couldn't even get Lisa's new name from her."

"I may still be able to find her. She's young and probably uses social media."

"Good. Give me a call as soon as you find something."

When she hung up, Dani pulled from her briefcase folders containing files of other cases she was working on. They were comparatively simple matters, as all turned on newly discovered DNA evidence. Such cases represented the heart of what HIPP did. So many inmates were languishing in jail—even on death row—because they'd been convicted before DNA testing was available. Now, HIPP would seek out the evidence files routinely kept by police precincts and, when they contained items from which DNA could be found, arrange for its testing. When it excluded HIPP's client as a perpetrator, Dani would file a motion with the court to free the wrongly convicted inmate. Often, the prosecutor joined in the motion. Sometimes, the prosecutor fought it. She opened her laptop, then spent the next few hours working on motions while waiting for the phone to ring. The longer it remained silent, the more nervous she became. She wouldn't go home until she heard from the court.

She kept glancing at her watch every ten minutes. By five o'clock, she gave up waiting. Court clerks rarely stayed past closing time. She put aside her work and changed into running shorts, then headed to the hotel's gym. She'd gotten into the routine of jogging after Ruth was born. Between the exercise and breast-feeding her baby, the pounds gained from her pregnancy plus the extra ten she'd put on over the years swiftly melted away, and for the first time in more than a decade, she was satisfied with her figure.

The exercise room was empty. Two treadmills, one bike, and free weights—pretty sparse, even for a hotel gym. She grabbed a towel, then got on a treadmill, set it at 6.0, and began jogging. She'd discovered that she was able to think through some of her thorniest issues while running, and so for the next hour, she thought about her upcoming argument before the Supreme Court of Georgia. She wished she had more in her arsenal. Bennington was correct—it was awfully difficult to prove an intellectual disability beyond a reasonable doubt, especially when the inmate has been institutionalized for so many years. When she'd taken Osgood's case, she'd hoped to first remove the shroud of death hanging over him. Then, she and Tommy would have time to thoroughly investigate the original crime and, hopefully, find proof of his innocence. But she now expected they wouldn't have that luxury. Tommy was right. They needed to begin that search in earnest.

At 8:45 the next morning, Dani received a call from the court clerk's office. She'd already showered and dressed and was availing herself of the hotel's free continental breakfast when her phone rang.

"A stay has been granted in *State v. Osgood*," the clerk said. "And oral argument is scheduled for two weeks from today."

Dani breathed a sigh of relief. She asked the clerk to fax a copy to her office, then hung up and called Tommy. After she filled him in on the stay, she asked, "Any luck tracking down Kelly's parents and Lisa?"

"Got the Bradens. They're living in a retirement community northwest of Orlando called The Villages. I'm still striking out with Lisa's info."

"Why don't we both catch a flight out today and meet up in Orlando? We'll go see the Bradens together."

"Hold on a sec." There was quiet on the phone for a few minutes, and then Tommy returned. "There's a two-thirty out of JFK, arriving at five forty-five. How does that work for you?"

"Sounds good. I'll coordinate a flight with that and text you the time."

As soon as Dani hung up, she checked the flights from Atlanta and booked a seat on a plane leaving at 2:15 p.m. She packed her bag, checked out, then decided to swing by the Hicks home once more before leaving for the airport. She drove up to the house but remained in her car, checking out the trees that flanked the residence. Just as she'd remembered, there were two tall trees in the front and another pair on each side of the house, but none in the back. Satisfied, she left five minutes later and headed south.

———

Dani had some time before her flight to Orlando, so once she arrived in Atlanta, she headed to the office of Dr. James Fein. She pulled up to a row of medical offices in West Midtown. Tucked in between a cardiologist and a pediatrician was Fein's dental office. She hoped he was the same man who'd testified about the bite mark on Kelly's arm at Jack Osgood's trial.

She walked into the reception area. A row of empty chairs was lined up against one wall, and on the opposite wall, a middle-aged woman sat behind a window, reading a magazine. Dani first said, "Hello," then ten seconds later, "Excuse me," before the woman looked up. Dani took out her card and handed it to her. "I'm hoping Dr. Fein can find a few minutes to speak to me in between his patients."

The woman looked over the card, then asked, "What's this about?"

"I believe Dr. Fein testified in the case of a man I'm representing. About bite marks on the victim."

"Sure. He did a lot of that years back. Not so much anymore."

"Is he in?"

The woman picked up the phone and spoke quietly into it, then nodded for Dani to go through the door. "His office is first room on the right."

"Thank you."

Dani entered the small office and found a slightly built man with just a few wisps of white hair left on his mostly balding scalp. As he stood up to shake Dani's hand, she noticed his back was bent. *The ravages of age,* she thought, then wondered why he still came into the office every day. He had to be at least in his seventies.

"Have a seat, Ms. Trumball. How can I help you?"

"My office is representing Jack Osgood."

He stared at her blankly, then asked, "Is he the one that took a girl from her bedroom, then killed her? Up north in Stone Ridge?"

"Yes, that's him. You testified at his trial that a bite mark on the girl's arm matched up with Osgood's teeth."

"That sounds familiar."

"Do you mind if I ask you a few questions about it?"

"Well, now, I haven't testified in over a decade. Doubt I'll remember much about your specific case."

"I'd just like to ask you general questions about your methodology."

"Go ahead."

Dani riffled through her briefcase and pulled out several sheets of photographic prints, each containing pictures of bite marks from various angles. Under each photo was a picture of a ruler, measuring the width and height of the mark. She handed the papers over to Dr. Fein and pointed out his name above the pictures and the notation at the bottom—*State v. Osgood, State's Exh. 36.* "Do you rely on pictures such as these when you compare the bite of a suspected perpetrator?"

Dr. Fein nodded. "Everyone's teeth wear down differently. They're as unique as fingerprints."

"Let's get to that in a minute. I just want to understand your methodology."

"Well, it's quite technical, but basically, when the police have identified a suspect and there's a bite mark on the victim, I make an impression of the suspect's teeth and do various measurements to determine whether it's a match."

"You know, there's been a great deal of controversy about whether it's true that teeth marks are unique. Is it possible that you were mistaken about the bite being made by Osgood?"

Dr. Fein narrowed his eyes and tightened his mouth. "I'm old, not addled, Ms. Trumball. I'm aware of the literature on the subject. Mistakes were made because the guy doing the analysis wasn't qualified. I knew what I was doing, and my opinion hasn't changed. Those bite marks were made by Jack Osgood. He murdered that poor girl."

———

Dani wished she could question Owen Richmond, the forensic dentist who'd testified on Osgood's behalf. Not that he'd been particularly helpful at the trial. Although he stated that the bite marks on Kelly's arm didn't appear to match Osgood's teeth, on cross-examination he admitted that he couldn't rule out Osgood. Unfortunately, Richmond had passed away four years earlier, so she couldn't probe his findings. Instead, she drove to the airport and flew to Orlando, arriving there shortly after four o'clock. She rented a car, then checked online for hotels near The Villages. There was a Holiday Inn nearby, and she booked two rooms for herself and Tommy. There was nothing to do but wait for Tommy's plane. She found the food court, bought a cup of coffee, and settled in. Two hours later, she and Tommy were on their way to find the Bradens.

"Should we go to their home first, or check in to the hotel?" Dani asked.

"They're retirees. It's going to be hit or miss finding them home. I say let's swing by their house before the hotel. Maybe we'll be lucky."

By the time they pulled up to the single-story, cement-finished concrete house, it was dark outside. Each home on the street had a lamppost in front illuminating the walkway. Hanging from the Bradens' lamppost was a metal plaque with the house number and the names Carl and Susan Braden. Under that, the name Molly. At the top of the plaque was a metal dog bone. "I guess they have a dog named Molly," Dani said.

They pulled into the driveway, walked up to the front door, and rang the bell. Almost immediately, the high-pitched bark of a dog rang out, but that was all. No footsteps. Dani peeked through the glass panels of the door and saw that the entrance foyer and living room were dark. They rang once more, but still the only response was the sound of a dog barking.

"Probably out to dinner," Tommy said. "We can wait here for them."

"No. Let's go check in, then get dinner ourselves."

As they drove to their hotel, Dani marveled at the size of the development. It seemed never ending.

"A hundred and twenty thousand, and still growing," Tommy told her. "It's a golfer's paradise. More holes than any place in the country. In the world, maybe. I've got a few buddies who retired here."

They checked in to their rooms, then backtracked to an Olive Garden they'd passed on the way. Once they were settled in their booth, drinks in hand—pinot grigio for Dani, Scotch on the rocks for Tommy—Tommy said, "You're hoping he's innocent, aren't you?"

"I always hope someone we take on is innocent."

"No, it's more than the usual client. With someone else, you'd walk away if you thought he was guilty. You won't with Osgood, will you?"

Dani knew Tommy was right. Perhaps, if his mother were still alive, if he had some relative who worried about him, it would be different for her. But he was alone in the world, and he needed someone in his corner. "Even if he killed Kelly, maybe he didn't understand what he was doing. I'm not saying he shouldn't be punished, but certainly not put to death, and maybe not even a life sentence. He's already served twenty-two years."

Tommy shook his head. "You're a marshmallow, through and through."

"I wasn't when I was a prosecutor." She'd spent five years as an assistant US attorney for the Southern District of New York. "I was tough as nails then. Motherhood changed me. Or maybe it was working at HIPP. I've just seen too much injustice now to let it slide off me. So, yes, I'd rather err on the side of freeing a guilty person than incarcerating an innocent one."

"So, the guilty ones would be free to commit more crimes."

Dani sighed. "It's not a perfect world."

Tommy picked up his Scotch and took another sip. "Well, maybe Osgood actually is innocent. There are two men I've been looking into for the crime."

"Who?"

"First, Kelly's boyfriend."

"He had an alibi."

"Yeah, his roommate. Not very reliable as far as I'm concerned. Friends cover for each other all the time."

"But why would he kill Kelly?"

"She was thinking of breaking up with him. Maybe she did, and he didn't take it well."

"That's a pretty extreme reaction."

"Still, worth checking out."

"I agree. Who else?"

"An itinerant worker. Was in both the Bradens' and the Hickses' homes, then disappeared."

"I like that possibility. Do you know where he is?"

"Not yet. But I'm working on it."

———

At nine the next morning, Dani and Tommy rang the doorbell of the Bradens' home. A woman answered—still dressed in pajamas and holding a cup of coffee—a small dog yapping at her feet.

"Yes?"

"Mrs. Braden?"

The woman nodded.

Dani handed her a business card. "I'm Dani Trumball, and this is Tom Noorland. We're representing Jack Osgood."

A frown passed over the woman's face for the briefest moment. "I've been expecting you. My sister told me you'd been to see her. Come on in." She held the door open, and Dani and Tommy entered. The open rooms were decorated in a tropical style, with casual furnishings and walls painted a sea-foam green. Out past the back wall of glass sliding doors was a screened-in lanai, and beyond lay the manicured fairway of a golf course.

"Mind if I take a few minutes to get dressed?"

"Go ahead," Dani answered.

Fifteen minutes later, Mrs. Braden emerged from her bedroom dressed in a pair of linen shorts and a sleeveless white blouse, with makeup expertly applied. Dani had seen pictures of Kelly in the files, and it struck her that Kelly had gotten her pretty looks from her mother. When Mrs. Braden sat down opposite Dani and Tommy in a rattan chair, Dani asked, "Is your husband home?"

"No, he's playing golf. Won't be back for hours."

"I know our visit must be difficult for you," Dani said. "After all these years, I'm sure you want closure. But we want to make sure that Jack Osgood truly is responsible for your daughter's death. From what we've learned, the police honed in on him very quickly, and sometimes when that happens, they don't look carefully at all the evidence."

"But my niece saw him."

"Your niece was five years old, awakened from sleep, and saw a man in a dark room."

"Still, there was other evidence that backed up her ID."

Dani knew she had to tread carefully. This was a grieving mother, no less so because of the passage of time. Her daughter's death would always feel like a sharp stab in the heart. She leaned toward Mrs. Braden. "If Jack Osgood killed your daughter, he should be punished for it. But for more than twenty-two years, he's continued to insist he's innocent. If there's some possibility that's true, wouldn't you want Kelly's real murderer to be apprehended? Wouldn't you want that person to pay for what he did?"

Mrs. Braden wiped back a strand of golden-blonde hair from her face. At her age, which Dani guessed was somewhere in her late fifties, it was no doubt a color that came from a bottle. "What is it you want from me?"

"I promise I'll keep this as brief as possible. I'd like to start with Kelly's boyfriend at the time, Greg Johnson. What can you tell me about him?"

"I didn't like him, but I don't think he'd ever have hurt Kelly."

"Why didn't you like him?"

"He was too old for her. You know, college boys want more from a relationship than I thought Kelly was ready for." She hesitated, then smiled weakly. "At least, more than I was ready for her to have."

"Why do you think he wouldn't have hurt Kelly?"

"Stone Ridge is a small town. I knew Greg and his family long before he and Kelly started dating. I can't imagine anyone there committing a murder."

"But Jack was from the same town. And you believe he killed your daughter. Before it happened, would you have thought him capable of that?"

"I'd like to say yes, because he was different from the other boys, but if I'm honest, then no. I wouldn't have thought it of him, either."

"So, let's go back to Greg. Did you ever see him display a temper?"

"No. He was all charm, all the time."

"How do you think he'd handle it if Kelly broke up with him?"

"Oh, I suppose he'd tell everyone it was what he wanted."

"You don't think he'd get angry?"

"Maybe. But not so angry he'd kill her."

Dani understood denial. Greg was a boy to whom Susan Braden had entrusted her daughter. If she'd been wrong in allowing Kelly to date him, then she'd open herself up to a flood of recriminations. Nothing she'd said, though, changed Dani's view that he was a person of interest. But there was still another. "I'd like to change gears here. Do you remember that you hired a handyman to do some work on your house shortly before Kelly's murder?"

"Did we? It was so long ago."

"His name was Tony. Tony Falcone. He repaired some shingles on your roof."

Mrs. Braden got up from her chair and stood over it, her hands resting on the head cushion. "I don't know what you want from me. You say Jack may be innocent; you ask me about other people, as though they might be guilty. I don't remember anything from back then. It all became a blur after Kelly died. She was everything to me, my whole world, my—" She stopped talking as tears ran down her cheeks. She reached into the pocket of her shorts and pulled out a tissue, then wiped away the wetness. After a few minutes, she sighed deeply, then returned to the chair.

"Do you have any children?" she asked Dani.

"I do. A son and a daughter."

"I doted on Kelly. I would have gladly died in her place if that were possible. When I lost her, I sunk into a deep depression that lasted more than a year. Drugs pulled me out of it. But I can't think about her or talk about her without feeling the loss all over, as if it were fresh."

"I'm sorry to have put you through this." Dani stood up, Tommy along with her, and said they'd leave her alone now. As they reached the door, Dani turned back. "If you think of anything, please call." She opened the door, and they walked out.

Just as they reached the driveway, she heard Mrs. Braden call out, "Wait."

"There is something," Mrs. Braden said when she reached them. "That worker, Tony. He told me he had a daughter, a toddler. Said her name was . . ." She stopped, bent her head down, and squeezed her eyes closed. After a moment, she looked up. "It was Abigail. That's it. I remember thinking it was the same name as one of my cousins. Do you think that's helpful?"

"It might be," Tommy said. "It just might be."

Chapter

11

1994

He wondered if it would feel the same if he did it again. If he killed another girl. But had the thrill come from the act of murder, or had the abduction been part of it? If a girl went with him willingly, would he get the same sense of excitement? Sneaking into a room in the middle of the night was risky—if he woke the parents or another child in the house, he could get caught. But maybe the risk was part of it. He had to test it. Find someone he could convince to go with him to someplace isolated.

It was past 11:00 p.m. when he entered the tavern. It was crowded with young people from the nearby college. It was important that the next one be in a different town. He couldn't have the local police putting things together. He walked up to two coeds sitting at the bar—neither was especially pretty, but not ugly either—and squeezed in next to them. When he caught the bartender's eye, he ordered a Budweiser on tap. After it was handed to him, he turned to the two and started a conversation. He had to shout over the music. It sounded like screeching to him, but he saw girls swaying their bodies to the pounding beat, so they must have liked it.

"You go to this college?" he asked the girls.

"Sure, don't you?" the nearer, less attractive of the two shouted.

"Nope. I'm finished with school."

"What do you do, then?"

"I'm a pharmaceutical rep. Go from town to town meeting with doctors. I'm supposed to persuade them to prescribe my company's drugs, then leave samples with them. Hey, what's your name?"

"I'm Bonnie, and this is Sasha."

He smiled brightly at the two of them. "Can I buy you girls another round?"

"Sure," they yelled in unison.

He focused on Bonnie, and not just because she was closest to him and they could talk without shouting. He suspected Sasha, the more attractive one, was used to boys' attention, so it would be harder with her. At least Bonnie had long blonde hair, he thought. Like Kelly's. "What year?"

"Sophomore."

"You know what you want to do when you finish?"

"Medicine. Hopefully my grades will be good enough to get into med school. If not, then physician's assistant."

"So, maybe one day I'll be visiting you to give you samples of my drugs."

Bonnie smiled at him. She looked nicer when she smiled. He noticed dimples in her cheeks. He kept chatting with Bonnie until some guy waltzed up to Sasha and pulled her away.

"Hey," he said, leaning in close to her, "want to get out of here? It's too loud to really talk."

Bonnie scanned the room, saw Sasha had been drawn into another group, then nodded.

He led her outside, then pointed to his car. "Let's go over to the park," he said. "It's quiet there."

Bonnie held back. "I don't know. I'm not really sure it's safe this time of night."

He laughed. "You're with me. No one's going to mess with someone my size."

He opened the passenger door for her, and she slid into the front seat. He walked around the car and got in, then drove toward the park. He'd scouted it out earlier, knew just where he wanted to take her. It would be isolated now, the joggers and bicyclists and rowers all out partying, or tucked safely in bed. Ten minutes later, he pulled into a parking spot. His was the only car there.

"Are you sure this is okay?" Bonnie asked again.

"Look up. Full moon, the sky crowded with stars. It's a perfect night for a moonlit walk, don't you think?"

She exited the car, and he took her hand. They began walking down the path heading toward the lake, talking easily. When they reached the lake, he pointed to a bench, and they sat down. He cradled her face in his large hands. "You're really nice. I like you."

She turned her face up toward him, ready to be kissed. He leaned in, and as his lips touched hers, he slid his hands downward, onto her neck, then squeezed. She tried to push his hands off, but he was too strong for her. Her eyes bulged as she tried to squirm away, until there was no more movement. He dropped her limp body onto the bench and gazed into her eyes, frozen in a horrified stare.

He didn't feel anything. No rush of excitement, no jolt of electricity, not even pity for the lifeless girl. Was it because she'd been a stranger to him before tonight? Or because she'd gone willingly with him? He didn't know. He felt a twinge of disgust toward himself, yet the memory of the surge he'd felt the first time lingered. He wanted to feel that again. Maybe he needed to replicate what he'd done before. Yes, that must be it. That's what he'd do the next time.

By the time Dani walked in her front door, she was beat. *I'm getting too old for this,* she thought. Before Ruth was born, she could fly out to a court, argue her motion or appeal, then fly home the same night. Now, traveling took a toll on her. She'd wanted Ruth so badly, and loved her intensely, yet mothering a baby when Dani was in her midforties was so different from when she'd just turned thirty and had given birth to Jonah.

Thankfully, both children were asleep. She plopped down on the sofa next to Doug and lay her head on his shoulder.

"Tough trip?" he asked.

"No more than usual. I'm just getting old."

"You're working too hard. You went back to handling cases from the outset too soon."

"I promised Bruce I would."

"You have to do what's right for you."

The problem, Dani knew, was that she enjoyed finding a client from the pile of letters on her desk, figuring out whether the person was truly innocent, then fighting with everything she had to prove it to the court. Writing appeals was so much more antiseptic—a cool-headed approach to marshaling the facts that had been handed to her and spinning them into a winning argument. She missed her family when she was away from home, but she missed the challenge when she handled only appeals. She felt tired now after days on the road, but it was a good tired, she decided. She knew she wouldn't give it up.

"How were the kids tonight?"

"Jonah's working on a new composition—a violin concerto this time. And Ruth walked all the way from the living room to the kitchen."

Great, Dani thought, as she slid down and lay her head on Doug's lap. *One more thing I've missed.*

———

Dani arrived at the office the next morning rested and ready to go. Her first priority was preparing for the oral argument before the Supreme Court of Georgia in eleven days. She hunkered down with her research and spent the next several hours making notes and organizing them into something that flowed. When she finished, she put it aside. She'd return to it two days before the court date and look at it fresh, rechecking the cases she wanted to cite and looking for any new cases that had just been reported. Now, there was no more she could do on Osgood's behalf until Tommy tracked down addresses for Lisa Hicks; Tony Falcone, the handyman, or his daughter, Abigail; and Greg Johnson, Kelly's former boyfriend.

She opened the packed folder on her desk containing letters from inmates seeking HIPP's help. Slowly, she went through each one, stopping occasionally to check out some claims on LexisNexis. Eventually, she chose William Dorney. He'd been convicted of the rape and kidnapping of two teenage sisters in their home based solely on their identification of him.

The two girls had been home alone when a man broke in through a basement window, tied them up, then sexually assaulted each in turn at gunpoint. Although he was in their home for almost two hours, they'd caught a glimpse of his face only before he blindfolded them. Nevertheless, they told the police that their captor looked like a former neighbor—William Dorney. Each girl identified Dorney in a lineup. Although rape kits had been collected, the DNA testing was inconclusive. Even though Dorney had an alibi—his claim that he was at work was corroborated by his employer—he was convicted and sentenced to two consecutive life sentences.

Dorney had maintained his innocence throughout his trial and his fourteen years in prison. Dani knew that in 75 percent of wrongful convictions, eyewitness misidentification was a primary or contributing factor. She turned to her computer and began a letter to him saying she would take his case.

At the end of the day, Dani stuffed papers to work on at home into her briefcase, then stopped at Tommy's desk on the way out. "Anything new?" she asked.

"You'll know as soon as I find anyone. Still searching."

Dani had expected it would be difficult to find both Lisa and the handyman. If Lisa was married, they didn't know her new name. And if the police couldn't locate Tony Falcone twenty-two years ago, it would be even harder now. But she'd thought finding Greg Johnson would have been easy. And it *had* been easy for Tommy to find him. Thirty-two Greg Johnsons, in fact, all within the right age range. He'd been busy tracking down each one to figure out which had been Kelly's boyfriend. So far, he'd hit dead ends.

She left the office, got her car, then started the commute north to her home. The leaves had finally begun to change, and as she drove north on the FDR Drive—the East River to her right, a brightly colored tree-lined walk to her left, tall buildings behind her and the expanse of the Triborough Bridge in front—she suddenly felt awash with gratitude that she lived near such a grand city. There had been times, since the terrorist attacks of September 11, 2001, when she and Doug had worried about working in a city that was a magnet for extremists. There had been times, because of that fear, they'd talked about moving elsewhere. But New York had always been her home. Tommy often talked about retiring to Florida when the last of his five children was in college, but Dani knew she'd never leave. Autumn in New York was just too beautiful to ever give up.

13

Once again, Dani was back at the Supreme Court of Georgia. When *The State* v. *Osgood* was called, both she and Gary Luckman moved to the front. Seven justices sat on the bench, only one a woman. The lack of women jurists at the highest courts in each state wasn't unique to Georgia. Despite a shift by law schools in the 1980s toward admitting more women, they were still underrepresented at the highest echelons.

Dani gathered her papers and moved to the lectern. "May it please the court, my name is Dani Trumball, and I represent Jack Osgood, who was convicted of murder in the first degree twenty-two years ago, and sentenced to die. His death warrant has been signed, and he is now scheduled for execution." Dani went through the facts of his case, and the history of his appeals, then continued. "Although Mr. Osgood has continually maintained his innocence, even assuming his guilt, he is ineligible to be put to death because he suffers from an intellectual disability that presented before the age of eighteen and which has resulted in limitations in his functioning. There is no dispute between the defendant's expert and the prosecutor's expert that, based upon intelligence tests, Mr. Osgood's intellectual functioning is significantly subaverage. The experts differ, however, with respect to Mr. Osgood's limitations in adaptive behavior. The prosecution's expert bases his determination on two factors: the nature of the crime, and reports of prison guards who come into contact with Mr. Osgood. The first factor should be given no weight. The State of

Georgia requires that a claim of mental retardation be backed up by demonstrable impairments in adaptive behavior. This court has never found that the ability to plan a crime is sufficient by itself to show adaptive behavior."

One of the judges broke in. "Aren't there any circumstances in which the planning of a crime can show there's no impairment in adaptive behavior?"

"I suppose there might be, if all the different areas that make up adaptive behavior are implicated. But that wasn't the case here."

"Give me an example where it might be the case."

"Well, if he were the ringleader of a group and planned a complex crime, assigning jobs to each member, obtaining the weapons and material needed to execute the crime."

The justices were quiet, so Dani continued. "The second factor—the reports of prison guards—is also insufficient. First, prison is a contained environment, and especially so on death row. Mr. Osgood is not required to perform any jobs, and his social interaction is limited. He does not need to care for himself, because the state cares for him by providing and laundering his clothing and preparing his meals. Furthermore, the United States Supreme Court decision in *Atkins v. Virginia* makes clear that the question is not whether Mr. Osgood now has limitations in adaptive functioning, but whether he had such limitations at the time of his incarceration. Defendant provided testimony from school officials and his employer that he had impairments in communication, social skills, self-direction, and functional academic skills. None of that testimony was contradicted by the prosecution. For these reasons, the defendant has shown beyond a reasonable doubt that, under the definition utilized by the State of Georgia, he is mentally retarded and may not have a death sentence imposed."

As Dani sat down, she saw Luckman stare at a handful of cards in front of him, then slowly stand and walk to the lectern, leaving the cards behind. Dani suspected he'd been caught off guard by her argument. He probably expected to contend that where there is a battle of experts, as there was here, the defendant didn't meet his burden of proving, beyond a reasonable doubt, that he had an intellectual disability. Now, he was forced to address Dani's claim that only Osgood's capabilities at the time of the conviction mattered.

"Your Honors," Luckman began, "Ms. Trumball would like this court to ignore all that is known about the defendant presently and hark back to a time when there is little known about his adaptive skills. His principal hadn't had contact with the defendant for six years. And his employer, who admitted that he'd been close to the defendant's mother and therefore possibly biased, was not privy to any behaviors outside the supermarket. Only Mrs. Osgood could give a full picture of his capabilities, and she is deceased. Given that, it is entirely appropriate for the court to rely on the assessment of the guards who monitor him twenty-four hours each day."

"But isn't it true that a death-row environment can't provide a true picture of his capabilities?" asked the woman justice.

"Perhaps. But the burden is on the defendant to prove he is mentally retarded. He simply hasn't done so."

Luckman finished the rest of his argument—more about the burden of proof—then he and Dani left the courtroom. Once again, Dani couldn't predict the outcome. And, once again, she'd already prepared a writ of certiorari to be filed with the US Supreme Court. This time, though, she wouldn't wait in Georgia for the court's decision. She flew back to New York, pessimistic about the outcome.

———

By the time Dani arrived home, her family had finished dinner. Jonah was entertaining Ruth in the living room, chasing her around the couch, pretending he couldn't catch her, then finally grabbing her and swinging her in the air. She laughed the joyous, high-pitched giggles that only a baby could make. As Dani watched them in the doorway, she marveled once again at how unpredictable life could be. For more than a decade, she'd believed her family was complete, never expecting she'd have another child. She and Doug had made the decision to stop with Jonah. Now, life without Ruth seemed unimaginable.

For the Braden family, life without Kelly also must have seemed unimaginable. Dani had seen pictures of the sixteen-year-old in the files—a beautiful, smiling girl with soft blue eyes and honey-blonde hair that fell in waves to her shoulders. They'd had to deal with the worst any parent could endure—burying a child.

Dani turned from the living room and joined Doug in the kitchen, watching as he loaded the dishwasher with the dinner plates and utensils. Once again, as so often before, she realized how lucky she was. So much of life seemed to be a matter of luck. Sure, she and Doug had worked hard, first in school and then at their jobs. But she'd been lucky to find a man who was such a perfect match for her. She'd been lucky that no tragedy had befallen her family, as had happened to the Bradens. She was lucky that she'd been born into a family that loved and nurtured her, unlike so many of her clients. She never took that luck for granted. She'd learned over the years that luck could disappear in an instant. Like losing a child. Or being convicted of a crime you hadn't committed.

14

Three days after her return to New York, Dani had something to smile over. She'd just hung up with the prosecutor in the William Dorney case. He'd agreed to retest the DNA, and it now conclusively excluded Dorney as the rapist. Even better, it turned up a match with another man who had been convicted of rape in a later case. Her client would go free.

A half hour later, her good mood vanished. The decision of the Supreme Court of Georgia had just come over the fax. It turned out Dani's pessimism had been warranted. The court upheld the lower court's finding. The majority wrote, "As we've previously ruled, the state identifies as mentally retarded those whose deficits are so clear as to be demonstrated beyond a reasonable doubt. In the current case, defendant has failed to overcome that burden." The sole dissenting opinion, written by Justice Mary Blackwell, said, "Georgia's requirement that defendants sentenced to death prove mental retardation beyond a reasonable doubt creates a risk that persons with such a disability will be executed. Such a circumstance should not be countenanced."

To compound Dani's distress, a letter arrived over the fax informing her that Osgood's execution had been rescheduled. It would take place in one week.

Within an hour, Dani filed her papers with the US Supreme Court, once again asking for a stay pending a ruling. There was nothing more she could do at the moment for Jack Osgood, so she began working on the cases of her other clients.

She looked up when she heard a knock on her open door and saw Tommy standing there.

"Hi, gorgeous."

"Hi, yourself. What's up?"

"Two things. First, I've tracked down Derek Whitman."

"Greg Johnson's roommate?"

"Yeah. Want me to interview him?"

Dani scrunched up her face. "Still no luck finding Greg?"

"Not yet."

"Let's hold off with Whitman. I'd prefer to interview Greg first. See if we can catch him with any inconsistencies. If you can't find him, then visit Whitman. What's the second?"

"Turns out the Bradens have a son. Adam Braden. Two years older than Kelly, and he, too, went to University of Georgia."

"That's interesting. There was nothing in the file about him. And neither the Bradens nor the Hickses mentioned him."

"Well, he probably didn't need to testify at the trial because he was away when his sister was killed. And I suspect the parents wanted to keep him out of the limelight. And still do."

"Do you have contact info for him?"

"Yep. Phone number and address. He lives in Atlanta."

"Why don't you fly out and meet with him? Maybe he can lead us to Lisa, since she's his cousin. Or even Greg."

Tommy nodded. "My schedule's flexible right now. I can go tomorrow."

"Good." Dani knew that tracking down proof of a client's innocence was like working a puzzle. Each piece that fit could lead to another piece. Step-by-step they'd work the puzzle, until a clear picture emerged.

When Tommy left, she returned to the case at hand: a nineteen-year-old man—really, still a boy—who'd been in jail in New Jersey for eighteen months on a possession-of-cocaine conviction. Although Dani hadn't met the young man yet, she had no doubt he was black. Among the wealthy titans of business in New York and the glitterati of California, cocaine was rampant, yet rarely did those mostly white men and women get arrested. Eddie Coleman had pled guilty and received a sentence of four to six years. Before he'd pleaded guilty, he'd already spent nine months in jail, unable to make bail. When a plea was offered, and his legal-aid attorney explained that he was facing ten to fifteen, he accepted. Normally, a guilty plea precluded reopening the case. But Eddie insisted to Dani that the white powder found in his pocket was benzocaine that he carried with him at all times because his seven-month-old son was teething, and it helped relieve his pain. Despite Eddie imploring his attorney to have the substance tested, neither the attorney nor the police ever did. And so, Eddie, if he was to be believed, was serving time when his only crime was being too poor to post bail, and having an overworked attorney who was too busy to push the police to test the powder. Now, Dani worked on papers to force the police to do just that.

Just before the end of the day, Dani's assistant, Carol, walked into her office and placed a copy of the *New York Times* on her desk, opened to page three of the Metro section. "I thought you might be interested in this," she said.

Dani thanked her and began scanning the article. A project run by the University of Michigan had shown a record number of exonerations in 2015—more than double that of 2011. One hundred forty-nine wrongly convicted people were freed. Forty percent had been convicted of a murder charge, and five of them were on death row. The average time in prison before exoneration was fourteen years. Twenty-seven of the cases involved a false confession. Dani knew from experience that once a suspect confessed, even if the confession was quickly withdrawn, jurors inevitably couldn't get past that. It was understandable. Twelve men and women who'd never been arrested, never been interrogated for hours on end, never made to doubt their own reality, rarely could understand why a person would confess to a crime he or she hadn't committed. Yet over and over, it happened.

The article went on to attribute seventy-one of the exonerations to the efforts of two individual district attorneys—one in Brooklyn, New York, and one in Harris County, Texas. Each had undertaken an effort to review questionable convictions. Imagine, Dani thought, if every county in every state made such an effort. Imagine, if just two counties found seventy-one innocent men and women serving time for crimes they didn't commit, how many others were in such a predicament throughout the country? She often thought about those numbers, and sometimes it overwhelmed her. Bruce regularly admonished her to distance herself from her clients, to avoid becoming emotionally affected by their plights, but she'd never been able to do that. When she freed an innocent client, she rejoiced. When she failed, she'd be despondent for days. And if the client she failed was on death row, when she'd been convinced of that client's innocence, she raged at a system so imperfect, so callous, that judicial economy trumped a person's life.

She shook her head, trying to dispel the anger that had welled up while reading the article. "You can't save the world, just one person at a time," Doug always told her. She turned back to her papers. Today, she would try to save Eddie Coleman.

15

1994

He knew he had to try it again, this time just like the first. He went to still another town, far away from the first and second, and checked in to a motel. Not seedy and not fancy. The kind of nondescript row of rooms that catered to traveling salespeople and cheating spouses. On the first day, he waited near the local high school, checking out the girls, finding the right one. As soon as he spotted her, with long wavy hair the same color as Kelly's, a tight cheerleader's body, and a look that said she was too good for the boys her age, he knew it had to be her.

He followed her home that day, saw where she lived, then for two days watched her house. Not always in the same spot. He didn't want to draw attention to himself, although his car was as nondescript as his motel. She had a mother and a father, and one younger brother. *Perfect,* he thought. Unlikely that she'd share a room with her brother. It had been messy business with Kelly's little cousin. No need to do that again. On the second day, when he watched the girl enter her home after school, he looked to see if a light went on in a front upstairs bedroom. It didn't. On the third day, after she came home, he left his car and slipped into her backyard. There it was—a light in the upstairs window on the left side of the house. He waited a little longer and heard loud music come from the room. It had to be hers.

At 3:00 a.m.—it needed to be that time—he removed the folding ladder from his trunk, walked into the girl's backyard, and placed it up against the wall. The lights in the surrounding houses were off, the street quiet. He'd brought tools to open a locked window, but he didn't need them. It was early October, and the night air still carried a warm breeze, but not so hot as to need air-conditioning. The window was open, with just a screen covering it. *Just like the first time. A good sign.*

He removed the screen, dropped it to the ground, and entered the bedroom. The full moon provided just enough light to reveal the twin bed, with the girl sleeping soundly under a light blanket. Soundlessly, he made his way over to her, then gently shook her awake. He needed her to see him; he needed to see the fear in her eyes before he choked her into silence. As her eyes slowly opened, at first confused and then terrified, she opened her mouth to scream. He was ready. He placed the webbing between his thumb and index finger on her windpipe and wrapped the rest of his fingers around the back of her neck. Then, with his thumb, he pushed down on her windpipe and held it there until her eyes closed, and her body went slack. With Kelly, he'd reacted instinctively, squeezing her neck until she'd passed out. He was lucky, then, that he hadn't killed her in the bedroom. Now, for this, he'd studied what he'd needed to do to knock out his victim without killing her. The killing would come later.

He scooped her up out of the bed, then threw her body over his shoulder. Then he eased open the bedroom door, scanned the empty hallway, and carried her down the stairs and outside into the autumn night. Once at his car, he laid her down on the backseat, took the rope he'd left on the floor, tied her hands and feet, then placed electrical tape over her mouth. When he was satisfied that even if she woke up, she couldn't do him any harm, he retrieved his ladder from the backyard.

He'd found a park with a little lake in the town. He would have preferred a creek, but he'd make do. Even though the streets were empty, he was careful to drive at the speed limit, to stop at every red light. When he reached the lake, he parked the car and carried the still-unconscious girl, then carefully laid her down on the grass and removed the tape across her mouth. He waited until she woke, and this time, when she started screaming, he didn't choke her at first. Instead, he placed his hand over her mouth and said, "I want you to be my girlfriend."

She tried to roll away from him, but he restrained her.

"If you stop fighting me, I'll let you go."

Slowly, she nodded, and he took his hand off her mouth.

"Who are you?"

"I'm someone who likes you. You're pretty."

She turned her face away from his. "You're crazy," he heard her whisper.

And so he choked her, tightly this time, squeezing the life out of her, biting her arm as she swung it in his face, just like with Kelly, feeling the arousal he'd felt with Kelly, feeling the power in his hands. Feeling godlike.

Tommy drove up to the two-story Craftsman-style house on a tree-lined street in Ormewood Park just after 7:30 p.m. He noted the late-model Acura MDX in the driveway and hoped that meant Adam Braden was home. He walked up the steps of the full-length front porch, rang the doorbell, and waited. A minute later, the door was opened by an attractive woman with a curvy body, dressed in jeans and a T-shirt, holding a toddler in her arms. She looked at him quizzically before saying, "Hello."

"Are you Mrs. Braden?"

"I am. And who are you?"

Tommy handed her his card. "I'm hoping that your husband is home."

"You're the one helping Jack Osgood, aren't you?"

"My office is, yes."

"I suppose if I tell you to leave him alone, you'll just keep coming back."

"I don't want to cause him any pain. But a man is going to be executed soon, and I just want to make absolutely sure he deserves it. I promise I won't take up much of your husband's time."

The woman hesitated, then opened the door wider. "Come on in."

Tommy stepped into the foyer. Straight ahead was the kitchen, and beyond that Tommy glimpsed what looked like a den, or family room. Three more children, two girls and one boy, were huddled around a TV, game consoles in hand.

"Adam," the woman called up the stairs, "that investigator is here to talk to you. The one your mom called about." She placed the toddler down on the floor, told her to join her siblings, then turned to Tommy and held out her hand. "I'm Sarah."

After Tommy shook it, she led him into the living room. Moments later, they were joined by Adam. He was built like Tommy—tall, carrying a little too much weight, but nevertheless sporting muscles that no doubt came from regular visits to the gym. Adam nodded to Tommy, then sat down on the couch next to his wife.

"I appreciate your talking to me," Tommy said. "You probably knew your sister even better than your parents. At least that's how it was when I was growing up. We'd keep secrets from the folks, but never from each other."

"I suppose that's true."

"Did your sister ever tell you she was worried about someone?"

Adam shook his head.

"What about her boyfriend?"

"Greg? He'd never hurt her. We were friends back then. Played high school football together. We all went to UGA together, pledged the same fraternity, rented a house together our junior and senior years."

"What do you mean, all?"

"Me, Greg, Derek, and Russ."

"Derek Whitman?"

"Yeah."

"Whitman went to high school with you and Greg?"

"That's right. We'd been friends since middle school."

Tommy searched through the notes Dani had made of the trial transcript. After each witness was a summary of their testimony and where they lived. Whitman had given an address in Athens, where the university was located. Why hadn't the defense counsel brought out where he grew up, that he'd been friends with Greg for years? It seemed all the more likely now that Whitman would lie for Greg. Give him an alibi, no matter what.

"Do you still keep in touch with Greg?"

"Not really. We drifted apart after I got married and the kids started coming." Adam looked toward the den, then turned back, his face paler. He lowered his chin to his chest. "We'd been so close, me and Kelly. After she was killed, I was lost. She was my only sibling, the only one I could talk to about family things. I never wanted my own kids to face that. So, we have four. If, God forbid, something happened to one, they'd have each other to lean on."

"How old are they?"

"The youngest is two and the oldest sixteen. Same age Kelly was when . . ." His voice trailed off.

"I know."

"She complains all the time that I restrict her too much. But I don't care. When she's older, has her own kids, she'll understand."

"I'm sure she will. I've got five kids of my own. I know how it is." Tommy already had two away at college. Tricia was next. She was sixteen, just like Braden's daughter, just like Kelly had been when she'd been murdered. He couldn't comprehend how any parent recovered from that. He knew he wouldn't.

Just then, a girl around ten, Tommy guessed, barreled into the living room, screaming, "Julie is hogging the Xbox! Tell her to stop."

Sarah stood up and led her daughter back into the den.

Tommy started to gather up his papers and stuff them back into his briefcase. "Just one more thing," he said as he stood up. "Do you have any idea where Greg is living now?"

"I heard he moved to Boston. That's all I know."

Adam walked Tommy to the front door and opened it. Before Tommy left, he asked, "How's your cousin doing? Lisa. Wasn't she hurt that night?"

"She's doing fine."

"No lasting injuries?"

"None, thankfully."

"And psychologically? Any trauma left over from that night?"

Adam lifted his shoulders in a half shrug. "Of course there is. For all of us. My sister died. And Lisa had been with her when she was taken."

"I'm sorry. I didn't mean to sound callous. I just wanted to see if she'd been able to get on with her life."

Adam's mouth curved into a smile. "She's doing well. Became a lawyer."

"I bet she's a prosecutor, right?"

"That's what we all expected, but no. She's a federal public defender."

"You get to see her much?"

"Family gatherings. She met her husband at law school. He was from Houston, and she settled there with him."

"Yeah? What's his name?"

Adam hesitated. "Look, everyone in the family knows what you're doing. If Lisa wants to speak to you, she knows how to reach you. I can't help you find her."

Tommy thanked Adam, then left. Adam was wrong. He had given Tommy a lead for finding Lisa. Even more important, he'd given him a possible lead for finding Greg. And he'd strengthened Tommy's suspicion that Greg was the real killer.

Relief washed over Dani. The US Supreme Court had issued a temporary stay of Osgood's execution. They still hadn't determined whether they would grant certiorari in his case, but for now, at least, he would remain alive.

She worked quickly to finish up anything that was pressing so that she could leave the office by 3:00 p.m. She had her coat on and was about to leave when a call came from the prosecutor in Eddie Coleman's case. She'd prevailed on him to test the white substance, still in the evidence files, that had landed Coleman in jail. "Got some good news for me?" she asked when she picked up the phone.

"Great news for you. A black mark for us. I don't know how this happened, but you were right. It was benzocaine. I'll start the paperwork to get Coleman released."

Dani thanked him, then quickly left the office as soon as she hung up. Today, she couldn't be late. It was Halloween, and Ruth's first time trick-or-treating. Dani had bought her a cat costume—a big, puffy black body, decorated with the face of a cat, orange-and-black striped tights, and a black headband with cat ears. Jonah insisted on wearing the same costume year after year—Superman—even though the children his age in the neighborhood now refused to wear anything more than a mask. Together, they'd join the other families with kids who lived on the block and go door-to-door. Dani loved seeing the costumes the other kids were wearing as much as she loved dressing Ruth and Jonah. It was her favorite holiday.

She walked in the door at twenty to four. Jonah's bus would drop him off at four, so she'd have a few precious minutes alone with Ruth.

"Hi," Doug said when he saw her.

Dani beamed. "What a nice surprise. I didn't expect you home yet."

"I left early."

"Don't you teach Con Law at three?"

"I canceled it. Didn't want to miss Ruthie's first Halloween."

Dani threw her arms around her husband and gave him a kiss. "I knew there was a reason I married you."

Dani found Ruth upstairs in her room with Katie. As soon as Ruth saw her mother, she threw up her arms. "Mama, Mama."

Dani picked her up and nestled her nose in the soft skin of Ruth's neck.

"I just bathed her," Katie said.

Nothing compared to the sweet smell of a baby, Dani thought as she held Ruth—fresh from the bath, baby powder all over her bottom. "Want to go trick-or-treating today?" she asked her.

Ruth nodded. It always amazed Dani how many words her daughter understood, even though she couldn't say them herself. Katie left to go home, while Dani stayed upstairs and played with her daughter. Five minutes before Jonah's bus was due to arrive, she dressed Ruthie in her costume, then brought her downstairs.

Doug couldn't hold back a laugh when he saw her. "That's about the cutest cat I've ever seen," he said.

"Don't let Gracie hear you say that." Gracie was their cat—fat, lazy, and terrified ever since Ruth had learned to walk.

When Jonah arrived, he quickly put on his Superman costume. Dani filled a bowl with candy and left it on the front porch. Then, with Ruth in a stroller, the family headed over to their next-door neighbor's home. Rose Marten, with two sons close in age to Jonah, always joined them as they walked door-to-door asking for treats.

Dani loved the block they lived on—homes built in the fifties and sixties but filled with school-age children. The families got together several times each year at one of the homes. Tonight, the Martens would host. After the trick-or-treating was finished, they'd all converge on their home for pizza, and the kids would look over their haul from the afternoon.

By the second house, the boys were running ahead, and Rose hurried to keep up with them. As Dani, pushing the stroller, quickened her pace, Doug placed his hand on her arm. "Let's hold back a bit. I have something to tell you."

Dani looked at him expectantly, waiting for him to speak.

"I got a call from a headhunter today. Stanford is looking for a new dean for its law school, and I'm on the short list."

Dani stopped short. "But that's in California."

"Is change bad? No snow, rarely freezing temperatures, an hour from San Francisco."

"I'll take snow over earthquakes."

"Seriously, Dani. It's a great opportunity."

Dani turned toward Doug. The smile that had been on her face as she'd watched the children disappeared. "I have a job here. One that I love."

"There are jobs there. Any place would be lucky to get you."

Dani knew she should be pleased for Doug. She knew she should be supportive of his goals. After all, he earned far more at his job than she did working for a nonprofit. Instead, she felt miserable. New York was home. Always had been. It was where they'd met and married. Where Jonah and Ruth had been born. And where Jonah was thriving. How could she uproot him and take a chance that across the country she'd find a school that was just as nurturing as the one he now attended? Where orchestras would recognize his musical talent? Where doctors were familiar with the medical risks associated with Williams syndrome? She took Doug's hand and turned him to face her. Her eyes bored into him. "I know it's selfish of me, but I don't want to move."

Doug crossed his arms. He took a deep breath and held it in before speaking. "I haven't been offered the job. They're looking at others. It's still the exploratory stage. But they want someone in place by July—August at the latest—for the incoming class. What's the harm if I go out for an interview?"

"The harm is you'll get the job, and want to take it, and I'm the bad guy holding you back."

"Instead, you're the bad guy keeping me from being considered."

"That's not fair."

Doug looked away, but not before Dani could see that his cheeks had reddened. She knew it wasn't from the chill in the air. He always turned red when he was angry.

"Let's catch up to the kids," he said. "We can talk about it more tonight."

—

The conversation didn't go any better that evening. The kids were hyped up from the party and the sweets they'd collected and didn't fall asleep until after nine, delaying "honeymoon hour." By the time Dani and Doug settled down in the living room, they were both tired.

"Have you thought any more about Stanford?" Doug asked.

"Haven't thought about anything else all evening."

"And?"

"I haven't changed my mind. I don't want to move."

"You're just afraid of change, like I was afraid of the change a baby would bring. But look how well that's turned out."

Dani glared at him. "How dare you compare the two."

"I'm not saying the decision is the same. Just that both involve an adjustment to change."

"Don't you like teaching at Columbia?"

"I do. I've settled into it like an old comfortable shoe. Now, I want more. I want to be challenged, just like you are with every new case you take."

"There are plenty of law schools in the New York area. Apply to be dean at one of those."

"There aren't any openings at those. And other than Columbia, none have the prestige of Stanford."

It didn't matter to Dani that Doug was right. It didn't matter to her that he deserved a chance to advance. She just couldn't bear the thought of picking up her family and leaving everything that was familiar and safe. She took Doug's hand in her own and began stroking it. "Please, don't pursue this. I really want to stay here."

Doug pulled his hand away from hers. "You may get your wish. They may decide on someone else. But I'm going out there next week for an interview. It's already scheduled."

Dani couldn't believe he'd gone ahead before even discussing it with her. She stood up from the couch. "I'm tired. I'm going to sleep early." She turned and walked away without even finishing "honeymoon hour."

T hree weeks had passed since Dani had filed a writ of certiorari with the US Supreme Court. Each day she pounced on the mail as soon as it was delivered to her assistant, not waiting for Carol to go through it first. Today was no exception. As soon as the mail carrier arrived at their office, Dani grabbed the stack of envelopes. Sitting on top was a letter with the return address of the US Supreme Court. She handed the remaining mail to Carol, then retreated to her office. She sat down on her chair, still holding the letter in her hands, afraid to open it. If cert had been granted, that meant Osgood had time. Time for HIPP to continue its search for witnesses, time for HIPP to find evidence of Osgood's innocence.

After five minutes, she gathered up the courage to tear open the envelope. Dani's hands trembled as she stared at the single sheet of paper she held. *Certiorari denied.* Those were the only words she focused on. The US Supreme Court had refused to consider Osgood's appeal, and so the decision of the Supreme Court of Georgia was the final word. This man, with an IQ of 68, would be executed by the state. *It's so wrong, so very wrong.* One of the reasons behind exempting those with an intellectual disability from execution as a punishment stemmed from an understanding that those defendants had a reduced capacity to control impulses, and to learn from mistakes and experiences. In many respects, they were like children, and children certainly couldn't be executed, no matter how brutal their crimes. Dani didn't know with certainty that Jack Osgood hadn't murdered

Kelly Braden, but she was convinced that if he had, he hadn't known what he was doing. He certainly didn't seem capable of planning it.

She stood up from her chair and headed over to Tommy's desk, then sat down across from him. "The Supreme Court turned down Osgood's appeal."

Tommy frowned, then uncrossed his legs and sat up straight. "Damn. What now?"

"The state will schedule Osgood's execution again. We don't have much time. We've got to find Greg Johnson."

"Well, we're in luck there. I just located him ten minutes ago. Adam was right—he's living in Cambridge, just outside Boston. I was thinking of flying up there tomorrow. Want to come with me?"

Dani hesitated just a moment before answering, "I can't. Doug's away tonight and tomorrow. I don't want to be out of town while he's traveling."

"I didn't know law professors took business trips."

"It's not. He . . ." She took a deep breath. "He's interviewing for a job at Stanford Law."

"Are you serious?"

Dani just nodded.

"And if he gets it? You moving?"

"I don't want to."

Tommy leaned in toward Dani. "You're not talking about a separation, are you?"

"No. It won't come to that. Right now, he's just exploring the opportunity. Nothing's been offered."

"I'd hate for you to leave. We make a good team."

"I know." Dani stood up to leave. She held a finger to her lips and said, "Don't say anything to Bruce, okay?"

"Mum's the word."

———

Tommy waited to take the 4:00 p.m. shuttle up to Boston. No point in leaving earlier. Most likely, Greg Johnson was at work during the day. Tommy arrived at Logan airport at six, got a rental car, then drove into the city for dinner at the Parker House hotel. Its restaurant was his go-to anytime he found himself in Boston. He knew there were fancier places, maybe even those with better food, but he could never pass up the Parker House rolls. He didn't think he'd ever tasted rolls that could compare.

He finished dinner at 6:25 p.m., then retrieved his car and drove to Cambridge. With luck, Johnson would be home, and Tommy would be able to catch the last shuttle back to LaGuardia. He pulled up to the address. It was a sprawling single-family home on a tree-lined street. *Kid's got money,* Tommy thought.

He rang the bell and waited only moments before the door opened. Before him stood a middle-aged man, at least six feet two, dressed in a neatly pressed suit, with a tie loosened at the neck. All of Kelly's girlfriends had described him as handsome, but if that was once the case, his good looks had morphed into features that blended together in his bloated face.

"I'm not buying whatever you're selling."

"Are you Greg Johnson?"

"Yeah."

Tommy handed him his card, and Johnson glanced at it. "What's this about?"

"Kelly Braden's murder. My office is representing Jack Osgood."

The scowl on Johnson's face disappeared, replaced with a look of melancholy. "That's the son of a bitch who killed her, right?"

"He's the one who was convicted for it."

"What are you saying?"

"Can I come in and talk to you? It won't take too long."

Johnson hesitated, then opened the door fully. "I suppose it's okay." As Tommy stepped into the front hallway, with its stairs that swept around in a curve to the second floor, Johnson said, "You know, you should have called first. I'm not usually home this early. Just got back from a business trip."

"Oh, yeah? What do you do?"

"Senior VP for Atlas Insurance."

Tommy whistled. "Aren't they the biggest insurance company in the United States?"

"Second biggest."

"Do you travel a lot for them?"

"Used to. When I was working myself up the ranks. The whole East Coast was my territory. Now, just occasionally."

Tommy followed Johnson into the den, furnished with a dark-brown leather sofa and two leather club chairs, and wall-to-wall bookcases on two sides. When both were seated, Tommy said, "My colleague is trying to prove that Osgood didn't murder Kelly."

"Of course he's guilty."

"What makes you so certain?"

"Well, I . . . I . . . Didn't they find his bat? With her little cousin's blood on it?"

"Yeah. But Osgood said he'd lost it. Anyone could have found it and used it that night."

"Who else would kill her? The guy was weird."

"I'm not saying it wasn't him. We're just double-checking everything. And, you know, police always look at those closest to the victim first, so I've got to ask you some questions. I'm not trying to pin anything on you. I just need to rule you out."

"I was in my dorm room, fast asleep when it happened. My roommate saw me."

"Whitman?"

"That's right."

"You were friends with him from home, right?"

Johnson nodded. "We played high school football together."

"Tell me about you and Kelly."

"What's to tell? We were high school sweethearts. Then I went away to college, and frankly, it was going to end anyway. It seems silly now, just two years' difference in age, but back then, it felt huge."

"So, you were going to break up with her?"

"That's right."

"Some of her girlfriends said the opposite. That she planned to break it off with you."

Johnson laughed—a deep, hearty guffaw. "They're pulling your leg. Kelly was crazy for me. Visited me on campus every other weekend. I finally had to tell her it was too much, so she dropped it to once a month."

Was this true? Was Kelly's friend mistaken? Maybe Kelly hadn't wanted to admit that her boyfriend was pulling back from her. Still, Stacy had been her best friend. Tommy knew from his own daughters that they shared everything—good and bad—with their own best friends. There was something about Johnson that put Tommy off, something just a little too slick.

"The police records showed a call to you from the Hickses' phone the night she was murdered. Wasn't that from Kelly?"

"That's right."

"What did you two talk about?"

"Usual stuff—school, parents, mutual friends. I told the police all this back when it happened."

"She didn't tell you that night she wanted to break up?"

"You kidding? I told you, it was going to be the other way around. But I didn't tell her that night."

"How would you have felt if she ended it before you did?"

Johnson smirked. "Relieved."

"Whitman said he got back to the room sometime after three, and you were sound asleep."

"That's right."

"How long's the ride from the college back home?"

"Little more than an hour."

"So, if you woke up after Whitman fell asleep, you could have driven home and back before he woke up."

Johnson's face darkened. He started cracking his knuckles, not saying a word, then stood up. "I've been trying to help you, but it seems you just want to pin this on me. I loved Kelly once, and grieved when she died, and you can just go to hell." He stormed toward the front door and held it open for Tommy to leave.

Tommy left. There was nothing more he'd get from Greg Johnson.

———

As he flew back to New York, Tommy kept thinking about Tony Falcone, the missing handyman who'd worked at both the Braden and Hicks homes. He'd had no luck finding a trace of him, or anyone named Abigail Falcone in the right age range. Although Dani wanted him to be on the up-and-up, they weren't getting anywhere that way. He'd already tapped friends from his days at the FBI, and they hadn't come up with anything. Now, he had one last hope—his hacker contact. He didn't just hack into unsuspecting accounts. He used his computer skills for tracing people. Tommy didn't ask him too many questions about how he did it. All he cared about were results.

He wanted to find Falcone, find something that would tie him to Kelly's murder. Because so far, nothing he'd found said Jack Osgood hadn't committed the crime. That wouldn't matter to Dani. She hated the death penalty, hated its finality. Not him. If you took a person's life, you deserved to lose yours. Maybe he could see Dani's point of view that someone as slow as Osgood couldn't have understood what he was doing, and therefore shouldn't be executed, but that was as far as he'd go. If Osgood did it, he should stay behind bars for the rest of his life. Except that wasn't an option now. Either the state killed him for the crime, or they got him a new trial and raised enough reasonable doubt for an acquittal. He didn't like either of those choices. So, he hoped he'd find Falcone. Hoped that led to proving Osgood innocent.

———

Dani waited impatiently for the front door to open, and for Doug to walk in. The three-hour time difference between New York and California meant his plane wouldn't land at JFK until 8:30 p.m., eastern time. She glanced at her watch once more, as she'd done every five minutes for the last half hour—it was 9:35. His plane had landed on time, and she'd expected he'd be back already, but New York highways were always unpredictable. He'd told her little when he'd phoned from the San Jose airport—just that he'd fill her in when he returned.

She picked up the book she'd been trying to read, although her head wasn't in it. No matter how much she tried not to, all she could think about was Stanford University. Ten minutes later, she heard a car door slam, and moments after, the front door opened. She jumped off the couch and ran into Doug's arms. "I missed you." She was used to being the one who traveled, not Doug. Being home, with just the kids, had seemed out of kilter.

He wrapped his arms around her, tilted her head up, and kissed her. "Missed you, too."

"Hungry?"

"Nope. Bought something at the airport and ate on the plane."

After Doug hung up his coat, Dani took his hand and led him to the couch in the living room. There was a bottle of Chianti and two glasses on the cocktail table. She poured wine for both of them.

"So. Tell me everything."

Doug sighed deeply. He leaned into the couch and closed his eyes.

"You tired?" Dani asked.

He sat back up. "No. I just wasn't sure I wanted to get into it tonight. I thought maybe we could just cuddle."

"If it's bad news, I'd rather have it now."

"There's no news. It was just an interview."

"But you liked it?"

Doug took a deep breath. "Yes. I liked it very much. The new dean will have a great deal of autonomy in creating the vision for the law school moving forward."

"But you love teaching. Won't most of your time be spent on administrative tasks?"

"I'd still teach one class."

Dani turned away from Doug. How could she make him understand her deep fear of moving? It wasn't because she'd be leaving HIPP, although she loathed the thought of that. It wasn't because she'd leave her friends behind, although that, too, made her sad. It was Jonah. Her fears had always revolved around her son. Fears that had finally moved into the background, just a gentle buzz that reminded her to be extra cautious when it came to his welfare. Would he be able to make friends if they moved? Would they find a good school for him near San Jose? Once she obtained a new job for herself, would they find a sitter as kind and loving and reliable as Katie? Would the music community in Northern California recognize and laud Jonah's musical talent, his key to living a productive life? She could accept uncertainty for herself, but never for Jonah.

Her stomach felt tied in knots. "I don't want to move."

"I know," Doug said, and pulled her back into his body.

―――――

"How did it go with Greg Johnson?" Dani asked.

Tommy was sitting in her office, coffee cup in hand. He'd brought
Dani a cup as well, along with a blueberry muffin from the corner gro-
cer. There were hundreds of small shops in Manhattan that stocked
fresh fruits and vegetables, along with essentials and freshly baked
goods. Practically one every few blocks. But both Dani and Tommy
knew the one on their corner of the East Village was the best. Now
that Dani was jogging regularly, she allowed herself to indulge in one
muffin or doughnut every morning. It just seemed to make the coffee
taste that much better.

"Hard to tell. He claimed he was about to break it off with Kelly,
not the other way around, and got huffy when he realized I was
honing in on him. Maybe that means he didn't do it, or maybe he's
a good actor."

"Did you get anything helpful from him?"

Tommy shook his head. "If he killed Kelly, it's going to be damn
hard to prove. Unless we can shake Whitman's alibi. Even then, won't
we need more?"

"We need new evidence to get a new trial. If Whitman lied, and
fesses up now, that might be enough. And then—we don't have to
prove Johnson killed her. Reasonable doubt. That's all we need. It's
time to talk to Derek Whitman."

"Okay. I'm available. Also, I'm pretty sure I found Lisa Hicks."

"In Houston?"

Tommy nodded. "There are two federal public defenders out of
the Houston office named Lisa—Lisa Albans and Lisa Montague. I
cross-referenced both last names with graduates of Texas law schools
around the time Lisa should have graduated, and found Lisa Hicks
and an Ethan Montague at the University of Texas Law School. I'm
pretty sure that must be whom she married. I've gotten an address for
Lisa Montague in a suburb of Houston."

"Good. We can interview them both. First Whitman, then Hicks.
We'll leave tomorrow morning."

19

1999

He'd been so good about it. He'd known, after Osgood took the fall, that he needed to stop. It had been so damn hard. He understood what addicts must feel, trying to get off the booze or drugs. It was a need, deep and strong, one that wrapped itself around his insides and had to burst free. But he'd quelled it. For five years. Only lately, now that his life was settled, had it begun waking him up at night, covered in sweat, desperate to re-create that feeling, the one at the end, when he'd taken the girls' lives, when he'd felt suffused with power.

He didn't know where this need came from. He hadn't grown up pulling the wings off insects, graduating to torturing dogs and cats—the kinds of behavior he'd read about in serial killers. No, he'd cared about other people, other lives. Until Kelly, until that accident, he'd never thought himself capable of murder. But it happened with Kelly, and his life changed. His needs changed.

I can't give in, he thought. *It's wrong. So very wrong.*

Derek Whitman hadn't gone far afield from the town where he'd grown up. He still lived in Georgia, now in Columbus. Before heading to Whitman's home, Dani wanted to visit Osgood. She hadn't yet told him about the Supreme Court decision and thought it better to do so in person.

She and Tommy arrived at the prison just after 2:00 p.m. They didn't have to wait long for Osgood to be brought into the attorney visiting room. As always, he was led into the room with his hands cuffed and his legs shackled, then had the chains attached to a ring in the floor. After he was settled, the guard who'd accompanied him left the room, remaining just on the other side of the door.

Dani smiled at Osgood, then asked how he was doing.

"Okay, I suppose."

"Since your mother has passed away, I wondered if you have any other relatives?"

Osgood looked at her blankly.

"Is your father alive?"

"I don't know. I haven't seen him in a really long time."

"When was the last time?"

"Maybe when I was ten."

"Is there anyone else—maybe an aunt or uncle? A grandparent?"

"I don't think so."

Dani wished that weren't the case. With an execution looming, she thought it might be helpful for him to have someone familiar to comfort him. She wondered what had happened to his childhood home. Someone must have inherited it after Osgood's mother passed away. She made a mental note to check it out.

"Jack," she said, "I have some bad news. The Supreme Court turned down your appeal."

Osgood looked straight at Dani. "What does that mean?"

"It means, unless we can find some new evidence, the state is going to execute you."

"Execute?"

"Kill you."

Osgood buried his face in his oversize hands, and a loud wail filled the room. Dani waited several minutes before she placed her hands on his. "We're not stopping, Jack. We're going to keep looking for the real killer."

Osgood looked up. With the backs of his hands, he wiped the tears from his cheeks. "Do you know who he is?"

Dani shook her head. "I know this happened a very long time ago, but I want you to think hard. Try to remember anything you can about the night Kelly disappeared."

"When did she disappear?"

"Think back to when the police first came to question you. It was during the night before that, that Kelly was taken."

"Okay." Osgood seemed lost in thought as he first stared up at the ceiling, then down at the floor. "There wasn't anything special that night. Mama and I watched television, I suppose. That's what we always did, then went to sleep."

"Do you remember where your bat was when you went to bed?"

"No. Mama sometimes got angry at me because I didn't put it away. The policeman asked me for it when he came to the house, and that's when I saw it wasn't in my room."

"When had you used it last?"

Osgood shrugged. "I don't know. I liked to watch the Little League games down at the field. I think there'd been one the day before. Maybe I left it there?"

"Are you sure you didn't take it home with you?"

"Sometimes I'd forget it there, at the field, then Mama would get mad at me. I tried to remember to keep it with me."

"If you brought it home, where would you have put it?"

"I have a special box for it in my room."

"So, that's where it should have been?"

"Yes, unless . . ."

"Unless?"

"Sometimes after I watched a ball game, I liked to hit balls against the side of my house. Mama sometimes got mad at me because I'd leave the bat outside. Then it would rain, and that wouldn't be good for the wood."

"Could you have left it outside that night?"

"I don't know. Maybe."

Dani glanced at Tommy, busy taking notes. She knew that, without her asking, he'd dig through records to see if a Little League game had been played at the Stone Ridge ball field that afternoon before Kelly was abducted.

"The police also said there was a ladder in your garage," Dani continued.

"Mama used it when the dust in the corners of the ceilings got bad."

"What else was it used for?"

"Sometimes when a lightbulb needed changing."

"Would you change the bulb?"

Osgood blanched. "Not me. Never. I'm afraid of ladders."

"What do you mean?" Tommy asked.

"I mean, I won't go up on one. Not since I was eight years old, and I was helping my daddy clean out the gutters. I fell off and broke my arm. It hurt really bad. Mama and Daddy took me to the hospital, and they put a cast on. I would never go on a ladder since then."

Dani could feel her pulse quicken. "Jack, did you ever tell this to Mr. Bennington, when you were on trial?"

"I don't think so. Should I have?"

"Whoever killed Kelly climbed up a ladder to her room."

"Well, I told you it wasn't me. I told Mr. Bennington, too."

Under the table, Dani crossed her fingers as she asked the next question. "Did anyone other than your mother know you were afraid to climb a ladder?"

"Everyone knew."

"What do you mean, everyone?"

"Mr. Barnes, across the street. If Mama needed something too high up, then she asked him to get it. Mama told him why I couldn't."

"Anyone else?"

"Mr. Bennett, at the store. He knew I wouldn't go on a ladder to reach the high shelves."

Dani held back a smile. This wasn't enough to get a new trial. But it was enough to fully convince her that Osgood was innocent. She glanced over at Tommy and saw he was sitting back in his seat with a big grin on his face.

"Feel better?" Dani asked Tommy as soon as they got in their rental car.

"Much. Now I can go full steam without a guilty conscience."

"You weren't working it hard before?"

"I was. Just felt bad about it. Now, I don't. I can't believe it never came out at his trial that he was afraid of ladders."

"Maybe his mother was so stressed by his arrest that she wasn't thinking straight. Or maybe she did tell Bennington, and he dismissed it."

They chatted comfortably on the drive to Columbus. Dani had become so used to working with Tommy that he was like a member of her family. How could she leave him for California? Even if she found a similar job there, it wouldn't be the same with anyone else.

They pulled into Columbus just before 6:00 p.m. and headed to the Holiday Inn on Bear Lane, not far from the Peachtree Mall. They checked in, then headed over to Ruby Tuesday at the mall for dinner. When they finished, they drove to Whitman's home, arriving just after 8:00 p.m. He lived in a development of midsize homes that looked like they'd been built recently. Tommy parked in the driveway, then together they walked up to the door and rang the bell. When the door opened, a tall, muscular man with sandy-brown hair thinning at the top stood before them.

"Derek Whitman?" asked Tommy.

"That's me."

Dani handed him her card. "Do you mind if we ask you a few questions? It's about the murder of Kelly Braden."

"That's a name from the past. Why are you dredging it up now?"

"We're representing Jack Osgood, who was convicted of her murder."

Whitman tilted his head. "Isn't he dead yet?"

"No. His execution is scheduled to take place soon. Look, can we come in? We won't take up much of your time."

He held the door open for them, and they walked inside, then followed him into the living room. An attractive woman with short, blunt-cut auburn hair came into the room and asked, "Who is this, Derek?"

"They're looking into the murder of a girl I knew back in high school." He looked down at the business card in his hand. "This is Ms. Trumball, and this is . . ." He pointed at Tommy.

Tommy held out his hand to the woman. "Tom Noorland."

She shook his hand as she said, "Nice to meet you. I'm Maisie Whitman, Derek's wife."

"You can join us, honey. Kids okay?"

"They're in our room, watching TV." She took a seat next to her husband.

Dani let Tommy take the lead. Interrogations were his forte.

"I'll get right to the point, Mr. Whitman—"

"Call me Derek."

"Whenever a murder occurs, people closest to the victims are always investigated. One of those was Greg Johnson, Kelly's boyfriend. You gave him an alibi for that night."

"That's right. I was at a party, came in around three a.m., and he was sound asleep. I woke up at six thirty to take a leak, and he was still in his bed."

"Could you have been mistaken about the time you got back to your room?"

Whitman's nostrils flared, and he stuck out his chest. "Absolutely not."

"Greg was your friend even before college, wasn't he?"

Whitman nodded.

"And you knew Kelly as well, right?"

"Yes."

"Did Greg ever talk to you about Kelly?"

"Of course."

"How did he feel about his relationship with her?"

"It was cooling off. I think he wanted to be freer once he got to college."

"Did he tell her that?"

"Actually, he didn't get a chance to. She called him the night she died. Said she thought it better if they broke up."

"He told you that?"

"Yes. She called right before I left for the party."

"How did he feel about that?"

"Relieved."

"Are you certain?"

"Look, they were never going to make it as a couple anyway. He was the big football star in high school, and she was the pretty cheerleader who was gaga over him, but he treated her miserably. She deserved better, and everyone knew that. It just took her time to realize it."

Dani had been watching Whitman, evaluating his body language, trying to decide if she believed him. His last statement lined up with what Kelly's friends had said. And he was able to confirm Tommy's speculation that Kelly broke up with Johnson the night she died. Perhaps Johnson wasn't as relieved as he'd pretended to be. Someone who was used to the spotlight might not handle rejection well. Still, he had Whitman's alibi.

"Where was the party?" Dani asked.

"Alpha Tau Omega."

"Were you a member?"

"No. I went with some friends."

"Who?"

Whitman scrunched up his face. "You can't really expect me to remember that. It was more than twenty years ago."

"Did you leave with them?"

"Probably."

Dani stared hard at Whitman. "The time you got back to your dorm may mean the difference between freedom and death for Jack Osgood. If you can't remember their names, then I'll ask Tommy to check who was president of the fraternity back then, and he'll reach out to every single member to see if anyone remembers you leaving and what time it was."

Whitman reached behind him and began to rub the back of his neck. "Look, Greg was my best friend then."

"Are you saying you lied?"

He dropped his hand from his neck and gripped his leg, his eyes fixed on the carpet between his feet.

"Honey?" his wife said in a small voice.

He sighed and shook his head slowly, then finally met Dani's eyes. "It's true that he was asleep when I got back," he said very quietly. "But it was closer to one, not three. And I didn't wake up at six thirty. It was closer to eight."

Dani let the silence in the room linger for a while. Finally, she said, "You need to sign an affidavit with the real time."

"Hell, no. I'm not sticking my neck out for a perjury charge."

"Has the statute of limitations passed?" Tommy asked Dani.

Dani shook her head. "There isn't one in Georgia, not in connection with a capital offense. But you didn't testify under oath at the trial. At most, it would be obstruction of justice, and the time to charge you with that has long passed." Dani paused. "I am concerned, though, about the prosecution tearing apart your new statement because of the change. Spare us the effort of tracking down your friends, and tell me who else knows when you returned."

Whitman dropped his chin to his chest and slumped down on the sofa.

"We *will* find out on our own," Dani said. "But if you don't tell us now, it makes me think you have something to hide."

Without lifting his head, Whitman answered, "Russ. He roomed with us, too. We had a two-bedroom suite. Greg and I shared one bedroom, and Russ and Aaron the other."

"So they both saw you when you came back?"

"Not Aaron. He didn't hang out with us. But Russ, Greg, and I were all friends back in Stone Ridge. We all played football together, along with Kelly's brother, and all went to college together. Only Adam didn't want to room with us. He wanted to"—Whitman made air quotes with his hands—"broaden his experience. I went to the party with Russ, and we came back together."

"What's his full name?"

"Jessup. Russell Jessup."

"Know where he is now?"

"Yeah. We've stayed friends."

"So, we have an understanding. You're going to give us an affidavit, right?"

Whitman glanced over at his wife, sitting stiffly in her seat, then back at Dani and nodded, without saying a word.

Piece by piece, Dani thought. They had just found another piece to fit in the puzzle.

Early the next morning, Dani and Tommy drove to Atlanta, where Russ Jessup lived. The door was answered by his wife, yet another willowy blonde, with glacial-blue eyes. Dani twirled a strand of her own dark-brown curls and wondered if every woman in the South had blonde hair.

She invited them in, then called out to Russ that he had company. "Excuse me," she said as she left them standing in the foyer. "I have to finish making the kids' lunch."

Moments later, Jessup walked down the stairs. Dani introduced herself and Tommy.

"You're in luck," he said. "Tomorrow I head out for a three-day business trip."

"Oh? What do you do?"

"I work for a management-consulting firm, analyzing efficiency metrics."

Dani explained why they were there.

"That was a long time ago," Jessup said.

"True. But you knew Kelly. Her death must have had an impact on you. Most people, when something traumatic happens, they remember a lot of details."

"I guess."

"Derek has admitted to us that he lied to the police about the time he got home from a party, that he'd gotten back much earlier. Do you remember what time that was?"

Jessup's face reddened. "Are we in trouble?"

"No. Not if you're truthful now."

"Greg knew the police would question him. I mean, he was her boyfriend. And she'd broken up with him. Derek was just doing him a favor. We didn't think it was a big deal, since Greg would never have hurt Kelly."

"Well, that little deal contributed to a man spending twenty-two years on death row. A man who's probably innocent. Do you remember what time you really got back to the dorm room?"

"It was around one."

"And will you give us an affidavit to that effect?"

"Yes." Jessup took a deep breath. "It's the least I can do."

⁓

Dani finished up with Jessup, and then she and Tommy headed to the Atlanta airport for a flight to Texas. They knew exactly where Lisa Montague worked, and so once they landed, they took a taxi to her office. When they arrived, they were told she was in court.

"Do you expect her back today?" Dani asked the receptionist.

"Probably. She usually stops in the office before heading for home."

"Then we'll wait."

Dani didn't expect to get much from Lisa. She had only been five years old when the abduction took place and had received a head injury in the process. Still, she was the star witness for the prosecution, identifying Jack Osgood as the man who stood over her bed and struck her with the bat. They had to at least talk to her.

At 5:15 p.m., a striking young woman entered the office, dressed in a tailored navy suit with an emerald-green silk blouse that matched the color of her eyes. Her blonde, pixie-cut hair perfectly framed her heart-shaped face. As she approached the receptionist's desk, the woman sitting behind it said something to her, then pointed at Dani and Tommy. She turned and walked back toward them.

"I'm Lisa Montague. I understand you're waiting for me."

Dani and Tommy stood, then Dani handed Lisa her business card. The look of recognition on her face told Dani that her parents or cousin had forewarned her.

"Come on into my office," Lisa said. "We can talk there."

Lisa's office was much like Dani's—small, without a window, and furnished simply.

"You're here to talk about Jack Osgood," Lisa said when they were all seated.

"That's right."

Lisa leaned back in her chair, ran her fingers through her hair, then sighed deeply. "I suppose you find it surprising that I work the defense side."

Dani smiled. "I do. I would have thought you'd want to put away criminals."

Lisa took in a deep breath, then bent her head downward. "It's my form of penance."

"For what?"

She looked back up at Dani and Tommy and spoke softly. "I was so young when it happened. I loved my cousin very much. She was like a big sister to me."

"Did you grow up feeling responsible for what happened?"

"Not for Kelly's death. No. I felt responsible for Jack's conviction."

Every muscle in Dani's body tensed as she held her breath.

"For so long, I was certain it was him standing over my bed, and then—" She stopped, took another deep breath. "One night, when I was about ten, I woke up from a nightmare in the middle of the night. My father came into the room to comfort me. There was a full moon that night, just like when Kelly was taken. As he stood by Kelly's bed, the shadow he cast from the moon's light made him look like a giant. I realized at that moment that the only reason I thought it was Jack was because of his size. He was the biggest man I'd ever seen."

Dani held back a smile. When she'd returned to the Hickses' home earlier, she'd checked whether there were any trees in the backyard that would block the moon. She knew that the subtle light from its reflection could create a shadow that would enhance a person's size. "Did you tell your parents?"

Lisa shook her head. She wrapped her arms around her body, and Dani saw tears in the corners of her eyes. "At first, I was afraid."

"Afraid of what?"

"I was still a child. I thought maybe they would put me in jail for saying something untrue at the trial."

"But you grew up. You went to law school. You must have known he was still alive, waiting to be executed."

Now, the tears flowed freely down Lisa's cheeks. "What could I have done? I can't say it was Jack or wasn't him. I can only say I don't know who was in my room. My aunt and uncle are still devastated by their loss. I thought, how could I reopen their wounds when maybe it was Jack? They still had a bat that belonged to him, with my blood on it."

"Anyone could have picked up that bat."

"I know," Lisa said, her voice barely above a whisper.

⁀

Dani and Tommy flew back to New York with an affidavit from Lisa Montague. Dani now had to make a decision—file a motion right away for a new hearing, or wait. Under Georgia law, she'd have only one bite at the apple. She had Whitman's affidavit that he'd lied about the time he returned to his dorm room, and Johnson had lied about Kelly breaking up with him. Without more evidence pointing to

Johnson as the killer, she knew the judge wouldn't give those statements much weight. Lisa's recanting of her childhood identification of Jack Osgood as the man who hit her with his bat was significant, though. Was that enough? Even without more, she'd go ahead with a motion if it meant his execution would be stayed, but that wasn't automatic under Georgia law. If a stay were granted, it would give them time to keep searching for more clues, more pieces of the puzzle. If not, and the court ruled against her motion for a new trial, she would have thrown away Osgood's chance at freedom—at life.

It was past seven when they landed at LaGuardia airport, so Dani drove straight home. Ruth was already asleep by the time she got there, but Dani was able to spend some time helping Jonah with his homework. By 9:00 p.m., "honeymoon hour," she was wiped out. She lay cuddled next to Doug on the living-room couch and described to him her quandary.

"What do you think?" she asked him. "File or wait?"

"Has the date been set for his execution?"

"I just got word today—three weeks from yesterday."

"Then I don't see that you have a choice. If you wait until closer to the set date, and the judge doesn't issue a stay, then it won't matter if you find more evidence. It'll be too late."

"But if I go in now, with just what I have, I don't know that it's enough."

"It's a tough decision."

"What's the right decision?"

"There's no crystal ball. Trust your gut. It's always worked for you before."

On the drive to work the next morning, Dani found herself again bemoaning that she no longer had an associate attorney working with her on cases. For many years, she'd worked with Melanie Quinn Stanton, but now Melanie was seasoned enough to handle cases on her own. Dani missed having another attorney to bounce around legal strategy. Doug was helpful, in his way, but teaching law was far removed from practicing it. Especially in life-and-death situations.

She arrived at HIPP's office with two cups of coffee and two blueberry muffins in hand. She dropped her coat off in her own office, then made her way to Melanie's. As usual, Melanie was dressed in a stylish suit, with a turquoise blouse that deepened the blue of her eyes. Melanie always looked like she'd stepped off a model's runway—with her slim figure, beautiful features, and silky butterscotch-colored hair.

"Brought you a present," Dani said as she handed Melanie one coffee and a muffin.

Melanie smiled. "What did I do to deserve this?"

"Nothing yet. But I need to pick your brain, so I'm bribing you in advance."

Melanie took a sip of the coffee. "Go ahead. Pick."

Dani filled her in on the Osgood case, then finished with the dilemma she faced.

"Ugh. Tough choice," Melanie said when Dani finished. "But I don't think you can afford to wait."

Dani nodded. It was the conclusion she'd reached, but it was good to have confirmation from someone she trusted. She walked over to Bruce Kantor's office. "I need to hire a forensic dentist for the Osgood case."

Bruce frowned, then began tapping the pencil in his hand onto his desk. "How much will that set us back?"

"Around eight thousand dollars, including travel costs."

"We've already spent money on a forensic psychologist, and you and Tommy have racked up the travel expenses. Is it necessary?"

"It's essential."

He paused, then asked, "Do you truly believe he's innocent, or are you just trying to avoid the death penalty?"

"He's innocent. I'm certain."

Bruce shook his head slowly. "I don't know where we're going to get the money, but go ahead. I'll find it somewhere."

Dani returned to her office and began the task of preparing documents to request a hearing for a new trial.

CHAPTER
22

1999

He promised himself this would be the last time. It didn't matter that he'd promised himself that once before. He wanted to believe it was true, that he would only murder one last time and get it out of his system forever. He'd wait until he came across someone who reminded him of Kelly. He traveled enough with his job that it could be anywhere. It didn't need to be a college town.

It took less than two weeks to find the right person.

He was on a business trip in Florida, traveling from Jacksonville to Tallahassee, when he stopped in a drugstore to pick up some Advil. She was in the same aisle. Long blonde hair, pretty, young. She looked up at him and smiled as he passed her, and he saw eyes almost as blue as Kelly's. He quickly paid for his purchase, then waited in his car for her to leave. He thought she looked too young to drive, and he was right. He followed her as she walked to her home three blocks away, then waited to see if a light went on in an upstairs bedroom. When it did, he knew he had his next target.

He drove three towns away and purchased a folding ladder, then returned to her block at 3:00 a.m. Her window was closed, but he had the tools he needed to open it. Quietly, he slipped inside. He took out his pocket flashlight and found her bed. For a while, he just stared at her, marveling at how pretty she was. He kept telling himself to leave, to climb back outside, pretend he'd never been there. He knew what he was going to do was despicable. But his excitement had already started to build. *Just this last time,* he thought as he went through his ritual—first waking her, then choking her, then carefully carrying her out of the house to his car.

Later, after it was over—after he'd experienced the thrill that was unlike anything else he'd ever felt, after he was suffused with the knowledge of his own power and had returned to his motel room—he broke down and cried. *I have to stop. I can't keep doing this. Never again. Never again.*

23

Dani was back in Lawrenceville, Georgia, in Judge Beiles's court-room. Once again, Gary Luckman was seated at the prosecutor's table. This hearing was without a jury. Only Judge Beiles would deter-mine whether Osgood was entitled to a new trial. When the bailiff announced the judge's arrival, everyone in the courtroom stood until she was seated on the bench.

"Everyone ready?" the judge asked.

Both Dani and Luckman answered, "Ready."

"Okay, Ms. Trumball. This is your motion. Call your first witness."

Dani called Lisa Montague. The bailiff held the door open for her, and she strode inside, then took her seat in the witness box. After she was sworn in and had given her name and address to the court reporter, Dani asked, "Would you state your maiden name?"

"Lisa Hicks."

"And are you the same Lisa Hicks that the defendant, Jack Osgood, allegedly struck with a bat the night your cousin was abducted?"

"I am."

"Tell us what you remember from that night."

"I remember everything up until I was hit. I don't actually remember being struck."

"That was twenty-two years ago, and you were only five years old at the time. How could you remember that night?"

"It was the worst thing that had ever happened in my life. And as soon as I woke from my injury, I was asked about it—over and over.

It was imprinted in my memory. I don't think I'll ever forget it. I can tell you today the television shows we watched before I went to bed. I can tell you the color of the nail polish Kelly had put on my fingers. What we ate for dinner."

"Do you remember telling your mother that it was Jack Osgood who'd been in your room?"

"I told my mother that I thought it could have been Jack. I didn't say it with certainty."

"You testified at Jack's trial, didn't you?"

"Yes."

"At his trial, you said it was Jack Osgood, right? Not that it could have been him."

"I did."

"I'd like you to think back to that night, and tell the court exactly what you remember."

"I'd gone to sleep before Kelly. At some point, I was awakened by some noise, and I saw a man next to Kelly's bed. He was holding Kelly in his arms. I cried out, and he laid Kelly back on her bed, then turned toward me and took a step closer. I don't remember anything after that."

"The man who turned toward you, do you still say that it was Jack Osgood?"

"I don't know who it was."

Dani let that statement hang over the courtroom before she asked the next question. "Are you saying that you lied at Mr. Osgood's trial when you identified him as the man in your room?"

"No. Back then, I believed it was him. But years later, I realized that what I'd seen was someone big, very big, and Jack was the biggest person I knew. At least, I thought I'd seen someone very big."

"What do you mean?"

"I'd seen the shadow cast by the moonlight streaming through the window, and it hit me years later that a shadow could make someone appear bigger than he was."

"Just to be clear, are you now recanting your testimony that you saw Jack Osgood in your bedroom that night?"

"Yes. I am."

"Thank you, Ms. Montague. I have no further questions."

Luckman stood up and walked toward the witness. "I have just one question. Can you say right now that it *wasn't* Jack Osgood in your bedroom?"

Lisa shook her head. "I can only say that I don't know who it was."

"So, it could have been the defendant, right?"

"Yes, that's possible."

"Thank you. You can step down now."

Dani next called Captain Ed Cannon. She knew this was risky. She'd subpoenaed Cannon but hadn't spoken to him, and she'd learned from Tommy that he was firm in his belief that Osgood was guilty. Still, she had just a few questions to ask him. He walked into the courtroom, dressed in his captain's uniform, and took his seat. "Captain Cannon, were you involved in the investigation of Kelly Braden's murder?"

His intense eyes bore into Dani as though she were his mortal enemy. "I was," he answered, his voice clipped.

"When the defendant's bat turned up, traces of Lisa Hick's blood were found on it, right?"

"That's correct."

"Were any fingerprints found on the bat?"

"No, the defendant wiped it clean. Except for the blood. There were still traces on the bat."

This was a hearing before the judge, not a jury trial. If it had been the latter, she would have objected to his reference to the defendant. Whether Osgood was the one to wipe the bat clean was a conclusion for the jury to determine. If she got a new trial for Osgood, she'd have to be on her toes with this witness. He was already showing that he'd be prickly.

"Thank you." As Dani started to return to the defense table, Luckman announced he had no questions for Cannon.

"I call Dr. David Bagley," Dani said. Bagley headed to the witness chair with long strides. The navy suit he wore looked custom-tailored and fit his slim frame perfectly. The deep blue served as a striking contrast to his full head of wavy, silver hair and goatee. He was sworn in, then gave his name and address to the court reporter.

"What is your profession, Dr. Bagley?"

"I am a licensed dentist, and a professor at New York University College of Dentistry. I am also a forensic odontologist."

"What is a forensic odontologist?"

"It's the forensic science that applies dental science to identify unknown human remains, and to analyze bite marks that occur during the commission of a serious crime, such as rape or murder."

"What kind of training did you receive to be a forensic odontologist?"

"First, I received my DDS from Columbia University College of Dental Medicine. After ten years of practice, I received training from the New York Society of Forensic Dentistry as well as the American Board of Forensic Odontology."

"As a result of that training, have you been called upon to identify human remains?"

"I have."

"In what circumstances?"

"I was utilized to identify remains from the September 11, 2001, attacks on the World Trade Center, as well as several plane crashes."

"Have you ever testified in a criminal trial about bite marks on a victim?"

"I have, yes, many times."

"Please describe how you would go about analyzing a bite mark on a deceased victim."

"First, the mark is excised from the body, and then photographs of the mark are enlarged to life-size. When a suspect is identified, a model of his bite mark is taken, and that model is compared to the photographs. The American Board of Forensic Odontology, or ABFO, has created guidelines to use for the comparison, including a scoring system."

"Did you examine the model of Mr. Osgood's teeth and the photographs of the victim's bite mark that were introduced at his trial?"

"I did."

Luckman stood up. "Your Honor, it seems that Ms. Trumball is bringing up an issue from the defendant's trial that was already fully addressed. A forensic dentist testified on his behalf, and the jury heard him. The purpose of this hearing is to determine whether there is some new evidence, not relitigate old evidence."

Dani turned to the judge. "This witness is going to testify as to facts that were unavailable at the time of the defendant's trial. I'm merely laying the groundwork here."

"I'll give you a little latitude," the judge ruled, "but I expect you to move on quickly from the past."

"Thank you." Dani turned back to the witness. "Dr. Bagley, at Mr. Osgood's trial, the state's forensic odontologist testified that it was scientifically conclusive that Jack Osgood bit Kelly Braden. Did you reach the same conclusion?"

"I did not, nor could any other forensic odontologist."

"Why is that?"

"Because no forensic odontologist can attribute a bite mark to an individual with any accuracy. The little scientific research that's been done has all been subsequent to Mr. Osgood's trial, and it's shown bite-mark analysis to be junk science."

"Can you explain?"

"There are two assumptions in bite-mark analysis. The first is that human teeth are as unique as DNA. The second is that this unique print can be recorded on human skin. Neither assumption has ever been proven scientifically."

"On what do you base that statement?"

"In 2009, The National Academy of Sciences was commissioned by Congress to report on the state of forensic science in the courtroom. It found there was no evidence of a scientific basis for identifying one individual and excluding all others based upon bite-mark matching."

"Have there been any studies that have proven the reverse? That those two assumptions are false?"

"In fact, yes. An extensive study was undertaken by a group of professors at the University at Buffalo School of Dental Medicine over the last decade. They examined more than one thousand human dentitions and studied hundreds of bite marks in cadavers. Using computer analysis and applied statistics, they attempted to match the bite marks to the correct dental impressions. The results showed that a single bite mark could match numerous individuals, thus creating a high likelihood of false positives. They also found that no two bite marks from the same set of teeth were the same."

"Is there any controversy over the source of marks on human skin?"

"Yes. With any bite-mark analysis, a mark must first be identified as a bite mark, and then that the mark came from human teeth. A test given by the ABFO itself, not too long ago, presented to its members a series of photos of marks in human skin. There was considerable disagreement, including among the most experienced of its members, as to whether the marks depicted were bite marks and whether they came from humans or animals. Of the one hundred cases looked at by thirty-nine certified bite-mark analysts, they reached the same conclusion only four times."

"Are there others, to your knowledge, who consider bite-mark analysis to be junk science?"

"Yes. Many dentists who previously testified in criminal trials about a bite mark are now recanting their testimony. Just last year, a high-ranking member of the White House Office of Science and Technology Policy called for the end of bite-mark evidence in criminal trials because it can't stand up to scientific scrutiny. And a few months ago, the Texas Forensic Science Commission, which is made up of scientists, forensic dentists, and law-enforcement authorities, voted to recommend a ban on bite-mark analysis until there is scientific research to support such testimony. Of course, it's only a recommendation, and not binding on courts, but it is expected to have a significant impact on its admissibility."

"Thank you, Dr. Bagley. I have no further questions."

Luckman stood up and walked to the witness. "Dr. Bagley, would you agree that the ABFO is the primary organization for training and setting standards in the field of forensic odontology?"

"I would."

"And are you a member of the ABFO?"

"I used to be. Not any longer."

"Weren't you asked to leave?"

"Yes. Because I didn't agree with them."

"Wouldn't you characterize yourself as an outlier?"

"No."

"But doesn't the ABFO still stand behind bite-mark analysis as an effective means of identifying perpetrators of a crime where there is evidence of a bite mark?"

"They do. But I would say they are the ones who are outliers, in that their blind insistence is contrary to the scientific evidence."

"Yet, don't most courts in the United States continue to accept testimony concerning bite marks?"

"I expect that to change, given the recommendation of the Texas Forensic Science Commission."

"Please answer my question. Do most courts today accept testimony about bite marks?"

"As far as I know, yes."

"Thank you. That's all I have for you."

Dani stood. "I have no other witnesses, Your Honor. The defense rests."

"Mr. Luckman?" Judge Beiles asked.

"I call Dr. Michael Forbes." A small man entered the courtroom, also dressed neatly in a suit and tie, with black-framed glasses worn across his narrowly set eyes. The court reporter took his oath, and he gave her his name and address.

"Please state your background."

"I received my DDS from Ohio State University College of Dentistry, have been trained in forensic odontology, and have been president of the American Board of Forensic Odontology for the past five years."

"Dr. Forbes, there has been testimony that bite-mark analysis is 'junk science.' Do you agree?"

"Absolutely not. Admittedly, there have been some errors, but by and large, those come about when practitioners try to find a match when there's insufficient detail in the bite mark. We've instituted rigorous standards to be followed, and when they are, a competent odontologist can, where there's enough information in the bite mark, match it to a set of teeth."

"Yet, isn't it true that the ABFO's own study found a great deal of disagreement?"

"The reports have exaggerated our disagreement. Again, with a detailed bite mark, matches can be accurately made."

"What about the report of the Texas Forensic Science Commission?"

GARY PUBLIC LIBRARY

"It's just a recommendation. Courts, even Texas courts, aren't bound to follow it."

"Thank you." Luckman turned toward Dani. "Your witness."

Dani approached Dr. Forbes. "Would you agree that DNA evidence is scientifically proven to be accurate?"

"Yes, it's been proven to be for many years now."

"Are you aware of any instances in which a conviction based on bite-mark analysis was overturned when DNA subsequently exonerated the prisoner?"

"I am. It's occurred a few times."

"Would you be surprised if I told you it was more than twenty-five times?"

"No."

"Would it surprise you that in one of those cases, the odontologist testified that the chance of someone else making that mark was four point one billion to one? Or that in another case, the expert said that the defendant's teeth matched the bite mark to a reasonable degree of scientific certainty? And in another case, that the chances were a million to one that someone else made the bite mark? And that in each of those cases, the expert was proven wrong by DNA?"

"When that happens, invariably it was because the odontologist wasn't sufficiently trained, or wasn't diligent enough. We at the ABFO work hard to ensure those people understand their mistakes and correct them."

"Do you believe that everyone's teeth are unique?"

"I do."

"What scientific tests can you point to that support that notion?"

"Through the experience of a body of analysis."

"Subjective analysis, right?"

"I suppose."

"Thank you. You can step down now."

GARY PUBLIC LIBRARY

As he left the courtroom, Luckman said, "I have no more witnesses, Your Honor."

"Okay. Let's take a break for lunch now, and I'll hear closing arguments at two thirty."

In the past, when Dani was on trial or arguing an appeal, she had a junior associate with her. Now, she was alone. She left the courthouse and wandered down the streets looking for a place to grab a bite. She hated eating by herself, but she had no choice. On the second block, she spotted an inviting café and went inside. A table for two by the window was empty, and she grabbed it, then pulled out her phone and began scrolling through her e-mails and texts. There were two texts from Tommy, both asking her to call him as soon as she could. She was about to dial his number when the waitress came over with a menu. Dani thanked her, then called Tommy.

"What's up?" she asked when he answered.

"I have a lead on Tony Falcone."

Dani brightened. "Where is he?"

"North Carolina. And listen, if I have the right guy, he just got out of jail three years ago for raping a young woman."

"Are you serious?"

"Yep. He was convicted eighteen years ago and sentenced to fifteen to twenty."

"How come no one was able to find him before this?"

"Because he went by different names. His real name is Axel Bonetti, but he's gone by three or four different names. Maybe more, but that's all I've found."

"How did you track him down?"

There was a hesitation on the phone before Tommy answered, "Don't ask how. I just did."

Dani knew she'd never change Tommy. Despite his years with the FBI—or maybe because of that—he was a risk-taker, doing whatever it took to get what he needed, even if the methods were sometimes questionable. She'd tried to pull him back over and over, to no avail. Still, perhaps she was complicit, since she never hesitated to use the information he gave her.

"Are you heading out there?"

"Yeah. This afternoon. I hope to see him tonight."

After she hung up, she tried to tamp down the excitement bubbling up in her. Tony Falcone—or Axel Bonetti, or whatever he was called—had been a person of interest from back when the crime occurred. To learn that he'd been imprisoned since then—and for a violent crime—intensified that interest. Dani wanted to believe that Tommy would find something incriminating, something that would point to him as the man who'd climbed up a ladder on a moonlit night and taken Kelly Braden from the bedroom. But she knew from years of searching for clues that it wouldn't be easy to prove. And, if she didn't win this hearing, she might never get the opportunity to try.

Promptly at 2:30 p.m., Judge Beiles took the bench and called on Luckman for his closing argument.

Luckman stood. "Your Honor, Georgia law is clear that there is a very high burden on a defendant who brings an extraordinary motion for a new trial based on the discovery of new evidence. He must prove that he only learned of this evidence after the trial, and it was not because of his lack of due diligence; that it's so material that it would probably produce a different result if it had been introduced at his trial; that it's not cumulative; and that it's not evidence in which its sole purpose is to impeach the credit of a witness at his trial. Failure to demonstrate any one of these requirements must result in a denial of a new trial. Defendant has introduced two specific witnesses that he claims constitute new evidence. The first is Lisa Hicks Montague, who has recanted her testimony from the trial in which she identified the defendant as the man in her room who attacked her. The Supreme Court of Georgia has made it clear that recantation testimony should be given very little weight without proof that the witness's trial testimony was the purest fabrication. Lisa Montague didn't lie at the trial. She testified as to what she believed to be true at the time. Her changing her mind now doesn't come close to meeting the requirement for admitting recantation testimony. Furthermore, Ms. Montague is not now saying that the defendant wasn't the man she saw. She's saying she doesn't know who it was. As such, it would not be so material as to likely change the outcome of the trial. The next allegedly new evidence is testimony from a bite-mark analyst, calling into question the testimony given by Dr. Fein at the defendant's trial. As such, its effect is to impeach the credit of Dr. Fein, and for that reason is not considered evidence to justify a new trial. For both these reasons, the defendant's motion must be denied. Thank you."

Luckman sat down, and Dani stood. "Your Honor, Jack Osgood was convicted of the murder of Kelly Braden and assault of Lisa Hicks, and sentenced to die, because of three pieces of evidence, and only three pieces of evidence. First, Lisa Hicks, then five years old and awakened from her sleep, testified that Mr. Osgood was the man she saw in her darkened room. Today, she has admitted under sworn testimony that the only reason she thought it was her neighbor was because of his size—he was the biggest man she knew. The State has argued that the recanting of her testimony should be given no weight because we haven't shown that her testimony at the trial was the purest fabrication. Although that might be relevant in most circumstances, it should not be so when the witness was only five years old at the time of her testimony. She was too young to appreciate the importance then of being certain of what she saw. Second, the State dismisses the testimony of Dr. Bagley as simply attempting to impeach the prosecution's expert on bite marks. That's not the case at all. The State's expert testified about the science of bite-mark analysis. That science has changed. When Dr. Fein testified, there had been no scientifically based research of bite marks made on human skin. When Dr. Fein testified, a highly respected forensic science commission hadn't made a recommendation to halt bite-mark analysis in criminal proceedings until there is science to support its admissibility. Both of those circumstances shed a new light on bite-mark analysis, a light that didn't exist at the time of the trial. Finally, the only other evidence tying Mr. Osgood to the attacks was his bat, with traces of Lisa Hicks's blood. The same bat that had his initials carved into it, yet was wiped clean of fingerprints. Just three pieces of evidence, and now two have been called into question. There can be no doubt that had Ms. Montague not testified she saw Mr. Osgood in her room, and had the jury heard testimony that the scientific community recommended a moratorium on bite-mark analysis because of its lack of a scientific foundation, there is a high probability the verdict would have been different. For these reasons, the motion for a new trial should be granted. Thank you."

"Okay, counselors," Judge Beiles said, "you'll have my decision within a week."

"Your Honor," Dani said, "Mr. Osgood's execution is scheduled to take place in ten days."

The judge nodded. "Thank you for reminding me. I hereby order the execution stayed, pending my decision."

There was nothing left for Dani to do but pack up her bags and head for home.

T ommy pulled up to the vinyl-sided ranch home just north of Asheville, North Carolina, a little past 7:00 p.m. Even in the dark, the light from the lampposts showed that the paint around the windows was peeling, and toys littered the front lawn. A beat-up, blue Chevy Colorado was parked in the driveway. He walked up to the front door, rang the bell, then waited. He always enjoyed looking at landscaping when he visited other homes, but just some scraggly burning-bush hedges grew under the front windows.

This didn't seem like the South, Tommy thought, as he zipped up his jacket. It was almost as cold here as it had been when he left New York.

Moments later, the door was opened by a thin woman dressed in tight-fitting jeans with holes by her knees. Her dull brown hair was pulled back in a ponytail, and bangs framed her gaunt face. A toddler, no more than two, had his arms wrapped around her legs.

"Who are you?" she asked.

"Is Axel home?"

"Who wants to know?"

Tommy handed her his card. She held it close to her face and squinted as she read the words.

"What do you want with Axel?"

"Just to ask him a few questions."

"He ain't done nothing wrong."

"I didn't say he did. Is he home?"

The woman turned and screamed out, "Axel! Someone here for you."

Tommy heard loud footsteps, then a large man appeared at the door. He was at least six two and heavily muscled. *Prison muscles,* Tommy thought.

"Axel Bonetti?" Tommy asked.

The man nodded.

"Did you once go by the name of Tony Falcone?"

Bonetti's eyes narrowed, and his mouth turned down in a frown. "Not in a long time. Why you asking?"

"Mind if I come in so we can talk a bit?"

"Matter of fact, I do. We can talk right here." He turned to the woman. "Go on in now, Carly, and take A.J. with you." When they were gone, Bonetti stepped outside, closed the door behind him, and sat down on the front stoop. He took out a cigarette from a pack in his shirt pocket, lit it with a lighter, took a deep puff, then asked, "So, what is it you want from me?"

"Do you remember doing odd jobs in Stone Ridge, Georgia, about twenty-two, twenty-three years ago?"

"I did odd jobs in a lot of places back then. Can't remember every one."

"This one was special. A girl disappeared from a home you worked on. Someone took her from the bedroom and killed her."

Bonetti broke out in a smile. "Well, hot damn, you're here because you think it was me."

Tommy stared at him. "You think this is funny?"

"No, sir, not what happened to that poor girl. I remember her. A pretty thing. Read about it in the papers. What's funny is you wasting a trip coming all this way. I was long gone when she disappeared."

"You were sent to prison for rape."

"A misunderstanding. Girl said yes, then changed her mind when her daddy found out about it."

"That's not what the jury thought. Why don't you tell me where you were when Kelly Braden was murdered, and I'll check it out?"

"You remember where you were on a particular day twenty years ago?"

"You said you were long gone. Where'd you go after Stone Ridge?"

"Here and there. It was a good haul. Probably went on a bender for a few weeks, then headed here to North Carolina. Asheville was always good for picking up work."

"Anyone you remember working for back then?"

"I barely remember what name I used back then."

"Why did you keep changing your name?"

Bonetti shrugged. "Why not? I enjoyed trying on different names then, seeing what fit best. My daddy was a mean SOB. I didn't particularly like carrying his name."

Tommy spent another half hour grilling Bonetti, trying to lock down dates and places he traveled to after leaving Stone Ridge, hoping to get something concrete he could latch onto. He came away with nothing. He would call Captain Cannon and give him Bonetti's address. Maybe he could shake something out of him.

———

The next morning, as soon as Tommy arrived in the office, he placed a call to Captain Cannon.

"I need your help," Tommy said when Cannon got on the phone.

"How?"

"I located Tony Falcone, although he goes by the name Axel Bonetti now."

Tommy heard a whistle on the phone. "How'd you manage that?"

"I had a source track him down. Here's the interesting thing. He was in prison fifteen years for raping a girl."

"I can guess what's coming. You want me to interview him."

"That's right. I just got back from seeing him, and he claimed to have no memory of where he was back then, but maybe you'd have more success."

"Look, I told you before, Osgood is guilty. I don't have the man-power to send my guys out on a wild-goose chase."

"But he raped a girl. Doesn't that tell you something?"

"That's not the MO for Kelly Braden."

"But it says he's capable of violence."

"I'm sorry, Tommy. I can't help you."

"My colleague just finished a hearing on a new trial for Osgood. She thinks it looks good for him. If that happens, she's going to bring up Bonetti. I've seen her in court often enough to know that if no one checks him out, she'll point fingers at the poor investigation. I'm just telling you this to give you a heads-up."

Tommy heard Cannon sigh. "I'll visit him. One visit. If some-thing seems fishy, I'll put a detective on it. If not, then it ends."

"That's all I'm asking for."

CHAPTER 25

J udge Beiles was true to her word. One week after the hearing
ended, her decision arrived at HIPP's office over the fax. Dani held
her breath as she began to read. She skimmed through the preliminary discussion of the facts, then read:

> *Defendant claims that the recantation by Lisa Hicks*
> *Montague and the scientific studies that now place into*
> *question the reliability of bite-mark analysis constitute*
> *new evidence which, if presented to the original jury,*
> *would likely change the outcome of the verdict. I have*
> *to agree. Although in most cases, a witness recantation*
> *would require affirmative proof that the witness lied at*
> *the original trial, that standard should not be applied to*
> *the testimony of a young child. Where, as in this case, the*
> *child provided a reasonable explanation for her incorrect*
> *trial testimony, she should be permitted to recant it. With*
> *respect to the bite-mark evidence, although the certify-*
> *ing association of forensic odontologists still stands by the*
> *reliability of that evidence, this court cannot ignore the*
> *scientific studies, unavailable at defendant's trial, which*
> *prove otherwise. Given the paucity of other evidence at*
> *defendant's trial that ties him to the murder, I hereby grant*
> *defendant's motion for a new trial, which shall begin five*
> *weeks from this date. Bail is set at one million dollars.*

Relief washed over Dani, the same feeling she always got when she'd taken a step closer to stopping the executioner's hand. It was so much preferable to the dread that enshrouded her when death had taken a step closer. She rushed out of her office to Tommy's desk. "We won the motion! Osgood will get a new trial."

Tommy broke out in a big smile. "That's great, Dani. So, what now? The state still doesn't have anything more tying Osgood to the murder. Should I stop looking into Bonetti? Or even Johnson?"

Dani thought a moment. "No, keep looking. I don't want to be caught flat-footed if they come up with something. Besides, I always feel better when we don't just free our client, but put behind bars the person who really deserves to be there."

"Okay. I'll keep going."

As soon as Dani returned to her office, she picked up her phone and dialed the GDCP. She doubted that Osgood had the resources to raise bail, but she needed to let him know of the judge's decision. When the prison answered, she asked for the social worker assigned to death-row inmates. A minute later, she was connected with Jesse Symons.

"How can I help you?" Symons asked when he answered the call.

Dani told him of the court's ruling and asked him to let Osgood know. "I don't suppose you know of any relatives Osgood might have?"

"I've only worked here for the past five years, and I don't think anyone's visited him during that time. Hold on, let me look up his file." A minute later, he was back. "I know he has no siblings, and his mother is deceased. His father abandoned the family when he was ten. I don't see anything in the record of any other relatives."

"I've been wondering about something. Osgood mentioned once that his favorite snack is peanut M&M's. I'm certain the prison doesn't hand that candy out to inmates, so can you check and see whether he has any funds on account with the prison commissary?"

"Sure. What are you thinking?"

"I'm just wondering if anyone has deposited money in it for him. If yes, then maybe it could lead to a relative."

"I'll get back to you on it."

Dani thanked him and hung up. Twenty minutes later, Symons called back. "I found something interesting," he said. "Osgood had been getting regular monthly deposits of fifty dollars until his mother died eight years ago. Then, seven months later, five thousand dollars was deposited into his account, and nothing since then."

"Do you know who made the deposit?"

"I do. Someone named Harry Osgood. He must be a relative. Do you know who he is?"

"No. But I'm going to find out."

As soon as she hung up, Dani buzzed Tommy and gave him this new assignment, then turned to the files on her desk. She would prep the witnesses for Osgood's trial the week before it began. In the meantime, there were new inmates seeking her help.

She leafed through the letters, looking for one she hoped could be resolved with DNA testing. When she reached the last one in her folder, she immediately knew she'd found her next client.

To whom it may concern,

My name is Luther Manning, and I've been in Riverbend prison in Nashville coming up on thirty-two years. I was twenty-three years old when they said I raped and killed a woman. I never did such a thing. Her boy, he was four years old back then, described someone who looked like me to the police, but it wasn't me, I promise. I've been real sick for some years now. Started as lung cancer, and now it's in my brain. I don't want to die in prison. I want to die at home, with my mama and papa. They know I'm innocent, but I want their friends to know their son is

innocent, so they won't look down on my parents. Can
you help me? I don't think I have much time left.

Dani turned to LexisNexis and looked up his case. Like Manning
wrote, he'd been imprisoned in Tennessee after his conviction for the
rape and murder of a woman in her home. The only witness was her
four-year-old son. The child had described only one man raping and
killing his mother, yet eventually the police arrested three, including
Manning. The two others, Evander Houseman and Al Williams, eventually confessed and implicated Manning and were sentenced to life. At
Manning's trial, Houseman recanted and claimed he'd only confessed
and pointed to Manning because he'd been threatened with a death
sentence. It didn't matter. Manning was convicted, although the jury
couldn't agree on the death penalty, and so he received a life sentence.

Dani prepared a letter to send back to Manning, then another to
the Metropolitan Nashville Police Department, asking them to investigate whether any DNA evidence remained in the case file. If there
were, it could be the magic bullet that hadn't existed thirty-two years
ago, holding the potential to exonerate Luther Manning and bring
him the peace he sought as his death grew near.

By the time Dani arrived home, the temperature had dropped, and
with snow in the forecast, the air felt damp. The chill seemed to go
straight through to her bones, and she looked forward to starting a
fire in the living-room fireplace and filling Doug in on her good news.

Ruth ran into her arms as soon as Dani came through the front
door and buried her face in Dani's chest. Doug wasn't home yet, but
Katie had prepared a casserole that could be quickly heated up when he
arrived. He'd left a message at home that he needed to finish some work
before he could leave. The children had already eaten, and Katie had

given Ruth a bath. Dani nuzzled the top of Ruth's head and breathed in the smell of her baby shampoo. At times, she couldn't understand why she was so lucky, when so many others weren't. It was luck that her children were safe. She had no doubt that the Bradens were careful parents, that they'd done all they could to keep their daughter from harm. But they had been unlucky, and their lives had changed irrevocably because their daughter had crossed the path of the wrong person.

Was that person Jack Osgood? Dani felt certain it wasn't. Over the years, she'd gotten good at recognizing when a client was holding back. Osgood didn't seem to have deception in him. Greg Johnson? Maybe. *More likely Axel Bonetti,* she thought. Or someone they didn't even have on their radar. The mission of HIPP was to free the wrongly convicted, not to identify the true perpetrators. Still, Dani had learned over the years that even when DNA proved an inmate's innocence, a stigma remained attached to the person when no one else was charged with the crime. Perhaps it was because of the need of the victim's family for closure. All Dani knew was that she felt an added layer of satisfaction when she and Tommy handed over to the authorities the man or woman who deserved to be imprisoned.

By the time Doug returned home, the children were already asleep. Dani popped the casserole into the microwave, then poured Doug a glass of wine. "What kept you so late?" she asked.

"I needed to finish up the article I'd committed to for the *Law Journal.*"

"I thought that wasn't due until the end of the week?"

"I got a call from Stanford. They'd like me to come out there again. They've narrowed it down to me and one other. I'm leaving after work tomorrow."

Dani realized Doug was on a runaway train, and there was nothing she could do to stop it. Although it was now "honeymoon hour," she suddenly felt exhausted. "I'm tired, Doug. I'm going to turn in early."

"You okay?"

Dani nodded, even though she wasn't okay. She was miserable.

The phone had already rung four times. *Pick up. Pick up.*

"Hi."

"It's me."

"I know. I saw the caller ID. What's up?"

"It's going to be in tomorrow's papers. Judge Beiles just ruled—Jack Osgood's going to get a new trial."

There was silence on the other end of the phone. When he spoke, his voice was tight. "Why are you telling me?"

She squeezed her eyes shut and whispered, "I thought you'd want to know. "

"You thought wrong."

She hung up the phone. Was she mistaken to call him? They'd never spoken about it. Maybe the fear she'd harbored about her brother all these years was just foolish thinking. Maybe working for the court had made her jaded, made her think the worst of everyone. Maybe she was wrong about her brother. That would be good. Yes, very good.

He'd kept his urge in check for so many years, but now, it kept bubbling up to the surface. It was that damn investigator, reminding him of that first girl, what it felt like, the rush of excitement. He'd breathed easy when Osgood was convicted for his crime. It had been a wake-up call for him, forcing him to acknowledge how he himself could have been facing the death penalty. It had convinced him to stop, hard as it was. He'd slipped only once since then. Still, there had been three others, three murders that no one had ever been charged with. He'd gotten away with it then, and probably could again. If he were careful. The risk was taking a girl from her home. But he'd learned that it was that very risk that added to his excitement.

He took out his map and decided first which state, then which town. He preferred small towns, not big cities. People seemed so much more distrustful in big cities, so much more careful. It was easy for him to get away. He was always on the road. He'd find just the right girl, then follow her. This time, he'd choose someone who lived in a one-story house. He was older now, not as strong as he once was. Maybe someone without siblings. That, too, was safer. Less likely to wake up others. Maybe one with just a mother, the father gone. He could find out a lot by observing his target for a few days. If the first one he picked wasn't just right, he'd choose another.

He shook his head. *I can't do this again. I'm married. A father. I know it's sick.* He told himself over and over that it was in his past. He'd gotten it under control. But he knew the truth.

28

It took a week for the Nashville police to get back to Dani, but it was worth the wait. Semen had been left on the victim's body, and it was still in the evidence kit. Dani now represented not only Manning, one of three men convicted of the rape and murder of a woman while her four-year-old son watched, but his alleged accomplice, Houseman, as well. Sadly, Williams, the third man, had already died in prison. Dani had just gotten off the phone with ADA Chuck Davies, who had agreed to DNA testing, when Tommy walked in her office.

"What's up?" Dani asked.

"I just located Harry Osgood. He's living in Atlanta."

"Great. He's a relative, right?"

"He's Jack's father."

His father. The man who walked away from his ten-year-old son and never looked back. Not the relation she was hoping for. "Did you talk to him?"

"Not yet. But I've done a little digging. Turns out he and Jack's mother were never divorced. When she died, he showed up and claimed the entire inheritance."

"Did she have much? Jack's legal bills must have been large. It was a death-penalty case."

"There was no mortgage on her house, and it sold for four hundred seventy thousand dollars. Plus, she had a hundred seventy-five thousand dollars in IRAs, and a vested pension paid out six hundred thirty thousand dollars."

Dani's jaw dropped. "Not what I expected at all. But didn't her husband own the house with her?"

"Nope. It was her family's home. She inherited it from them. And I checked—the pension and the IRAs listed Jack as the beneficiary, with no alternate."

Dani turned to her computer and did a quick check online. "The most his father should have gotten was a year's worth of maintenance. Everything else should have gone to Jack."

"Seems like his father took all of it. Less five thousand dollars he put in Jack's prison account."

"I think we need to pay a visit to Mr. Osgood. Do a little arm-twisting. There should be enough to get Jack out on bail."

"Just what I was thinking."

———

Two days later, Dani and Tommy were back in Georgia. They drove up to the bungalow-style home in the Candler Park section of Atlanta. It was on a tree-lined street of one- and two-story homes, none of which looked the same. Four steps led up to the wide front porch, with three white pillars contrasting the painted gray brick of the house. A Lexus SUV sat in front of the separate garage.

Tommy knocked on the door, and a few moments later, it was opened by a gray-haired woman with an apron tied around her waist and a warm smile on her face. "Hello, can I help you?"

"We're looking for Harry Osgood," Dani said. "Does he live here?"

The woman held out her hand. "I'm Maria Osgood, his wife." She held the door open wider. "Please, come in." She turned and called, "Harry, it's for you."

A large man walked down the steps from the second story. Instantly, Dani recognized him as Jack's father. They had the same build, the same droopy eyes, and the same square jaw.

"How can I help you folks?" Osgood said when he neared them.

Dani held out her card. "We represent your son, Jack."

There was silence in the room as Maria grabbed onto Harry's arm and pulled herself close to him.

Finally, Harry spoke. "He hasn't been my son in a long time."

"He's always been your son, Mr. Osgood." Dani had tried to keep her anger in check, but she knew it had spilled over into her tone anyway.

"You can't put his violent behavior on me. I was gone from his life long before he killed that girl."

"No one is blaming you for Kelly Braden's death. My colleagues and I aren't even blaming Jack. We don't believe he killed her."

Osgood's mouth fell open, and he grabbed his wife's arm. "Are you serious?"

"Completely."

"Well, I'll be damned." He paused and shook his head. "Still don't know what you're doing here, though. There's nothing I can do for him."

They still hadn't moved from the front foyer. "Do you mind if we sit down and have a talk?"

Maria looked up at her husband, and he nodded. She led them into the kitchen, where it looked like she'd been in the process of loading a dishwasher. The kitchen table was cleared, and they all took seats around it.

"Would you like some coffee?" Maria offered. "Some water?"

Dani and Tommy shook their heads.

"Mr. Osgood—," Dani began.

"Call me Harry."

"We've been successful in getting a new trial for Jack."

"That's good."

"But he's still in jail waiting for that trial."

"I suppose that makes sense."

"No. It doesn't. He's been on death row for more than twenty-two years, for a murder that he probably didn't commit. He shouldn't have to stay a day longer while he waits for the new trial."

"That's up to the judge, isn't it?"

"No, Harry. It's up to you."

Harry scratched his cheek as he frowned. "How so?"

"It appears that you took all of the proceeds from his mother's estate."

Harry blanched. "Now, I had every right to. I was her husband then. Never got divorced. I kept asking her to sign the papers, but she downright refused. She knew me and Maria wanted to make it legal, but that woman was stubborn as a mule. So, yes, I took the money. Wasn't going to do Jack any good, with a death penalty hanging over him."

Dani sat back in her chair and stared at him, her dislike of the man deepening by the moment. "You knew your son was in prison. You knew his mother had died, yet you never once visited him."

"I told you before. I didn't think of him as my son anymore. Not since it was clear he was a retard."

"He was still your son."

"Maybe some men can handle that. I couldn't. He'd just keep getting under my skin, and I'd blow up at him. He was better off without me."

Dani wished she could be someplace else rather than listening to this sad excuse for a man. Everything about him made her skin crawl. Was it because of Jonah? No, she decided. She'd think him repulsive even if she didn't have a son with special needs. She looked over at Maria, who sat very still, her hands folded in her lap, her eyes downcast.

"You can justify your abandonment all you want, Harry," Dani said, "but I don't care about your excuses. The only thing I care about is raising one million dollars for Jack's bail. And you have that money."

Harry leaned back in his seat and folded his arms across his chest. With a defiant tone, he said, "You're wrong about that. Maybe I did once, but it's been used."

"That was a lot of money to use up."

"Used it to start my business. The rest paid for my kids' college."

"You have other children?"

His expression softened. "Two daughters. Bright as can be."

"You can put up ten percent and give your house and business as security for the rest. That way, Jack could get out."

"And go where? He has no one."

"He has you."

Harry bent his head down and shook it slowly. After a minute, Maria put her hand on Harry's arm. "It's the right thing to do, honey. You know it is."

Harry just kept shaking his head.

"You know that money rightfully belongs to Jack," Dani said.

Harry looked up. "What if I come up with the ten percent? Can you find someplace else for him to go?"

Dani thought about it. Jack had no other relatives that she knew about. There had to be group homes that he'd qualify for, and frankly, he'd be better off there than with this man. Problem was, they often had waiting lists. "I'll look into it. But on two conditions."

"What's that?"

"That you pay the fees for it. And you visit your son. He needs you."

Harry took a deep breath. "Okay. Make the arrangements."

~

As soon as Dani returned to the office the next day, she began looking for a bail bondsman in Gwinnett County and a group home for Jack. There were halfway houses for prisoners released on parole, but she didn't want him in that environment. Since he was on death row, he'd been sequestered from the rest of the prison population. Now wasn't the time to throw him in with what might be a rough crowd. Instead, she searched for homes that catered to those with a developmental or intellectual disability. Jack Osgood might not need such a home on a permanent basis—he wasn't so impaired that he couldn't care for himself—but after twenty-two years behind bars, it would likely be too frightening for him to be cast out on his own. A group home would give him a chance to acclimate to a technological world that was in its infancy when he was first convicted. And, perhaps more important, it would provide him with a social environment, something that would no doubt be difficult for him to find on his own after so many years locked up. There was one big hurdle, Dani knew. Most group homes would be reluctant to take someone who'd been convicted of murder and sentenced to death.

Finding a bail company was easy. She'd located someone with a quick search on Google. She told him to hold off until Osgood had a place to go, and after three hours of searching, she had come up empty. Even where there was an opening, they wouldn't take someone from prison. There were just two more on her list to try. She dialed the number for Kenny's Place and was put through to Amy Shore.

"My name is Dani Trumball, and I'm calling to see if you have room for a forty-six-year-old man with an IQ of sixty-eight."

"Where's he been living up till now?"

Dani paused. This was always the stumbling block. She took a deep breath, then went on. "He's been at GDCP for twenty-two years."

"I'm sorry. We don't take anyone who's been convicted of a crime."

"I'm an attorney with the Help Innocent Prisoners Project in New York City. I've looked into his case and believe that he was wrongly convicted. A judge has just ordered a new trial for him, and he can make bail, but he has no one left. He needs someplace safe to live."

"Twenty-two years. He must have been convicted of something serious."

"Murder."

Dani heard a sharp intake of breath. "Oh, my. I wish we could help you, but it wouldn't be fair to our residents."

It was the same answer she'd gotten from every facility she'd called. "I've met with him many times. He's a gentle soul, and over the years has always maintained his innocence. The evidence against him was minimal, and the primary witness, a five-year-old girl, has now recanted her testimony."

"Still—"

"Please." Dani stopped, just long enough to control the quiver in her voice. "Please, he's been punished long enough for something he didn't do. Don't punish him again because of those false charges."

There was silence on the other end for a beat. "How certain are you that he's innocent?"

"Ninety-nine percent."

More silence. Then, "We do have room." Dani could hear a sigh. "We'll take him on a probationary basis, at least until his new trial. After that, we'll see."

Dani thanked her profusely, then placed a call to Osgood's father. "It's a go," she told him.

Winning Osgood's permanent freedom was still far away, but now, he would at least be free in the weeks leading up to his trial.

J ack Osgood has been released from prison," she told her brother.
"Did you know?"

"Why are you telling me this?"

"Because I want you to be careful."

"Don't sound so melodramatic. Why would I care if Osgood is
free?"

"I know what you did."

There was silence on the phone. A minute passed, then, "What
is it you think I did?"

"I'm your sister. I know you."

He asked again, "What do you think I did?"

"It was you. You killed her."

He laughed loudly. *Too loudly,* she thought.

"You're being ridiculous."

"I found it," she said, her voice just a whisper.

"Found what?"

"Your shirt. With blood on it."

More silence. "I cut myself shaving."

"No. You killed her."

There was silence on the phone, just the sound of her brother
breathing. Finally, she asked, "Are you still there?"

"What are you going to do?"

"Nothing. You're my brother. I love you. Just be careful, that's all."

"I always am."

A week after Osgood moved in to Kenny's Place, Dani called him. "How are you finding things?"

"Everything is strange to me."

"Like what?"

"The TVs are so big. It's like a movie theater. And the phones are so small. And . . ." He paused. "I'm not used to being with other people. They're nice, though. They try to help me. Especially Mrs. Shore. And Doris."

"Who's Doris?"

"A lady. She talks to me."

"Is she one of the residents?"

"Yes."

It had been a long time since Osgood had interacted with a woman. A friendship with Doris could be very good for him—it could help bring out the socialization skills he'd need to live outside prison. Or, it could be very bad—engendering in him more excitement than he could handle at this time.

"Have you done anything special since you got out?"

"Mrs. Shore took a few of us to a movie."

"That's great. What did you see?"

"It was a new Star Wars movie. I don't remember the name."

"Did you like it?"

"It was really good. And it was in three-D. I'd never seen that before."

"What else have you done?"

"I go for a walk every day. And last Saturday, there was a high school football game not too far from the house. It was good, but I really miss baseball. Maybe I'll still be free in the spring, and I can watch the games on TV."

That was Dani's hope as well. "Has your father come by yet?"

"No."

Dani wanted to scream at the man. They'd had a deal. She wanted more than money from Harry. She wanted him to support his son, not just financially but emotionally. Jack should know there was someone in the world who cared about him. Although his absence made it clear he didn't.

She chatted a bit more, then hung up. Not five minutes passed before her assistant buzzed her to say that ADA Chuck Davies was on the phone.

"Tell me you have good news for me, Chuck."

"I do. The DNA excluded all three of the men. And"—he paused—"it pointed to someone else. A guy we caught for raping another woman in her home, in the same county, two years later."

Dani smiled. The magic bullet had worked again. If only DNA were available in every case. It certainly would have helped Osgood if the bite mark on Braden's arm had left saliva. But, with her arm submerged in the creek for more than twenty-four hours, any saliva that might have been there was washed away.

"So, you'll join me on a motion to dismiss the convictions?"

"Absolutely."

"Thank you, Chuck. I wish every prosecutor cared about justice more than racking up wins."

"Oh, I think most do. Every profession has a few bad apples."

As Dani hung up, she couldn't help but think the legal profession had more than its fair share of those.

Tommy was just packing up to head home when a call came from Captain Cannon.

"Have you seen Bonetti yet?" Tommy asked.

"Just got back from interviewing him."

"And?"

"And nothing. His memory wasn't any better for me than for you. But Tommy, I still think you're grabbing at straws. There's no reason to think he's responsible for the Braden murder."

"He was in prison for raping a girl."

"Braden wasn't raped. And rape isn't murder."

"Still—it's a violent crime."

"He claims the girl's father pushed the prosecution."

"Are you going to speak to the girl?"

Cannon hesitated before answering. "Look, I told you I'd check out Bonetti. I did. That's the end, as far as I'm concerned."

"At least give me the name of the girl. I'll check her out."

"You know I can't do that. They keep the names of rape victims private for a reason. I'm not going to violate that privacy because you're off on some fool's errand."

Tommy's frustration was palpable as he hung up and left the office. If Cannon wouldn't help him, he'd have his source track down the girl's name. He knew Dani hated it when he went outside accepted lines, and using his hacker source was definitely in the no-no column. But he wouldn't have found Bonetti without him.

On his drive home, he kept thinking about Kelly Braden. He didn't want to focus only on Bonetti and exclude other possibilities. That's what the police often did: hone in on one suspect and forget to do their jobs. He still liked Johnson for it, but he shouldn't stop with him, either. Since he and Dani were convinced Osgood was innocent, he needed to expand the search for possible suspects. Bonetti was one, Johnson another, but he needed to start from the beginning. Go back to Kelly's friends, mine them for details of Kelly's life. Whom she hung out with, who wanted to hang out with her but was excluded. Who didn't like her. Who liked her too much. It was only a few weeks until the new trial. He needed to give Dani ammunition for it.

CHAPTER
31

Thank goodness for the Internet. It made life easy in so many ways. Although he didn't learn the exact address Jack Osgood had gone to after his release from prison, he learned enough. He found out that Osgood went to a group home in Atlanta. From that, he discovered only three such homes. One a halfway house for prisoners just paroled, the other two for developmentally disabled adults. He tried each, pretending to be a reporter. The first two said he wasn't there; the third, that he wasn't available for an interview. Bingo. Although he preferred small towns, he'd make an exception if it meant Osgood's proximity would turn the police's spotlight Osgood's way. Osgood had taken the fall for him once. If he chose carefully, Osgood could take the fall again. It seemed serendipitous that the resurrection of his urge coincided with Osgood's release from prison.

He'd gone for so many years, keeping his craving in check. Only once after Osgood's conviction did he weaken, and that was more than fifteen years ago. Since then, with a wife and children of his own, he'd controlled it. He wondered why it had come back so strong again. Was it just because of the investigator? Or was it because he was now middle-aged, saddled with a mortgage and credit-card debt, and feeling weighed down by responsibility? The feeling of empowerment that surged through him at that moment when the girl's eyes locked on his own, when she knew her life was in his hands, when he made the decision to end it—the memory of that feeling had kept him awake at night these last few weeks. Maybe he just needed one more time, one more kill, and it would satisfy him. Maybe.

He told his wife he'd be gone for the week, traveling for his job. The first two days, he watched the group home, watched for Osgood. The house looked like every other one on the block, maybe just a bit larger. A white, vinyl-sided, two-story colonial with a manicured lawn and blue shutters framing the front windows, the color matching the front door. Each day Osgood left the house and took a walk. *That's good,* he thought. He can leave the house and go out on his own. That was important.

The next day, he parked his car a few blocks away and waited for the school bus from the high school. The first day, no one got off that was worthy of him, so he quickly got in his car and followed the bus to its next stop, and then the one after. It was at the third stop that he spotted a potential target—long blonde hair and a trim figure, just like Kelly's. He wasn't close enough to see the color of her eyes, but he would've bet they were blue. He watched to see the house she went into, then waited to hear which room the loud music came from. It was always the same with teenagers, he thought. Straight into the room, slam the door, and turn on the music. She lived in a two-story, her bedroom on the second floor. He would have preferred a ranch. He decided to wait another day, start following the school bus a little farther away from the group home, maybe find a girl just as good who lived in a one-story.

As soon as she stepped off the school bus the next day, his breath caught. The same blonde hair and trim figure as the others, but this one wore a cheerleader's uniform, just as he'd seen Kelly wear. He knew it had to be her, even if she lived in a two-story, but when he followed her home and saw her walk into a ranch house, it confirmed that he was meant to do this once more. He was meant to take her life.

32

W hat's that?" Jack asked Doris, pointing to a screen on her lap.
"It's an iPad."

Jack picked the beautiful, strange thing up and turned it over and around. "What does it do?"

"Lots. You can look up almost anything. You can play games on it. You can read books on it. You can even watch movies on it."

Jack liked Doris. Of all the residents, she was the friendliest to him and didn't make him feel stupid when he asked her questions. She was pretty, too. She had a heart-shaped face, with wide-set brown eyes that always looked friendly. Her brown hair was shiny and matched the color of her eyes. She wasn't heavy, but she was a big woman, with broad shoulders and wide hips. He thought that fit with him, since he was a big man. She was younger than he was, by at least ten years, but that didn't seem to bother her. "Can you show me how it works?"

Doris smiled and invited him to sit next to her on the couch. For the next hour, she taught him how to use it. There were so many things he had to learn. Everything felt different from when he worked for Mr. Bennett. Everyone seemed to walk around with a phone in their hands. Even in the movie theater, when Mrs. Shore took some of them, he looked around and saw people punching letters on their phones. When they watched television in the house, someone could press a button on the remote control, and the TV show would freeze, and then magically start up again. One of the men in the house played games on the television with someone who wasn't even there. It made his head dizzy, the amount of things that were new.

The biggest change, though, was his missing mother. Before Dani told him she'd died, he always thought of her sitting in their kitchen, baking his favorite cookies and waiting for him to come home. He missed her so much. Whenever he thought of her, his eyes would well up a little bit.

At least Doris tried to make him feel better. He felt comfortable with her, more comfortable than he'd ever felt with the girls in high school. Yes, he liked Doris a lot.

———

Once more, Tommy's hacker had come through for him. He'd just given Tommy the name of the victim raped by Axel Bonetti. He was in luck. Although the rape had occurred when Becky Rostoff was a coed at Emory University in Atlanta, she now lived in Hoboken, New Jersey, just on the other side of the Holland Tunnel. He and Dani had already racked up high expenses on this case. He knew Bruce would frown on another flight for something that was just a hunch. Now, he'd be able to drive to her home.

When he was finished at work, Tommy called Patty to let her know he'd be home late, then retrieved his car from the parking lot and headed west to the tunnel. When he got close to it, traffic slowed to a crawl. Par for the course. It was always impossible getting out of Manhattan after 4:00 p.m. Sometimes even after 3:00 p.m. He inched his way forward, the radio blasting classic rock to drown out the honking all around him. He never understood why drivers bothered to honk their horns when it was clear the cars in front weren't able to go any faster. Still, in New York City, it was commonplace.

He finally got through the tunnel and made his way to Rostoff's apartment building, a new high-rise that overlooked the Hudson

River. He hadn't called in advance. He suspected she'd be reluctant to dredge up something so unpleasant from her past, and he didn't want to give her the chance to brush him off. Still, when he saw the building, he knew he'd have to get past a doorman.

He parked his car, then walked over to the entryway. A doorman held open the door, which led to a desk in the lobby with a concierge behind it. "I'm here to see Becky Rostoff," Tommy said.

"Name?"

"Tom Noorland."

"Is she expecting you?"

"She's not." Tommy took out a business card and handed it to the concierge. "I'm here about a case. I'm hoping she can help me with it."

The concierge picked up the phone on the desk and punched in four numbers, then announced Tommy to the person on the other end. There was some hushed give-and-take between them, and then he hung up and said, "Apartment 1206. Elevators are ahead on the left."

Tommy's knock on the door of 1206 was answered by an attractive woman still dressed in a power suit—navy pin-striped with a lilac silk blouse. Her brunette hair was worn short, with a soft wave throughout.

"I just got home from work," she said. "What's this about?"

"Do you mind if I come in?"

"Maybe. First answer my question."

"There's a possibility that the man who raped you eighteen years ago murdered some teenage girl years before that."

Rostoff flinched. She opened the door wider, and Tommy stepped inside. The living room was immaculately decorated, with each piece of furniture either black or white. Accent pieces in bold red added a splash of color. The wall of windows in the living room provided an expansive view of the Hudson River, with the Manhattan skyline on the other shore. Tommy took a seat on the leather sling-back chair, and Rostoff sat adjacent to him on the modern white sofa.

"Do you mind if I ask you a few questions about what happened to you?"

"Go ahead."

"Would you tell me what happened with Bonetti?"

Rostoff just stared at Tommy, her eyes fixed on his face yet distant, as though she were seeing someone else.

"I know this is difficult," Tommy said.

She bent her head down, then softly said, "I was so young then, so trusting. I met him in a bar. He was older, maybe late twenties, but handsome. I could see his muscles under the tight T-shirt he wore. He bought me a drink, and we talked, and then he suggested we go for a drive, go someplace quiet to talk. I knew I shouldn't go, but he seemed so nice, and I admit, I was excited by him. I thought we'd kiss, maybe a little more, but I'd keep my clothes on. I didn't want more. We drove to a lake. Within minutes, he was all over me, pulling at my blouse, my pants . . . I kept saying no, but it didn't matter. Finally, I kneed him in his crotch, and when he loosened his grip on me, I ran out of the car. He ran after me, threw me down on the ground, and raped me."

"He claims that you wanted to make love, that it was your father who forced you to press charges."

Rostoff opened the first button of her blouse. Just below her neck was a two-inch scar. "I kept fighting him when I was on the ground. He took out a pocketknife and warned me to stop. When I didn't, he slashed me. I gave up then."

"I'm sorry that happened to you."

"Is that what happened to the girl who was killed? Was she raped and cut with a knife?"

"No. She wasn't raped, but that doesn't mean Bonetti didn't kill her. He was violent with you. It shows he had it in him."

"I hope you prove it was him. I hope he goes back to prison. I hate knowing that he's walking around again, maybe raping another girl."

Tommy nodded. "I'm going to do my best."

———

It was after eight when Tommy finally arrived home.

"Eat yet?" Patty asked him.

"Nope. I'm starved."

While Patty heated up his dinner, Tommy stopped by the bedrooms of his three children still at home. Tommy Jr. and Emily were away at college. Brandon was next, then Tricia, and last, now just thirteen, was his baby, Lizzie. In five short years, she'd be off to college, too, and they'd be empty nesters. He almost couldn't wrap his head around it. It seemed like their house had always been filled with children—their own and their kids' friends. Their place had been the magnet, always welcoming, always filled with the aroma of something cooking. He kissed Brandon and Lizzie hello, then walked back downstairs.

"Where's Tricia?"

"A late band practice. She'll be back any minute."

"Who's picking her up?"

"No one. She's walking back."

"You know I hate that. It's dark out."

"She's sixteen already. She can take care of herself."

I bet that's what the Bradens thought of Kelly. He shook his head, trying to rid it of the dark images that kept popping up since he'd started on this case.

He sat down at the kitchen table, and Patty set his dinner plate in front of him. When he'd met his wife, she'd been working as a project coordinator at the Bureau, but she left after Tommy Jr. was born, and she'd been a full-time mother ever since. Patty ran everything at home, and because of that, Tommy had been able to flourish in his own career. Every day he was grateful she'd made the choice she did.

As he ate his dinner, he thought about Axel Bonetti. Kelly hadn't been raped, and she hadn't been cut with a knife. Still, Tommy thought that Bonetti could have been the one to kill Kelly. Although Tommy placed him at the top of his list, Johnson was still on it, and others could be added. Proving who, though, twenty-two years after the crime, was going to be damn hard.

———

Dani, Doug, and Jonah were seated at the round table in the ballroom of the Hilton Westchester in Rye Brook, with the president of the board of the Westchester Philharmonic and her family. They had rented Jonah a tuxedo for the occasion, and he looked dashing. The ballroom was huge and ornate and mostly filled. Dani estimated that more than six hundred people were in attendance. A string quartet had played throughout dinner, which had been better than Dani had expected for a fund-raising event.

The time had come for speeches. The president rose from her chair and made her way to the lectern. She thanked everyone for attending and for their generous contributions to the orchestra. "Without your support, we would not be able to provide the residents of Westchester County and its neighbors the gift of orchestral music." She continued to thank various donors, the other members of the board, the conductor, and the members of the orchestra. When she finished, she said, "Most of you know that we instituted an honorarium this year for a youth musician. Our first honoree, Jonah Trumball, is a gifted composer, and our orchestra was honored to be the first to perform his *Symphony of Spring*. Please join me in applauding young Mr. Trumball."

The room broke out in applause as Jonah stood. The president motioned him to come to the microphone. When he reached her, she handed him a certificate, then pointed him to the mic. This was the moment Dani had dreaded. She'd prepped Jonah on his words of acceptance, but she never knew what he might come out with.

"I want to thank the Westchester Philharmonic for this honor," he began. *So far, so good.* "Music is in my head most of the time. It swirls around until I put the notes on paper." *Still okay.* "And when it's complete, I feel assuaged." *Uh-oh.* He meant content or happy or satisfied. But this was Jonah—using a word just a little bit off. "Thank you very much."

Wrong word or not, the room once again applauded vigorously as Jonah returned to his seat, a smile on his face so big that it almost matched Dani's.

Her name was Alison. He'd heard a friend call to her when she got off the bus. Now it was 3:00 a.m., the same time he'd taken Kelly from the bedroom.

He knew by now everything had to be the same.

The lights in the house had been off for hours, just like every other house on the block. He grabbed his tools from the passenger seat of his car, then slipped out and made his way to her bedroom window. He slipped in a pry bar near the latch and applied increasing pressure until he heard the lock pop open. He waited but heard no stirring inside the room. He slid the window open, then eased his bulk through it—not the easy task it had once been. Once he'd gathered himself in her room, he flipped on his flashlight and looked around. Alison was asleep in her bed. It was a girl's room, with pink walls and flower decals making a border just under the ceiling. Up close, he could see she looked different from Kelly, but that was all right. He bent over her bed, then gently shook her awake. Her eyes opened slowly, but once she saw him, she opened her mouth to scream. He was ready, though. He clamped a hand over her mouth, then wrapped the other around her neck, squeezing just tight enough for her to lose consciousness after several thrashing moments.

He lifted her from the bed. Although the years had weakened him, he was still strong enough to carry her. Carefully, he opened the door to her bedroom, then tiptoed down the hallway to the front door, opened it, and walked to his car. He laid her down in the backseat, then tied her hands and feet and placed a strip of duct tape across her mouth. When he was finished, he drove his car to the isolated marsh he'd scouted out earlier.

When he arrived at his destination, there was little light from the quarter moon and mostly starless night. He placed a hiker's light around his forehead, then opened the door to the backseat and retrieved his prize. His pulse raced, and he bit down a smile in anticipation of what was ahead. He laid Alison down on the ground and pulled the tape off her mouth. She remained unconscious. He could wait. It wouldn't start to get light for another two hours. Besides, he enjoyed looking at her, at her silky blonde hair and toned body, shown to perfection in the boxer shorts and tank top she wore. At her youthfulness. Everything about her was perfect. Just like Kelly.

Forty minutes later, she began to stir. He waited for her to open her eyes, and when she did and saw him, she let out a scream, and that was his cue. The time to strangle her for real, to wring the life out of her perfect body. He straddled her body as his hands tightened on her neck, his excitement reaching a peak at the exact moment her body became limp. Before he left her, lifeless, he bit her arm, halfway between her elbow and shoulder, just where he'd bitten the others. And with that bite, he once again felt like a god.

O h, it's the most terrible thing," a breathless Amy Shore told Dani over the phone. "The police were just here. They took Jack away. A girl was murdered two nights ago, just a few blocks away. And she was taken from her home in the middle of the night. They must think Jack did it. Oh, I just can't believe it. He seems like such a sweet man."

Dani was speechless. She had been certain Jack was innocent. She quickly took down the name of the police station, then called and instructed them to stop their questioning of Osgood, that he was represented by counsel and she would be on a flight down that day.

As soon as she hung up, she walked over to Tommy's desk. "We have a problem," she said. "Osgood has been arrested. Another murder. Can you fly down with me today?"

Tommy nodded, and Dani asked her assistant to make the travel arrangements. She left the office to run back home and pack a small bag of essentials, then met Tommy at LaGuardia airport for a 2:30 p.m. flight. On the plane down, she could barely talk to Tommy, she was so distraught at the news.

They arrived at the police station at 4:30 p.m. and were led to Osgood's cell. He sat on a stool, hunched over, wringing his hands. He looked up when he heard the key unlock the door.

"Jack, are you all right?" Dani asked as she and Tommy stepped inside the small cell.

"They think I killed a girl."

"I know."

"I didn't touch anyone. I don't even know who it is."

"Her name is Alison Grant, and she lives twelve blocks away. Maybe you saw her on one of your walks?"

He shook his head vigorously. "Are they going to send me back to prison?"

"Probably."

"Then I won't see Doris again."

Dani saw tears well up in his eyes. "You'll still have a new trial on Kelly's murder. And they have to prove you committed this murder. If we win both trials, then you won't stay in prison."

Osgood ventured a small smile. "I really like her."

Dani was confused. Was Osgood referring to Alison? "Who's that?"

"Doris."

The sudden tightness in her neck disappeared as quickly as it had arrived. In just a few weeks, Osgood had formed a relationship with a woman. Maybe the first one he'd ever had a chance to have before being locked up. She reached over and patted his hand. "Did you tell the police anything when they brought you here?"

"I told them I didn't hurt anyone."

"Did they ask you to write anything down?"

"No."

"That's good. Now, I need to ask you some hard questions, and I need you to tell me the truth. Did you take that girl from her bedroom?" Most criminal-defense attorneys never asked their client whether they'd committed the crime. If they answered, "Yes," then they couldn't be put on the stand. But Dani worked for an innocence project for a reason. It wasn't in her makeup to help a guilty person go free. If Osgood committed this murder, she'd help him find another attorney, and then she'd back out.

"I don't even know where she lives."

"Kelly was taken from a bedroom, too."

"I remember. That's what they told me."

"And this girl, Alison, she had a bite mark on her arm, just like Kelly did."

"But I didn't bite Kelly."

"Did you leave the house late at night, after everyone was asleep, maybe to take a walk?" The police hadn't said they had a witness, but Dani had to make sure she wouldn't be surprised if someone stepped forward.

Osgood shook his head vigorously.

"Okay, Jack. I spoke to the police here. They think you killed Alison, and they've placed you under arrest. Tomorrow, they're going to take you into court, and I'll be there. The judge is going to read what you're charged with, and ask you if you plead guilty or not guilty. When he asks that, you answer, 'Not guilty.' Okay? You understand?"

Osgood nodded, his head hung down.

"In the meantime, if anyone but us asks you any questions, I don't want you to answer. Just say, 'I want my attorney.' And if anyone asks you to sign something, then say, 'No.'"

As they walked out of the police station, Tommy said, "The location of the bite mark on the arm was never made public. Alison was bit in the exact same spot."

"You think Osgood is guilty?"

"Actually, I don't. But I think someone wants the police to believe that. Someone who's the real killer of Kelly Braden."

The next morning, Dani appeared in the Superior Court of Fulton County. At 9:30, a string of prisoners was brought in to Judge Max Kahn's courtroom and settled in the jurors' box. Osgood was among them. When his case was called, Dani moved to the front of the room, gave her appearance, and Osgood was unshackled and seated next to her. The judge read the charges, then asked for Osgood's plea. Dani nudged him to stand, and she did as well. Loud and clearly, Osgood said, "I'm not guilty. I didn't kill anyone."

"Bail?" the judge asked the district attorney.

"The People ask for a remand, Your Honor. The defendant has recently been granted a new trial after serving twenty-two years for the murder of another young woman, also taken from her home. It's too dangerous to return him to the outside."

"The reason defendant has been granted a new trial is because the evidence that convicted him was tainted," Dani responded. "We believe he is innocent of that crime, as well as the current one, and a new trial will show that. He's already been wrongly imprisoned for more than two decades and shouldn't have to endure any more time behind bars. He has posted bail of one million dollars in the earlier case, and we think that should be applied to this allegation as well. It is a sufficiently high amount to ensure he will return for every court appearance, which is precisely what bail is meant to do."

"The similarity of the two crimes concerns me," Judge Kahn said. "I'm going to have to side with the prosecution on this. Defendant is remanded." With that, he banged his gavel, and Osgood was led away.

Tommy had spoken to Stacy Carmichael the previous night and had gotten the names of three people—two girls and a guy—who'd traveled in the same circle as Kelly and Stacy. One was still in Stone Ridge, one in a neighboring town, and the guy, in Atlanta. At 7:30 a.m., Tommy rang the doorbell of Jonathan Ross, hoping to catch Ross before he left for work. Ross answered the door, already dressed in a suit and tie. Tommy handed him his card and explained why he was there.

"I don't think I can help you," Ross said. "Kelly wasn't really my friend. I only knew her because of Greg."

"How well did you know Greg?"

"We were close back then. We stayed close during college, even though we went to different schools, but then drifted apart. Haven't spoken to him in years."

"Do you know how he felt about Kelly before they broke up?"

"He was crazy about her. I mean, she was hot. Most of the guys were jealous that he was the one to hook up with her."

"Did you speak to him after Kelly's body was found?"

"Yeah, we were all calling each other. We couldn't believe anyone would do that to her."

"How did Greg sound?"

"Broken up. We all were."

"Let's say for a moment that Jack Osgood didn't kill Kelly. Is there anyone you can think of who might have wanted to hurt her?"

"No. If not Osgood, then it had to be some stranger, right?"

"Did you ever see anyone in your group act violently?"

Ross paused for a moment, then frowned. "Are you really thinking it might have been one of us?"

"No, not just your crowd. Maybe someone in school who had a beef with her. Or just the opposite—someone who wanted her for himself."

"Like I said, a lot of guys liked her, but it was hands off because she was Greg's girl. And I don't know anyone who disliked her."

"Anyone in particular who had a crush on her?"

Ross shook his head.

Tommy asked a few more questions, then left. He drove up to Stone Ridge, went through the same round of questions with the two women who'd been part of that group, and got the same answers. If Kelly had been on someone's most-wanted list—whether for hate or love—he'd been pretty adept at keeping it to himself.

Dani had expected to prep Derek Whitman the day before Osgood's retrial, but she was here in Georgia and so decided to take care of that now. The trial was only a week away. She doubted Whitman would forget what they'd go over in that time. She'd called his cell number and arranged to meet him after he returned from work.

"I'm not really comfortable with this," Whitman said once they were settled in his living room.

"You only have to tell the truth."

"Greg was my friend. I don't want him to get in trouble."

"And what if your friend murdered Kelly Braden and got away with it because you lied for him?"

"He didn't do that."

"Maybe not. But you lied to the police, and now you need to set it right."

Whitman fidgeted in his seat, averting Dani's gaze.

Dani could hear the sounds of children shouting at one another coming from upstairs. "Your kids?"

"Yep. It's their crazy time. Homework is done, and they're over-tired, so they go at each other." He turned toward the stairs to the second floor and called out, "Keep it down up there!"

"Kelly was someone's child."

Whitman ran his hands though what remained of his hair and sighed. "I'll tell the truth. Go ahead."

Dani spent the next half hour going through his testimony, not just listening to his answers but watching his body language, giving pointers now and then. She then switched to the prosecutor's role, peppering him with questions she thought he'd be asked.

Just as they were finishing up, Maisie Whitman came down the stairs, a frown on her face. "I could use some help up there," she said to her husband.

Dani stood up. "I'm leaving now. Thanks for letting me take up Derek's time. I know how hectic bedtime can be."

"Well," said Maisie, "he travels so often for business. I'm used to handling it on my own, but when he's here, I could use a break."

"I understand completely."

Whitman walked Dani to the door. Just before stepping outside, she asked, "What do you do for a living?"

"I'm an accountant. I work for a company that sends me out to different businesses to audit their books. We cover the Southeast—North Carolina to Florida, and west to Kentucky and Tennessee. It's hard for my wife, handling the kids alone. She works as well—in marketing—so when I'm away, she doesn't get any downtime."

"Sounds like you're an understanding husband. That's half the battle."

"I try to be."

Dani thanked him, then left. He'd been shaky at first, but in the end, she thought he'd make a fine witness.

CHAPTER
35

Think, Tommy admonished himself at his desk in HIPP's office. *You're missing something.*

He kept going back over the same suspects, but he wasn't getting any closer. Before he'd left Stone Ridge, he'd stopped back at the police station and gone over Kelly's murder file once more, this time looking for something that could tie in to the murder of Alison Grant. He'd found nothing.

If his instinct was right, whoever murdered Kelly had killed Alison as well. That meant he had to have been in Stone Ridge twenty-two years ago, and in Atlanta now. He pulled out his interview notes. Bonetti still worked as an itinerant handyman, traveling where needed. Asheville was only three and a half hours from Alison's home. He could easily have gotten there, then home before his wife even noticed him gone. Or, he could have said he was going out on the road to scare up some work and been gone for days, even a week.

Greg Johnson was more of a stretch, living in Massachusetts, but he worked as an executive for a large insurance firm, with responsibility for the East Coast. It wouldn't be so hard for him to arrange a business trip to Atlanta.

Tommy picked up his phone and dialed his hacker contact. "Can you track someone's credit-card purchases?" he asked.

"Sure. Whose do you need?"

Tommy gave him Johnson's and Bonetti's names, then the five days leading up to Alison's murder. "I just want to see if either of them was nearby during that week."

"No problem. I'll get right on it."

Tommy had hoped to expand his search beyond those two, but so far, none of Kelly's friends had given him any leads. He had to go with what he had and hope something would pop up.

———

"Greg, it's Derek."

"Wow, haven't heard from you in ages. How's it going?"

"Fine. Listen, I want to give you a heads-up. I'm going to be testifying in Jack Osgood's new trial. I don't want to, but I have no choice."

"Yeah? About what?"

"About my alibi for you."

There was silence on the other end of the phone.

"I had to tell Osgood's attorney the time I really got back to the room."

"Why's that?"

"She was going to check with others at the party. Someone might have remembered, and then I'd be caught in a lie. It wouldn't look good."

"You know I had nothing to do with Kelly's murder."

"Sure. I guess Osgood's attorney wants to create some doubt, you know, to get Osgood off."

"Well, thanks for letting me know."

There was a coldness to Johnson's voice, but Whitman couldn't blame him. He said good-bye and hung up, and hoped that he wasn't going to end up hurting Johnson. Even though they were no longer in touch, they'd once been close friends, and Whitman was certain he didn't deserve to have a finger pointed at him as a killer.

Dani had spent the day on the telephone prepping the remaining witnesses for Osgood's trial. She arrived home in time to greet Jonah as he got off the school bus, then spent an hour playing with him and Ruth before she started to prepare dinner.

Cooking was a shared responsibility between Doug and her, and sometimes even Katie, when both were late getting home. As she was about to take what she needed from the refrigerator, Dani glanced over at the kitchen table, where Katie had left the day's mail. She picked up the pile and began to leaf through it, sorting the bills from the junk mail, when she stopped and stared at the envelope in her hand. It was addressed to Doug, and the return address was Stanford Law School. *Job offer or polite rejection?* she wondered, anxious to know which. Doug wasn't due to return home for another hour, at least. Should she open it? It's what she wanted to do. Her finger hovered over the back of the envelope; then she placed it under the flap, ready to slide it open. She stopped. It was Doug's right to learn the verdict. Instead, she turned to the refrigerator and took out the package of chicken cutlets.

As soon as Doug got home, Dani handed him the envelope without saying a word. He hung up his coat first, then took Dani's hand and led her into the living room. When both were seated, he opened the envelope and slid out the single sheet of paper. He read it silently, then looked up at Dani.

"They've offered me the dean's position, beginning in August."

Dani sighed deeply. "What are you going to do?"

"It's a big raise. Very big. I want to accept it."

"And me? The kids?"

"I've been thinking about that. I want you to come with me. I want the kids with me. But if you really don't want to leave, I can fly home every other weekend. And maybe once a month, you and the kids can go there. Spend the year getting a feel for the place, maybe checking out schools for Jonah, trying out nannies for Ruth."

"And what about my work?"

"There's an innocence project just a half hour away, at the law school at Santa Clara University. They may have an opening. Or, I could start an innocence-project clinic at Stanford, and you could head it."

"You haven't even accepted the position, and you already assume nepotism would go unnoticed?"

Doug's face reddened slightly. "Actually, I'd already discussed that possibility with the president. He had no problem with it."

Dani leaned back into the soft cushion of their worn couch. She loved this house. She loved her job. Yet, this was clearly important to Doug. Of course, it would be. Maybe having a long-distance marriage wasn't a bad idea. Maybe during that time, she'd find a great school for Jonah, a great nanny for Ruth, great doctors for both, a great job for herself. Maybe during that time, Doug would find that he hated being dean, that he hated being away from New York.

"I'll think about it," she said, then returned to the kitchen to set the table.

CHAPTER 36

Dani was back at Gwinnett County Superior Court, ready for the retrial of Jack Osgood in the murder of Kelly Braden. Hanging over the proceeding was the new charge of murder. Dani had spent the morning arguing before Judge Beiles that the prosecution should be barred from making any mention of Osgood's arrest in connection with the Alison Grant murder. The prosecutor, Gary Luckman, had argued the reverse. "It's highly relevant," he'd insisted over and over. "The same MO and identical bite marks."

"That might suggest the same person committed both crimes," Dani had retorted. "It doesn't mean that person is Jack Osgood. An arrest is not a conviction."

Eventually, Dani had prevailed. Osgood would be retried solely on the murder of Kelly Braden, without any mention of Alison Grant. If they were successful, he'd still face trial for Grant's murder. Unless, before then, they somehow, miraculously, uncovered the real killer. And Dani was convinced that wasn't Osgood.

She made a halfhearted motion to move the trial even farther away from Atlanta than Gwinnett County, to avoid jurors who'd read about Osgood's new arrest. She knew she was unlikely to succeed, and as expected, the judge turned her down. It meant she'd need to be extra careful to find jurors who were unaware of Alison Grant's murder.

The rest of that day and the next, Dani picked a jury. Seven women and five men—*a good mix,* she thought. Women would be more sympathetic to Osgood's intellectual limitations.

On the third day, the trial began. Jack Osgood sat by her side, dressed in a neat suit and tie. Amy Shore was in the gallery, along with Doris Waring, the resident at the facility who had befriended Osgood.

It was the first time Dani had met Amy in person, and she'd thanked her profusely for taking Jack in.

"Now that I know him," Amy said, "I can't believe he'd ever hurt anyone. It infuriates me that he was picked up for another murder."

Doris had remained seated and hadn't said a word, but Dani could see tears in her eyes.

After opening statements, Luckman began with Captain Ed Cannon. He described the steps taken by the police that led to the arrest of Osgood, emphasizing the bat with Lisa Hicks's blood and Jack Osgood's initials. He skimmed over Hicks's identification of Osgood. Luckman already knew that would be challenged. He made no mention of the bite mark on Braden's arm—Judge Beiles had already ruled that she wouldn't allow any expert testimony on its source.

When he finished, Dani stood. "Your Honor, I'd like to reserve my cross of this witness for my direct case."

"Okay."

Luckman called next the medical examiner. His testimony was straightforward—Kelly Braden's cause of death was asphyxiation as a result of strangulation. The doctor testified that based on the marks around Braden's neck, the killer was a man with large hands. Dani had no questions for him.

Next, Luckman had a crime-scene technician testify as to the examination of the premises, as well as the site where Braden's body was found. On cross-examination, Dani had only one question. "You testified that the perpetrator climbed a ladder placed on the outside of the house to reach the second story. How high was the climb on the ladder?"

"About nine feet."

Luckman followed up with a DNA technician, who testified that the blood found on Osgood's bat belonged to Lisa Hicks. When it was Dani's turn, she asked, "Did you find any fingerprints on the bat?"

"No. It was wiped clean of prints. But there were traces of blood that remained."

"So, can you say with any certainty that it was Jack Osgood holding the bat when it was used to hit Lisa?"

"No, I guess not."

Luckman called several residents of the neighborhood where Osgood lived. Two had been children at the time of the murder; two had been older. Each testified that they'd been afraid of Osgood, that he'd walk down the street swinging his bat, staring at them with a face that was frightening. Dani asked each one if Osgood had ever harmed, or attempted to harm, them or anyone they knew. Each said no.

When Dani finished her cross of those witnesses, Judge Beiles said, "This seems like a good time to break for the day. We'll begin again tomorrow at nine thirty." She gave the jurors instructions not to discuss the case with anyone, and not to watch any newscasts of the trial or read any newspapers about it.

Dani returned to her hotel and changed into jogging clothes, then headed to the gym. She was in luck—there was one open treadmill. She stepped on it, did some light stretching, then set it to 6.0—a nice, easy pace. As she settled into her run, she freed her mind of all else but this trial. She felt comfortable that the prosecution didn't have enough evidence to prove Osgood's guilt beyond a reasonable doubt. And, without a conviction in this case, Osgood's arrest in Grant's murder was shaky. Still, juries were unpredictable. They wanted justice for the victim. If she couldn't hand them someone else who killed these women, they might decide, even without more evidence, that Osgood was guilty.

Tommy was still in the office when his hacker source called him with results. "Got something good for me?"

"Something good, and something surprising."

"Spill."

"The only credit cards Bonetti uses are for gas, but it seems he was in North Carolina the whole time. But, keep in mind, it's only about three and a half hours from there to Atlanta. Less, if he drives fast."

"How about Johnson?"

"According to his credit-card charges, Johnson was on a weeklong trip through North and South Carolina and Georgia when Grant was killed. On the night she died, he stayed at a hotel in Augusta, Georgia. It's a little more than a two-hour drive from there to Atlanta."

"So, either could have killed her."

"I don't think so. Here's the surprising thing. I decided to check state-police databases for similar unsolved murders. I found two—both teenage girls, taken from their homes in the middle of the night, both strangled but not raped. Here's the kicker—both had bite marks on their upper arms. One in Clemson, South Carolina; the other in Madison, Florida."

"My God!"

"One was six months after Osgood's arrest. He hadn't been convicted yet but was incarcerated. The other was five years later. Bonetti was already serving time for rape then."

Tommy was a black-and-white kind of man. He didn't like gray. And he didn't like helping guilty people go free. After he'd heard from Osgood about his fear of ladders, he'd been pretty sure he was innocent. Now, he was certain.

———

Halfway through her sixty-minute run, Dani's cell phone rang. She picked it up to check who was calling—if it was Doug, she always took the call—and saw it was Tommy. She slowed the treadmill to 4.0, then pressed "Answer."

"What's up?"

"You sitting down?"

"Nope. On the treadmill."

"I think you need to stop."

Dani slowed it down gradually until it came to a halt. "Okay, I'm off."

Tommy filled her in on his conversation with the hacker.

A surge of adrenaline rushed through Dani. "You have to go down there right away. Talk to the police who investigated the cases. This could push away any lingering doubt in the jurors' minds. We need them to send someone to testify about those cases."

"I'll see if there are any flights down tonight. If not, I'll leave first thing in the morning."

"Good. And Tommy?"

"Yeah?"

"I don't know how you're getting your information, and I don't want to know. But I wonder if there's a way for you to find out where Greg Johnson was when those other two women were murdered."

"I'm already on it."

Before court started the next morning, Dani called Meghan Milgram, the psychologist who'd testified that Osgood was intellectually disabled. When she answered, Dani asked, "What can you tell me about serial killers?"

"A lot. Can you narrow down your question?"

"I think whoever killed Kelly Braden has killed three other teenage girls. Kelly was the first, so I think it's possibly someone who maybe lived in Stone Ridge, someone who knew her. I'm hoping you can tell me if there's a specific personality profile that fits a serial killer."

"It's not so simple. Do you have time to come in and talk to me?"

"I'm in court today, on Osgood's retrial. Can we meet for dinner tonight?"

"Sure."

They set up a place and time, and then Dani headed into the courtroom.

Osgood was brought in from the holding cell, once again dressed in a suit and tie. And, once again, Amy Shore and Doris Waring were in the gallery. A few rows in front of them sat Kelly's parents, Susan and Carl Braden, along with her brother, Adam. After the judge was seated, the jurors filed in. When everyone was seated, Judge Beiles asked Luckman if he had any more witnesses.

"Just one. I call Lisa Hicks Montague to the stand."

Dani knew Luckman had to call her. Even if her memory now differed, she had once claimed Osgood was the man in her bedroom. He took her through that early identification, made just days after the attack, then asked if she still believed it was the defendant. When, as he expected, she answered "No," he got her to say that she didn't know that it *wasn't* him who hit her with a bat.

There wasn't much for Dani to do with this witness. She just asked her a few questions to elicit why her testimony had changed from Osgood's first trial, then ended with, "Just to reiterate, you now say that your statement twenty-two years ago, that you saw Jack Osgood in your bedroom, was incorrect."

"Yes."

"Thank you. You can step down now."

Lisa exited the stand, then took a seat next to her aunt and uncle.

Luckman stood up. "The People rest, Your Honor."

They had put on a poor case. Without a bite-mark expert and with Lisa's changed memory, there wasn't much else they could do. Dani stood and asked the judge for a directed verdict—taking the decision away from the jury because it was clear that the State hadn't met its burden of proof. Such motions were rarely granted, but in this case, Dani thought she had a good chance.

Luckman stood up to argue against the motion, but Judge Beiles raised her hand to stop him. "I'll reserve decision on your motion. You can both argue it at the end of the trial."

Dani was pleased that Beiles had not immediately ruled against her. She called her first witness, Captain Ed Cannon, and once he was seated, she walked over to him. With his eyes narrowed and jaw set, Cannon seemed no more warmly disposed toward her than the first time she'd questioned him.

"When did your investigation focus on Jack Osgood?"

"Pretty much from the beginning. The Hickses' neighbors all thought he was strange, which raised our suspicions, and then, two days later, Lisa Hicks identified him as the man in her room."

"Was there anything else that made you suspect him so early?"

"The bat. Lisa had been hit with something hard, and we kept hearing that Osgood often had a bat with him. When we asked to see it, he claimed he'd lost it. That didn't seem believable to us."

"So, is that when you arrested him?" Dani knew that another reason for the early focus was that the forensic dentist had claimed a match between Osgood's teeth and the bite mark on Kelly's arm, but Cannon had been warned not to mention it.

"We were getting ready to when some kids found the defendant's bat. There was blood on it, so we decided to wait for the test results. It came back matching Lisa Hicks. That's when we arrested him."

"And how much later was that from the night of Kelly's disappearance?"

"Just over four weeks."

"During those four weeks, did you investigate the possibility that someone else had abducted Kelly?"

"Of course."

"And whom else did you consider?"

"Well, in a homicide, you always look at those closest to the victim first. So we had to rule out her parents, and of course, her aunt and uncle, since they were in the same house."

"Anyone else?"

"She had a boyfriend, but he was away at college."

"What was his name?"

"Johnson. Greg Johnson."

"What school was that?"

"University of Georgia, in Athens."

"And how long is the drive between Athens and Stone Ridge?"

"About an hour fifteen."

"So, Mr. Johnson could have driven to the Hickses' home and gotten back to school for classes the next day, couldn't he?"

"We checked him out. He had an alibi."

"Who?"

"His roommate. Derek Whitman. He came back to the room around three a.m., and Johnson was fast asleep."

"Wasn't that still enough time to drive back and kill Kelly?"

"No. He needed about two and a half hours for the drive back and forth, then time to get into the bedroom, take Kelly out to Wilson's Creek, which was twenty minutes away, then kill her. Figure three and a half hours minimum. Whitman said he woke up at six thirty, and Johnson was still sound asleep."

"What if I told you that Whitman returned to his room at one, not three? And that he woke up at eight. Would that change things for you?"

"I suppose it would give Johnson more time."

"Isn't it true that from the beginning you were focused on Jack Osgood?"

"We explored every possibility."

"But he's the only one you brought down to the station for questioning, right?"

"Yes."

"And that was one day after Kelly's disappearance?"

"Yes."

"Isn't it also true that once you focused on Osgood, you didn't continue to search for other potential suspects?"

Cannon shifted in his seat. If possible, his eyes seemed even more glaring now. When he spoke, Dani could detect the annoyance in his voice. "We did a thorough job. Osgood's bat was missing, and his mom had a ladder. When his bat was found, we knew he was our man. He is the one who killed Kelly Braden."

"Let's talk about the bat. Isn't it possible that the real killer found the bat outside Osgood's house and picked it up? Then discarded it after he'd killed Kelly? After all, Osgood's lawn is right next to the Hickses' home, and there's no fence dividing the two properties."

"Sure, it's possible. But unlikely."

"Wasn't the bat wiped clean of fingerprints?"

"Yes."

"If Osgood's initials are on the bat, why would he bother to wipe off his fingerprints?"

"He's not too smart. Probably didn't think it through."

"Thank you. I have no further questions."

Cannon stepped down from the stand and took a seat in the gallery. He seemed to studiously avoid looking at Dani.

Dani next called Ted Bennett. Although he was now seventy-six, he walked spryly down the aisle and took his seat in the witness box. His gray hair was thin at the top, but his body was trim and his eyes sharp.

"Mr. Bennett, are you currently employed?"

"Been retired for six years now."

"Prior to your retirement, where did you work?"

"I managed the A and P in Stone Ridge for thirty-two years."

"Are you familiar with Jack Osgood?"

"Yes, I've known him since he was a little boy."

"Did there come a time when he worked for you?"

Bennett nodded. "After he left high school, I took him on. He was about sixteen then. Always showed up on time and worked hard."

"What duties did he perform?"

"Mostly stock, unpacking items as they arrived, stacking them on the shelves. Sometimes, if there was a spill, he'd sweep or mop it up."

"Could he reach the top shelves without a ladder?"

"He's a tall boy, but no, back in the warehouse, a ladder was needed. I used someone else for those shelves."

"Why is that?"

"'Cause that boy just wouldn't get on a ladder, no matter how hard I pushed him. Said he was afraid of ladders."

"Do you know why?"

"He fell off one helping out his daddy, before he left the family. I think he was about eight years old then. Fell off a ladder and broke his arm. I guess that left its mark on him."

"Thank you. I have no further questions."

Luckman stood but didn't approach the witness. "Mr. Bennett, do you know for a fact that the defendant never climbed a ladder after he broke his arm?"

"Can't say I do. But in the store, he was adamant that he wouldn't climb one."

"You never saw him outside the store, did you?"

"Once in a while, I'd visit his mother. We were friends. I'd see him then."

"How often would that be?"

"Maybe a few times a year."

"So, you have no way of knowing if the defendant really wanted something strongly, whether he'd climb a ladder."

"I suppose not."

"Thank you. That's all."

Bennett left the chair, and as he walked down the aisle and found a seat, Dani called Derek Whitman. Whitman headed to the witness chair with long strides, his head bent down. The navy suit he wore looked like it had seen better days. He was sworn in, then gave his name and address to the court reporter. Dani asked a few preliminary questions.

"Were you familiar with Kelly Braden?"

"Yes. We went to high school together."

"And did you also go to high school with her boyfriend, Greg Johnson?"

"I did."

"Where did you go to college?"

"University of Georgia."

"And with whom did you room your freshman year?"

"Greg."

"Greg Johnson?"

"Yes."

"Did the police question you after Kelly Braden was murdered?"

"They did."

"And what did you tell them?"

"I said that on the night Kelly was murdered, I returned to my dorm room from a party around three a.m. and Greg was asleep, and that when I woke up a little before six thirty a.m., he was still asleep."

"Was that testimony truthful?"

Whitman lowered his head, and in a weakened voice, answered, "No."

"Sorry, I didn't catch that," the court reporter said.

He lifted up his head, his cheeks and ears now a pale red. With his voice louder, he repeated, "No."

"In what respect was it not truthful?" Dani asked.

"I got back about one and slept until eight."

"Why did you lie to the police?"

He turned to the jury. "You have to understand. Greg was my best friend." His voice now sounded like he was pleading for absolution. "I didn't think he'd hurt Kelly, and so I didn't think I was doing any harm."

"Before you left for the party, do you know if Greg received a phone call from Kelly that evening?"

He turned back to Dani. "Yes, he did."

"Do you know what she said?"

Luckman called out, "Objection. Hearsay."

"I haven't yet asked for the content of the conversation. Counsel's objection is premature."

"Go ahead, Ms. Trumball," Judge Beiles said.

"I do," Whitman answered.

"How do you know?"

"Because I could hear Greg's end of the conversation."

"And what did you hear Greg say?"

"I renew my objection," Luckman said.

"Your Honor," Dani responded, "what Mr. Whitman heard was an excited utterance, a clear exception to the hearsay rule."

Judge Beiles motioned the attorneys to approach the bench, then quietly asked, out of the jurors' hearing, what Dani expected the witness to say. When Dani finished, the judge said, "Objection overruled." Luckman returned to his seat, and Dani asked Whitman the question once again.

"'You're breaking up with me?' He said it as a question," Whitman said.

"Did Greg seem upset?"

"Yes."

"Thank you. I have no more questions."

Luckman stood but remained at his table. "Back when the crime occurred, you told the police you returned at three a.m. You were lying then, isn't that so?"

"I thought I was just helping out a friend."

"And so you lied, right?"

"I suppose so."

"Why should we believe that you're telling the truth now?"

Whitman shrugged.

"You need to answer the question," the judge said.

"It's been a long time. I was a kid then. I'm not anymore. I understand the importance of being accurate."

"When you returned to your room, allegedly now at one a.m., was Mr. Johnson asleep?"

"Yes."

"When you awoke the next morning, was he still asleep?"

"Yes."

"Did anything in the morning look different than it had when you went to sleep yourself?"

"No. Everything looked the same."

"Were you still in your room when Mr. Johnson awakened?"

"Yes."

"Did he seem upset?"

"No."

"Did anything about him seem different?"

"No."

"Thank you. You can step down now."

Dani called Russell Jessup to the stand. He was a big man, like Whitman and Johnson. He strode down the aisle to the witness chair, took a seat, then brushed his hand through his wavy brown hair.

Dani began by taking him through the timeline of the evening. "Are you certain that you and Mr. Whitman returned to your dorm room at one?"

"Give or take five minutes, yes, I'm certain."

Luckman asked him a few perfunctory questions, mostly to demonstrate the unreliability of memory so many years later.

When Jessup left the stand, Dani stood up. "Your Honor, may we take a short break?"

The judge looked at the round clock on the wall. "Ten minutes."

Dani thanked her, then quickly walked outside the courtroom, turning her phone on as she did. She walked to the end of the corridor, away from other people, then dialed Tommy's phone. When he answered, she could hear the excitement in his voice.

"I think we hit something big," he said. "I'm at the Clemson police station, with Detective Lou Hammond. Their cold case—it's the exact same MO as Kelly."

"Give me the specifics."

"Sixteen-year-old girl, taken from her bedroom in the middle of the night, a bite mark on her arm midway between her elbow and shoulder. And get this: she was pretty, with long blonde hair, just like Kelly."

"And never solved?"

"Nope. No leads, either."

Now Dani's excitement matched Tommy's. "Can you get the detective to come here tomorrow to testify?"

"He's already agreed. He'd like to solve his case, and if there's a connection with Kelly's murder, that might help."

"How about the Florida case?"

"I'm heading there next. I'll call you when I'm done."

Dani returned to the courtroom, stopping by the Bradens to say hello. Carl Braden had his arm around his wife, whose dark circles under her eyes suggested she hadn't been sleeping much. "I know this must be very difficult for you."

"Then why are you doing this?" Susan Braden asked. "Jack Osgood killed our daughter, and you're trying to free him. He should have been put to death already." She practically spat the last words at Dani.

"Calm down, sweetie," Mr. Braden said. "We have to trust the jury to do the right thing."

"Mr. and Mrs. Braden, I know you want the person who killed Kelly punished. But shouldn't it be the right person? I promise you, after tomorrow you'll understand why I'm certain Jack Osgood didn't kill your daughter."

Just then, the bailiff announced the judge's entrance, and Dani moved up to the front.

After Judge Beiles had retaken the bench, Dani called Jack Osgood to the stand. Most defense attorneys don't want their client to testify. After all, it's the prosecution who has the burden of proof. But jurors often need to hear the defendant say he didn't commit the crime. They need to look at him, at his demeanor, when he says it. Other than Alison Grant's murder, which Luckman couldn't bring up, Osgood had never been in trouble. He was a good witness to take the stand on his behalf. Once he was seated, he scanned the courtroom. Dani saw his shoulders visibly relax when his eyes settled on Doris.

"Jack, did you know Kelly Braden?" Dani asked after he was sworn in.

"I saw her once in a while, when she visited her aunt and uncle."

"Did you ever talk to her?"

"Sometimes. She was nice to me."

"Did you climb up to Lisa's bedroom and take Kelly away?"

"I won't climb a ladder. And I did not take Kelly."

"Did you kill Kelly Braden?"

Jack shook his head vigorously. "I would never hurt Kelly. I would never hurt anyone. It would be wrong."

"Thank you, Jack. I don't have any more questions."

Luckman walked up to him with a stern look on his face. "Do you understand that you swore to tell the truth?"

"Yes, sir."

"Didn't you think Kelly was pretty?"

"Yes."

"Wouldn't you have liked her to be your girlfriend?"

Osgood blushed. "She would never like someone like me."

"But you thought about her being your girlfriend, didn't you?"

"No. I thought about a girl at the A and P being my girlfriend. Not Kelly."

"Isn't it true that you climbed up a ladder and took Kelly away, then killed her because she didn't want to be your girlfriend?"

"No." Osgood took a handkerchief from his pocket and wiped away beads of sweat from his forehead. "No, I didn't do that."

Luckman stepped back a little, then turned to the jury. "People say you're slow, don't they?"

"Some do."

"But you're not too slow to lie in order to save yourself, are you?"

"I wouldn't lie. I promised to tell the truth."

Luckman mumbled, "No further questions," then turned and walked back to his table.

After Osgood returned to the defendant's table, Dani stood. "Your Honor, I have one more witness coming tomorrow, possibly two. I only learned of these potential witnesses last night and was told one is available to testify. My investigator will be meeting with the second later today. Both are out of state, and tomorrow morning is the earliest one or both could be here. May we adjourn until tomorrow morning?"

"Your Honor," Luckman said, "I know nothing about these witnesses. I should have been informed of a change to counselor's witness list."

Dani turned to him. "I just learned during the break that Detective Lou Hammond from the Clemson, South Carolina, police department has testimony relevant to this case."

"This is a death-penalty case," the judge said. "I'm going to allow the defense latitude. We'll reconvene tomorrow morning."

Dani sat back down next to Osgood and patted his arm. She always hated to give a defendant hope. It was crushing when it didn't pan out. But she couldn't help herself. She didn't have Melanie by her side, and she needed to say this to someone. "I think we're going to beat this," she said with a smile. "I really think we will."

At 7:00 p.m., Dani sat down to dinner with Meghan Milgram in a French country restaurant with gingham tablecloths and a lit candle set in a round amber glass on each table. Every table in the small restaurant was full, many with people she recognized from the courthouse.

"It's my favorite place to eat in Lawrenceville," Milgram said. "For my money, it rivals any restaurant in Manhattan."

They placed their orders, and while waiting for their first course, Dani began. "I can't help thinking it's someone from Stone Ridge, someone who knew Kelly. Her boyfriend back then is the obvious one to look at, but I don't want to focus in on him if he doesn't fit the profile of a serial killer."

"Actually, serial killers tend to prey on strangers, not people known to them."

"If that's true, then we have no chance of finding who really killed Kelly."

Milgram nodded. "They tend to be caught in the act, or close to the time of their most recent kill. Not twenty-two years later."

Dani reminded herself that it wasn't her job to unmask Kelly's killer. With the witness Tommy was bringing to court tomorrow, she had plenty to create reasonable doubt. But, even if Osgood was acquitted of Braden's murder, he still had another trial to face. And that judge might not be as willing to bar testimony on bite-mark analysis. "So, you think it's unlikely that the murderer was someone Kelly knew?"

"I wouldn't rule it out completely. It's possible that Kelly's murder was an accident, that he didn't plan to kill her. But when he did, it triggered something in him that made him want to repeat the experience."

"What kind of trigger? It wasn't a sexual thrill. None of the girls were raped."

"It might have given him a sense of power, of control."

"What kind of person becomes a serial killer?"

"Don't get bogged down on profiles. Remember, they're compiled based on characteristics of previously known serial killers. There can always be an outlier, and then that person's profile will be added to the mix."

"Still, I'd like to know. If there's even a slight chance it was someone from Stone Ridge, it'll help me."

Milgram sat back in her chair. "All right. First of all, most serial killers wouldn't necessarily appear strange to others. They often have families, have jobs, and own a home. It's because they can blend in so seamlessly in a community that they're especially difficult to catch."

"But there must be something that causes a person to kill, and keep killing?"

"It's no surprise, I'm sure, that many come from unstable home lives, often with child abuse. Many times, aberrant behavior is evidenced from a young age—torturing small animals, for instance, or frequently starting fires. Antisocial behavior, from childhood on, is another frequent characteristic. Usually, there isn't one single thing that causes one to become a serial killer. It's a combination of biological, social, and psychological factors."

"So, I should rule out anyone who doesn't have any of those factors?"

"No, unfortunately. It's not that simple. Some of the newer research strongly suggests that head injuries in children and adolescents are linked to killing, especially injuries to the frontal lobe."

"Head injuries?" Dani straightened in her seat. "What about from playing football?"

"Well, more often, the injuries are from a car accident or from physical abuse, but yes, conceivably from a football injury. But I'd look for some other factor or factors as well, maybe an unstable family. Obviously, not everyone who suffers a serious head injury will become violent, but studies seem to show that those who do become violent often had some damage to their brain."

Interesting, Dani thought. *I'll have to let Tommy know.* The waiter came with their salads, and talk of serial killers was put aside as they ate. In the back of her mind, though, Dani kept wondering if it was just a coincidence that Greg Johnson, Kelly's rejected boyfriend, had played football.

———

The next morning, Dani met Tommy, along with Clemson detective Lou Hammond and Detective Peter Wilson from the Madison, Florida, police department. Dani had spoken to Tommy after she'd returned from dinner the night before and learned that the circumstances surrounding the second girl's death, like the first, were identical to Kelly's. She found an empty room, then spent a half hour going over the details of those cases. At 9:30, she and Tommy entered the courtroom. Osgood was brought up from the holding cell, the judge took the bench, and then the jurors were led in. When everyone was settled, Dani called Detective Hammond to the stand. She ran him through the cold case from Clemson, stopping periodically to highlight the similarities between his case and that of Kelly Braden, especially the bite mark.

When it was Luckman's turn, he asked Hammond, "Isn't it possible that the perpetrator in your case was a copycat? Kelly Braden's murder was well publicized."

"Maybe well publicized for twenty-two years ago, but it didn't reach us. Otherwise, we would have put it together as a similar crime."

"Still, let's say the perpetrator in your case had been living in Georgia and had followed the case. Couldn't he have traveled to Clemson and copied exactly what he'd read about?"

"It's possible."

"Thank you. You can step down now."

Dani called Peter Wilson next and went through the same questions related to the Florida case. When it was Luckman's turn, he, too, did the same cross-examination. When Wilson left the stand, Dani called Captain Cannon. He'd remained in the courtroom, following the trial ever since he'd finished his own testimony.

Luckman shot up from his seat. "Counsel has already had her cross-examination of this witness," he said to the judge.

"I'm calling him as a rebuttal witness, Your Honor."

The judge nodded. "Go ahead."

Once he was seated, the judge said, "You're still subject to the oath you took yesterday, Captain Cannon. Do you understand?"

"Yes, ma'am."

"Your Honor will do."

Cannon blushed as Dani went ahead with her question. "You've heard the testimony of Detectives Hammond and Wilson, correct?"

"Yes."

"Do you recall their testimony about the bite marks on the arm of each of those girls?"

"I do."

"And is their description of the location of the bite mark the same, or similar to, the location of the bite mark on Kelly Braden's arm?"

Cannon shifted in his seat. "Yes," he said.

"Now, prior to the trial, did the Stone Ridge police department release any information about the bite mark on Ms. Braden's arm?"

"No," he said more quietly, though still loud enough to be heard. "We held that back."

"As far as you know, did any media outlet report on the bite mark prior to Mr. Osgood's trial?"

"None that I'm aware of."

"And you heard Detective Hammond state that the murder in his case took place five months after Kelly Braden's murder, correct?"

"Yes."

"And how long after Braden's murder did the trial take place?"

"About seven months."

"Let's turn to the murder in Madison. That was five years after Ms. Braden's death, right?"

"Yes."

"And at Mr. Osgood's trial, there was a great deal of testimony about the bite mark on Ms. Braden's arm, right?"

"Yes."

"Were you in the courtroom for that testimony?"

"I was."

"Do you recall any mention at that trial of the location of the bite mark?"

"Yes. There was testimony that it was on her arm."

"Just her arm? Not where on her arm?"

"I don't believe so."

"Your Honor, I'd like to mark as defendant's Exhibit A the transcript from Mr. Osgood's trial, which will clearly show there was no testimony about where on her arm she was bitten."

"So marked."

Dani turned back to Cannon. "So, just to reiterate, although there was no mention of where on her arm Ms. Braden was bitten, in those other two cases, the bite mark was in the exact same area, right?"

Cannon looked over at Luckman with a sheepish look on his face. "That seems to be the case."

"Thank you. I have no further questions."

"Recross, Mr. Luckman?"

"Just a few, Your Honor." He walked up to Cannon. "If the victim had her arm up trying to ward off her attacker, where would her arm be bitten?"

"Just where it was. On the outer arm, midway between her elbow and shoulder."

"So, if those other girls had their arms up trying to stop an attack, is that where you'd expect them to be bitten?"

"Yes, it's the likely spot."

"Thank you. No further questions."

Dani stood. "The defense rests, Your Honor. I renew my motion for a directed verdict."

"I'll take that under advisement. Let's adjourn until tomorrow morning. If I deny the motion, be prepared with your closing statements."

Dani left the courthouse with Tommy and the two detectives. Once they were outside, she filled them in on the information Milgram had given her the night before concerning serial killers. "Now that it appears the cases are connected, will you reopen yours?"

Both Hammond and Wilson said they would.

"There doesn't seem to be an obvious connection among the three girls," Hammond said, "but we'll look more closely for one. Maybe we can identify someone who's been in all three communities. Or nearby at least."

"I know Dr. Milgram said it's probable that all three girls were strangers to the perp," Tommy said, "but I still think Greg Johnson should be looked at."

Dani flipped through her notes. "She did say the first could have been more spur-of-the-moment. Maybe the murder wasn't planned, and in that case, it could be someone she knew."

"I'll check him out," Wilson said. "Believe me, I'd like to solve this case as much as you."

"Ditto to that," Hammond chimed in.

⁓

The next morning, Dani and Tommy were back in court. Once again, Osgood was brought in to sit beside her. When Judge Beiles took the bench, she announced, "I rarely award a directed verdict, but in this case, it seems clear to me that the prosecution hasn't even come close to a threshold showing of guilt beyond a reasonable doubt. The paucity of evidence on its direct case alone would be sufficient for a dismissal of this case. But when one looks at virtually identical circumstances in two additional murders, including the striking similarity in appearance of the victims, both of which took place when the defendant was imprisoned, there can be no other result here than judgment in favor of the defendant."

Dani turned and hugged Osgood.

"What does this mean?" he asked.

"It means the judge said you're not guilty of killing Kelly Braden." A smile broke out on his face. "So, I can go back to the home?"

"Not yet. There's still a trial in the other case. But I'm going to see if we can get bail now."

As the sheriff's deputy took Osgood away, Dani was struck once again by how well she and Tommy worked together. She knew she was a good trial attorney, but a gun wasn't effective without bullets. And Tommy always provided her with the ammunition she needed. Whenever she asked for the impossible, he always seemed to come through for her. She couldn't imagine walking away from that. Yet, that's just what Doug wanted her to do.

The Bradens were waiting for her outside the courtroom. The strained look that Dani had seen on Susan Braden's face throughout the trial was gone. "I understand now," Susan said. "Just promise me—you'll try to find who really did kill our daughter."

———

As soon as the verdict was read, Cannon stood and left the courtroom. Tommy followed him out.

"What do you think now?" Tommy asked him when they were in the hallway.

"I'm thinking a guilty man just got off. I'm hoping the jury for the Atlanta girl corrects the mistake."

"Come on. You heard about those other girls. The MO is the same for all. And Osgood was in custody then."

"Osgood's bat. Lisa's blood on it. And Osgood's teeth matching the bite mark on Kelly's arm. The jury didn't get to hear that. That's why he got off."

"The jury didn't hear it because it's bullshit."

"Tommy, I think you're a decent guy. But you've been swayed by the work you do now. You want to believe everyone's innocent."

Tommy chuckled. "Just the reverse. I'm the one who always needs to be convinced."

"Well, you haven't convinced me."

"I'm meeting with Hammond and Wilson now. Why don't you join us?"

Cannon shook his head. "I've wasted enough time on this." He shook Tommy's hand, then strode down the hallway to the elevator.

When Lou Hammond and Peter Wilson exited the courtroom, Tommy sat down with them and gave them everything he knew about the Braden murder.

"Maybe we can find someone who did some work for each of the families," Hammond said. "Or had some business in each of the towns."

"How about Greg Johnson?"

"Since it's interstate, we can link in the feds. They might be able to track his movements. It's going back pretty far, so it's probably a long shot."

"Anything you guys can do, it's appreciated," Tommy said.

Hammond spread his arms out, his palms up. "Hey. Someone is killing teenage girls. We'll do everything we can to stop him."

The following morning, Dani returned to Superior Court in Fulton County. Craig Franklin, a local assistant district attorney, was by her side as she asked Judge Kahn to allow bail for Jack Osgood in the Alison Grant arrest.

"Your Honor," she began, "the only reason Mr. Osgood was arrested for that crime was because of his prior conviction for a markedly similar murder twenty-two years ago. That conviction has now been overturned. The police have no real evidence against Mr. Osgood. He's already been wrongfully imprisoned for most of his adult life. He shouldn't spend any more time behind bars without the State proving, beyond a reasonable doubt, that he committed this crime. We ask the court to set bail at two hundred fifty thousand dollars."

"The fact that he was acquitted doesn't mean he wasn't guilty," Franklin said. "The judge in Gwinnett County didn't allow the jury to hear highly relevant information that clearly implicates the defendant in that murder."

The judge leaned forward in his seat. "What evidence is that?"

"Bite-mark evidence. Judge Beiles wouldn't allow an expert forensic dentist to testify that the bite on Kelly Braden's arm came from Jack Osgood."

Dani jumped in. "There was a good reason for that. Bite-mark analysis has been found to be unscientific and unreliable."

"Not by the Supreme Court of Georgia," Franklin countered.

"Is that so, Ms. Trumball?"

"It's true so far. But there hasn't been a case that's gone to the Supreme Court of Georgia refuting bite-mark analysis in more than five years."

"Still, it has to give me pause. Bite-mark analysis has been a staple in my courtroom for decades. I'm not inclined to throw it out until the top court tells me I have to. I see no reason at this time to change my earlier ruling. Bail is denied."

Dani fumed as she left the courtroom. It was too unfair! She left the courthouse and made her way to the county prison. She needed to give Osgood the bad news. They'd both been so excited by yesterday's acquittal. He should be a free man now. Instead, because of outdated thinking and a group of dentists who refused to admit their own failings, he would remain in jail. It would be at least six months before he was tried for Grant's murder. Another six months without his freedom. Unless, before then, the real killer was unmasked.

Tommy was relieved that he was no longer alone in trying to find who'd killed Kelly Braden and Alison Grant. Two police departments, and maybe the FBI, had joined the hunt. That meant he needn't rely on his hacker source anymore. It always bothered him when he turned to John Doe, or JD—the name he always called him on the off chance someone listened in on his phone calls. After all, if Edward Snowden was to be believed, the government was listening to everyone's phone conversations.

He'd helped JD escape a federal rap for hacking once. It was back in his FBI days, and he'd seen a smart kid with a bright future who deserved another chance. Since then, his faith in JD had mostly paid off. He'd gone to college, made his parents proud with a straight-A average, and graduated magna cum laude. He now held a high-level job with a West Coast tech company, pulling down big money, and had put hacking behind him. That is, unless Tommy called in a favor. It always gave Tommy a twinge of guilt when he did so, but he justified it by the results he got—helping to free the innocent and identify the guilty.

He knew he should let Hammond and Wilson go about their jobs, but something kept nagging at him. He picked up the phone and dialed Emily Halstein, the principal at Stone Ridge High School. When she came on the line, he asked, "By any chance, is the school's football coach from 1992 still there?"

"I'm afraid not. He retired six years ago."

"Do you know, is he still in the area?"

"Moved to Florida, he and his wife. I think they're in the Tampa area."

"Can you give me his name?"

"Sure. It's Coach Webber. Fitz Webber."

"Thanks. I appreciate your help."

Tommy did a quick search and came up with a phone number for Fitzroy Webber in Saint Petersburg. He gave it a try but got voice mail. He didn't want to leave a message. Instead, he figured he'd try again later—only to forget, as he got bogged down in other matters.

———

Back in the office, Dani was still seething. It infuriated her that Jack Osgood remained behind bars because of discredited science. Nearly half of the DNA exonerations had been in cases where faulty forensics led to the wrongful conviction. She shuddered to think of the men and women still in prison, perhaps facing death like Jack Osgood, because some dentist or doctor or scientist or technician testified with certainty that their science assigned guilt to the defendant.

It would take years, maybe decades, for the courts in all the states to rectify the past mistakes and put a halt to the continuation of those errors. For Osgood, Dani would have to continue the fight against admitting bite-mark analysis—up to Georgia's Supreme Court, if necessary. Only, for Osgood's sake, she hoped it wouldn't be necessary.

She left work at 4:00 p.m. The light was already fading, and the darkness that would soon engulf the city matched her mood. By the time she walked in the front door, even Ruth's gleeful shouts of "Mama" did little to lift the heaviness she felt. She went through the motions of preparing dinner, and managed to keep a smile on her face for Jonah and Ruth, but once the children were asleep and she settled onto the couch for "honeymoon hour," Doug's first words were, "What's wrong?"

"You can tell?"

"Of course I can. We've been married almost twenty years."

Dani bowed her head. "Sometimes I think it's too much. That I should walk away from what I'm doing."

"Something happen today?"

"Nothing new. I'm just tired of fighting ignorance. Willful ignorance. Or maybe it's heartlessness."

"From prosecutors?"

"Oh, they're bad enough. I'm talking about judges."

Doug wrapped his arms around Dani and pulled her into his body. "Surely, not all judges."

"Of course not. It's just so damn frustrating that testimony based on junk science is still allowed." She straightened up and turned to look at Doug, her features set in a glower. "Out in California, a man was convicted of murdering his wife based on bite-mark evidence. Eleven years later, the same dentist admitted that there was no science to conclude that the defendant's teeth matched the bite mark. The judge ruled that as a result, the prosecution had no case and the remaining record showed he was innocent."

"That's good."

"Not so fast. On appeal, the California Supreme Court ruled that an expert could never be wrong or legally false because his testimony was merely opinion. That's insane. Jurors are so used to watching shows like *CSI* that they believe an expert's testimony is infallible. Especially when they say things like 'It's a match' or 'There's no chance of error' or even 'to a reasonable degree of scientific certainty.' To a juror hearing those words, it spells 'guilty.'"

"Our justice system isn't perfect. You know that. That's why you work for an innocence project."

"Only . . . it's wearing me down. I come home and see Ruth for such a short time before she goes to sleep. I miss spending time with her. And Jonah is growing up so fast. Before we know it, he'll be leaving us."

Doug began to rub Dani's shoulders. "You know, you don't have to work. Come to California with me. Take time off. A year, maybe more. Figure out what you want. It doesn't even have to be law."

Dani's eyes began to tear up as she once again leaned back into Doug. "I can't. It keeps me awake some nights, thinking about innocent people in prison. I have to keep doing this." She managed a wan smile. "I just needed to vent tonight. Tomorrow, I'll be ready to fight again."

CHAPTER
39

His chest tightened, and his stomach did somersaults as he read the newspaper article. He'd been traveling the day before and so missed reading it yesterday, but now he sat in his office, catching up. Two detectives, two different towns, two different states. It was so long ago. How could they have pieced it together? A drop of sweat from his brow dripped into his eye, and he took out a tissue to wipe it dry. He never should have given in to the urge. If it hadn't been for the latest one, that investigator wouldn't have gone looking. At the time, he'd gloated over Osgood taking the fall for him once again. It proved he was safe, impervious to arrest. But now—now they'd discovered the link. How long would it take them to realize it was him? Soon? Maybe never?

He thought about running away, but where? He had a family. They wouldn't follow him without questions, and he couldn't give them answers. Could he leave them behind? If he went to prison, he'd have no choice. He'd heard about people taking on a new identity, buying false documents, starting over. He wouldn't know where to begin to make that happen.

"Dinner's ready," his wife called.

He put down the newspaper and slowly lifted himself from the chair. He was still a big man, but some of the muscle had softened, and his bones creaked as he moved. Some would consider him middle-aged, but he still thought of himself as young. Only now, carrying the weight of his misdeeds, he felt old.

He walked into the dining room and gave his wife a peck on her cheek. His children were already seated, bickering among themselves. How could he survive never seeing them again?

As he watched them fight, he thought of his sister. They used to argue all the time, but they were devoted to each other. *Maybe she would know someone.* Someone to give him a new name, a new life. She had to come across plenty of criminals in her job at the courthouse. And she already knew about him, even though he'd denied it to her.

Yes, she would help him. As he sat down to eat, he resolved to call her tomorrow.

Three weeks passed before Dani got a response to her discovery request from the Fulton County District Attorney's office. She groaned when she saw a report from Michael Forbes. He was old school—in the camp of odontologists who were convinced, without any scientific evidence, that they could distinguish a human bite from an animal one, and definitively determine who made the bite mark. She glanced through the report, which had compared the mark on Alison Grant's arm to Osgood's teeth and found it a match. She leaned back in her chair and read it again, this time more slowly. Halfway through, she stopped, incredulous. Forbes had used the same imprint of Osgood's teeth taken twenty-two years ago. She didn't need training as a dentist to know that his bite would have changed over the years, especially over such a long period. Any dental work done, like caps or bridges, would surely result in a different bite mark. She jotted a note to herself to check with the prison dentist to see what work had been done on Osgood's teeth during the past two decades.

As she'd suspected, there was little else tying Osgood to the crime. A neighbor said she'd seen him walking on the block a few days before the murder. There was no hair or fingerprints left at the scene. A few footprints were found on the lawn under Grant's window, and the shoe size matched Osgood's. *More junk science,* she thought. All it should do is prove that a person wearing footwear of a certain size and make was present. But so-called experts would get on the stand and state with certainty that a shoe worn by the defendant made the print at the scene of a crime. Sometimes, when a shoe had been worn down in a unique way, it could provide markings that were useful in an identification. But Dani had taken Osgood shopping on his first day freed from prison and been with him when he'd purchased a new pair of Nike sneakers. There had to be thousands of men in the area with the same brand. *So, good luck getting that into evidence.*

Dani pivoted to the two other cases she had taken on—it would be at least six months for Osgood's case to get to trial. Both of the new cases had DNA available. Both, she expected, would be resolved quickly. Without DNA evidence, these men would continue to languish in prison. One had been behind bars for eighteen years, the other for sixteen. How did the system get so broken? Or, was it ever fixed? It seemed so simple on *Perry Mason*, where eyewitnesses were never wrong and the bad guy always confessed. Now, she knew that eyewitness testimony was the least reliable, and sometimes innocent people confessed.

But the system was broken beyond that. Technical testimony, for such a long time considered the gold standard in trials, was now being questioned. After decades of forensic examiners testifying in court that ballistic markings or fingerprints or shoeprints or tire tracks or bite marks could identify a perpetrator, The National Academy of Sciences had said, "Not so." At least, not with a high degree of certainty. Just recently, the FBI had conducted a postconviction review of its own hair-sample lab. In 268 cases in which the lab reported a match, the technician was wrong 96 percent of the time. Fourteen of those defendants convicted, in large part, because of that testimony had since been executed. Yet, Dani knew, courts continued to admit testimony from so-called technical experts. She was determined not to let that happen to Osgood.

She finished the motions she was working on, then went back to the discovery she'd gotten from Franklin and thumbed through it again. Up until Grant, each of the girls abducted from her bedroom and then murdered had been bitten on the upper arm. In each case, the arm had been submerged in water for a long period before the body was found, and the DNA had been washed away. There was nothing in the files she'd received about saliva in the bite mark, so she expected the same would be true with Alison Grant. Still, she had to check. She picked up the phone and called Franklin.

"So, I guess there was no DNA recovered," she said when he got on the phone.

"There was no rape."

"I mean from the bite mark."

She was met with silence on the other end.

"You still there?"

"They might have recovered a small amount. I'm not sure it will be enough."

Now it was Dani's turn for silence. Most prosecutors cared about justice. If they didn't believe the evidence supported a charge, they didn't bring one. Some counties had even instituted conviction-integrity units—prosecutors charged with going over certain past convictions to make sure the evidence wasn't flawed. Once in a while, though, she came across a prosecutor whose uppermost concern was winning. Franklin now struck her as that kind. "Has it been sent out for testing?"

"Not yet. We've been busy with other matters."

Dani exploded. "If that sample isn't sent to a lab today I'm going straight to the *Atlanta Journal-Constitution* and accusing you of purposeful obfuscating. And my second stop is to your district attorney."

"Don't get your britches all tied in a knot. We just do things in the South a little slower than you northerners."

"Today!"

"It's been getting readied to send out. I suspect it's on tomorrow's schedule."

"Today!"

Dani heard a deep sigh on the other end. "I'll do you a favor and see if I can fast-track it for you."

"So, it'll go out today?"

"Yes. But you know these labs are slow. Probably won't get the results back for a couple of months."

"Four weeks. Tell your lab if they don't have the results in that time, I'm going to the newspapers."

He chuckled. "I can see you're going to be a tiger in court. I look forward to going up against you."

"This isn't a contest, Mr. Franklin. A man's life is at stake."

"A man who took the life of a young girl."

"No. A man who's suspected of taking her life. And when those results come back, you'll see it's an innocent man whose life you've been playing with."

41

I need your help," he said to his sister when she answered his phone call.

"What?"

"I need to disappear."

Her voice, when she responded, was strained. "It *was* you. Oh, God. All of them?"

"Yes."

"What do you want from me?"

"You work at the courthouse. I thought, maybe, you might know someone who knows how to make up false identities."

She thought for a moment. "There is someone."

"I need it soon."

"It'll be expensive, I suspect."

"That doesn't matter. I have money."

"Get me some passport-size photos."

"Okay. I'll overnight them."

"I'll let you know when they're ready."

"Thanks. I knew I could count on you."

He could hear her sniffles. "I love you, you know," she said. "But promise me you'll stop. That this will be the end."

He wanted it to end. He was losing everything of importance to him—his wife, his children, a satisfying job. He wanted to be normal. He hoped he could be. "Yes," he said to his sister. "It won't happen again."

CHAPTER

42

Three weeks later, Dani was still waiting for the DNA results on the saliva found in the bite mark in Alison Grant's arm. Just before leaving the office to return home, she placed a phone call to Osgood. It was easier to reach him at a county jail than the state prison, so she only had to wait five minutes before he got on the line.

"How are you holding up?" Dani asked him.

"It's different here. I'm not locked up by myself all day. I'm with everyone else."

"Are they bothering you?"

"No. I'm big. I guess they think I'm strong, too. Some of them call me names."

"What names?"

"Retard."

"I'm sorry."

"I'm used to that. They called me the same when I was in school."

Dani wondered if verbal bullying would ever stop. It had gone on when she was in school, and probably had when her parents and grandparents were young as well. But longevity didn't make it right. She'd heard some educators excuse it as a rite of passage, something that kids had always done. She'd also heard some schools had adopted a zero-tolerance policy, but often that backfired, bringing more abuse on the bullied kid when the aggressor faced consequences. She didn't know the answer. She was just glad Jonah went to a school where everyone was different, and everyone accepted those differences.

"Doris came to visit me. Two times," Osgood said.

"That's nice. I'm sure it was good to have a visitor."

"I like her. I think she likes me."

Dani hoped that was true. This man had spent half his life in prison unfairly, and now that freedom was in sight, he was once again the target of a careless police investigation that was choosing expediency over thoroughness. He should be living in that home, solidifying a relationship with Doris. He should have his father in his life, helping soften the loss of his mother. There were so many *shoulds*. Dani hoped the most important one would come back soon—the DNA testing that should show someone else had murdered Alison Grant.

Dani felt bone-weary by the time she arrived home—late as usual. She always tired more easily in the winter months, when the days were short and darkness came too quickly. She wondered if it would be different on the West Coast, where the milder weather might compensate for the reduced sunlight.

Katie had left the family a lasagna in the oven, and as soon as Dani opened her front door, the delicious smell of garlic greeted her. Thank goodness Doug liked garlic as much as Dani did. Her best friend was married to a man who couldn't tolerate the odor and had banished it from their kitchen. Dani couldn't imagine going through life without it.

Ruth rushed up to greet her, holding her arms up in the air to be picked up. Dani was happy to oblige and planted kisses all over her daughter, causing Ruth to erupt in giggles. Doug was already home, and after they exchanged their news of the day, they called Jonah down for dinner.

They'd finished the meal, and Dani was serving dessert, when Jonah said, "I think we should all move to California. It would be an exploit."

Dani had to stop and think what he meant. Usually, she had no problem understanding his word substitution, but now she was stumped. "What do you mean, Jonah?"

Doug jumped in. "Are you saying it would be an adventure?"

"Yes. Completely."

Dani glanced over at Doug. They purposefully hadn't discussed his job offer with Jonah, figuring they'd wait until it was closer to the time for him to leave. Doug shrugged his shoulders.

"Who talked to you about California?"

"Nobody. I attended to you talking to each other. I think we should all stay together. That would be exceptional."

"Wouldn't you miss your friends? And Katie?" Dani asked.

"Yes. But I would miss Daddy more."

Dani sat back in her seat, numb. She felt the forces closing in on her, pushing her to leave New York, to move to California. Pushing her to leave HIPP.

———

Something kept niggling at the back of Tommy's brain, but he couldn't lock down what it was. Something he'd said he'd do later, only now he couldn't remember what. It frightened him, these lapses in his memory. He'd always prided himself on having a mind like a steel trap—once it was part of his consciousness, it stayed there. He'd never had to write it down. Lately, though, he'd sometimes forget the simplest thing—where he'd placed his keys, the name of the person who'd asked him to leave a message for Patty, even the name of someone he'd known from his kids' soccer games. He'd told Patty that it worried him, but she just laughed. "You're not far off from sixty. It's common to forget things. It happens to me all the time." But it didn't happen to Tommy. And he didn't like it one bit.

He'd kept in touch with Hammond and Wilson, but they hadn't gotten very far. They were checking down leads of anyone who knew the murdered girls and who might also have been where the other girls were murdered. It was a slow process, especially since, as cold cases, they didn't warrant a lot of manpower. Still, they'd promised Tommy they wouldn't give up.

Four teenage girls, abducted and killed. All of the girls had long blonde hair. All were good students, not part of a party scene. Tommy looked over at his own teenage daughters, both sitting at the dining-room table and doing their homework, insulated from the ugliness in the world. There were times when he thought they should be warned beyond the usual—don't get in cars with strangers, don't give anyone you don't know your personal information, don't drink and drive, don't do drugs. The litany most parents tell their kids. Sometimes he wanted to say, "There are sick people in the world. Always look behind you. Be suspicious of everyone." But he didn't want his children to go through life afraid.

A muscle in his jaw twitched. *At least they have dark hair.*

As soon as Jonah's school bus pulled away, Dani began her five-mile jog. Katie was in the house with Ruth, and she had a little more than an hour before she needed to leave for work. The temperature hovered around the freezing mark, typical for New York in the winter, but she'd dressed in layers and welcomed the briskness on her cheeks. She ran toward Bronxville Lake, then did a loop around it. Running cleared her head and helped her work out problems. Usually, they were problems with cases. Which ones to take, how to persuade a prosecutor to test DNA, what arguments to make to convince a jury her client was innocent. Today, all she could think about was California. And Jonah. When did he become so grown up? She thought she'd been worrying about Jonah's needs when she fought going with Doug to Stanford, but now she realized it was about her. Her need to stay in New York. Her wish to continue working at HIPP. She'd been selfish. Yet, even recognizing that, she still found it hard to acquiesce. She shook her head. There was time to figure out what was best. Months before Doug would leave.

Her thoughts turned to Osgood. He seemed like such a sweet-tempered man. People who knew him back before his arrest said the same thing about him. How could they have thought he was capable of murder? She knew the answer. It was because he was different. And different made people uncomfortable. The group residence she'd found for him was a place where no one judged him. She hoped the DNA results came back soon. Dani was certain they would exonerate her client, and then he could return to the residence. He might not have a father who cared about him, but there, he had friends who did.

She finished her run, then showered and dressed for work. Before she left, she sat down with Katie.

"Doug's been offered the position of dean at Stanford Law School."

Katie's eye's widened. "That's great for him. I bet you're proud."

Dani lifted her shoulders in a half shrug. "Sure. But it's California. I don't want to leave New York."

"Oh, Dani, we all need to sacrifice for our family sometimes."

Of course, Dani knew that was true. She glanced up at the ceiling, then back at Katie. "You wouldn't be able to take care of Jonah and Ruth." Her lower lip trembled. "I'd really miss you."

Katie wrapped her arms around Dani and pulled her close. "You'll always be my second family," she whispered in Dani's ear. "Even if you live across the country." She let go of Dani, then stepped back. "Besides, Ralph's been complaining that I don't spend enough time with him. Now, he can get his wish."

———

It came to Tommy as soon as he awakened that morning—the task he'd put off for later and then forgotten. As soon as he arrived in the office, he placed a call to Fitz Webber, the Stone Ridge High School football coach when Johnson played on the team. It was picked up on the third ring.

"Are you the Fitz Webber who coached football at Stone Ridge High School back in 1992?"

"The very same."

Tommy introduced himself, then asked, "Do you remember Greg Johnson?"

"I coached football for twenty-six years, and I remember every one of my boys. Not just the starters but the benchwarmers, too."

"By any chance, do you remember if Johnson ever got a concussion playing football?"

The coach laughed. "A concussion? Boy, that kid just about specialized in getting knocked out. Must have had three or four while in high school. A real trooper, though. He'd get knocked out, sit on the bench a quarter, then go right back in. You got to understand, we didn't know then about the lasting effects of too many concussions. Nowadays, we'd make him skip a few games until he was all better. But—"

"Thank you," Tommy said, interrupting him. He had the feeling Webber enjoyed talking and would keep going all morning if allowed. "That's all I needed to know."

"I remember he and his best friends used to have a bet going on who would get more concussions before they graduated. The three of them were thick as thieves."

"His friends?"

"Derek Whitman and Russ Jessup. I think it was Jessup that won the bet. He beat Johnson by two."

———

Tommy hung up the phone, stunned. Ever since the psychologist had told Dani the connection between head trauma and serial killers, it had further fueled his belief that Greg Johnson had murdered his girlfriend. His call to the football coach had been to confirm what he'd suspected—that Johnson had sustained at least one concussion on the football field. Now, for the first time, he had to consider both Whitman and Jessup as well. Both of them knew Kelly; both knew she'd broken up with Johnson the night she died. Maybe one of them had thought it was his chance. Maybe he'd never expected it to get out of hand. Maybe, maybe, maybe. He could speculate all he wanted. What he didn't have was facts.

He walked over to Dani's office and told her what he'd learned.

"That's good, Tommy. Maybe Hammond and Wilson can check all of their movements when the murders occurred."

"They've already got someone at the FBI going over credit-card receipts for Johnson. I'll ask them to add Whitman and Jessup to the mix." Tommy knew it wouldn't be quick. Getting records from every possible credit-card company, especially gas cards, was time-consuming. These weren't computerized back when the earlier murders occurred.

"See if you can confirm whether either of them had a thing for Kelly," Dani said. "And, keep in mind, Milgram said that when there's head trauma, it's likely that another factor is present as well. Maybe you can find something in their backgrounds, some instability."

Tommy returned to his desk and pulled out his notes on the investigation. He found the phone number for Stacy Carmichael, Kelly's best friend, and dialed. "This is Tom Noorland," he said when she answered. "I'd like to ask you a few more questions about Kelly."

"Sure."

"You mentioned that Derek Whitman and Russ Jessup were part of your group. Do you happen to know if either had feelings for Kelly?"

"I'm sure they did. All the guys did. But they all knew she was off-limits."

"How well did you know the families of the kids in your group?"

"Some better than others. Most of the girls, we'd hang out at each other's homes, so I knew their families pretty well."

"How about Greg's?"

"I'd met his parents a few times."

"What were they like?"

"Nice enough, I suppose. Look, what are you trying to get at?"

"Was there any scuttlebutt about how they treated each other? Or Greg?"

"Just seemed like a normal family to me. They doted on Greg, I remember. He was their only child."

"How about Derek Whitman? Know his family?"

"Sure. Nice folks. They moved to Florida two years back."

"Any scuttlebutt about them?"

"Seemed normal to me."

"What about Russ Jessup's family?"

"Just his father. His mother left them when Russ was ten. Ran away with another man."

"How do you know that?"

"Oh, everyone in town knew. Six months later, they got into a car accident, and both died. His father was so broken up that Russ pretty much raised his sister."

There it is, Tommy thought. *The extra something.*

CHAPTER

44

His sister had come through. It had cost a bundle—$25,000 for a new life. He would become Patrick Barnes. But he'd gotten more than a name, more than a driver's license and Social Security number, a credit card in his new name. More than an address where he'd lived the past twenty years, an address far removed from Columbus, Georgia. He'd gotten a history. Patrick Barnes graduated from the University of Arizona with a 3.8 average. He'd gotten his MA in business administration from the University of Texas, graduating summa cum laude. A search of those school records would confirm those lies. He'd worked as an analyst for a consulting business located in Houston and founded by his father, recently deceased. When his siblings demanded their share of his father's estate, he sold the business, pocketing a handsome profit for all the children. Now, he was ready to offer his considerable skills to another consulting firm, willing to relocate anywhere in the United States.

For another ten grand, he could get a death certificate sent to his wife, with a police report about his fatal car crash. That way, she could collect on his life-insurance policy. One million dollars, a benefit of his job. Well worth the money, he thought, to know his family wouldn't be left destitute.

He didn't need to implement his plan yet. No one had come back asking him questions. Maybe it would all blow away; maybe he'd overreacted. But still, it was comforting to know that he had a way out. He didn't want to leave his family; he loved them. But, if the police were closing in, he knew now he could disappear. And then he would be safe.

Y ou need to add another name to your list," Tommy told Lou Hammond. "Russ Jessup."

"Who's that?"

"He shared a dorm suite with Greg Johnson at college. Also a friend from Stone Ridge. He knew Kelly. He knew she'd broken up with Johnson."

"Still, why him?"

"It's a hunch. But listen, he has a job that requires travel. Some management-consultant company. Check and see if he was anywhere near the towns when those girls were killed."

Tommy heard a sigh at the other end. "You know it's probable that it was a stranger. Not someone who knew her."

"Yeah, I know. Still, he's worth checking into."

"I'll let my FBI contact know. But my guess is he'll be way down on the list of people to check out."

Tommy hung up, frustrated. He'd been relieved that law enforcement was now on the case. Trying to close their own murders would lead to Kelly's killer, and that meant he could leave John Doe alone. But he didn't want to wait for the FBI to get around to checking out Jessup. He picked up the phone and called the hacker. "I just have one more thing for you to do."

Two days later, Tommy got the answer he was looking for.

"The first date you gave me," JD told him, "the one killed a few months after Kelly Braden, the student at Clemson University—all three guys were still students then. All three had gas credit cards, but for Johnson and Whitman, the charges were all near the University of Georgia. Athens is about an hour-and-a-half drive to Clemson, maybe less if you have your foot on the pedal. Now, I didn't find any gas charges right there, but in the few days leading up to her death, Jessup filled up his tank an unusual number of times. And once, it was only twenty miles from Clemson."

"Interesting."

"There's more. The second one, years later, was killed in Madison, Florida, right? By then, Jessup was working as a business analyst and had a company credit card. He used it that week for a stint in Tallahassee, less than an hour away from Madison."

Tommy felt his excitement rise. "And how about Alison Grant?"

"Well, Atlanta is his hometown. I got into his company's HR records, and it turns out he called in sick for the three days leading up to Grant's murder."

"This is great. Thanks, once again."

"I'm not finished."

"What do you mean? You told me there were only two others with the same MO."

"That's true. But when I was checking Jessup's gas charges, I noticed another anomaly. A few weeks before the Clemson murder, he filled up his tank near Auburn University, in Alabama. I decided to check the record of unsolved murders near the college around that time, and there was one. The very same night Jessup's car was there. She wasn't abducted from her room, but her friends described her talking to a guy at the bar who was built like a football player."

"Damn. It has to be Jessup. I'm gonna find the proof and put that bastard away."

"I hope you do. Because if you don't, I suspect he's going to keep on killing."

⁓

"I can't get his DNA on just your hunch," Hammond told Tommy. "I need more than that."

Tommy knew he couldn't reveal the information gotten from his hacker. Dani had learned not to ask questions, but a cop would be suspicious. "Why don't you see if he'll give it to you voluntarily? Just to rule himself out."

"Because if he's the one, that might spook him. Let's wait to see if we can place him in the vicinity of the murdered girls."

Tommy hesitated a moment. "Look, I can't tell you how I know, but I've already confirmed he was nearby each time."

"If you want us to act, you need to be more specific."

"I can't. You need to trust me."

"Sorry, Tommy. We need to go through the steps ourselves."

"By then, he could have murdered another one."

"You're just going to have to be patient."

Patience wasn't part of his DNA. He could manage it when it was part of a plan—like a stakeout. But waiting for the feds to comb through decades of credit-card receipts and then maybe, only maybe, deciding they had enough to compel Jessup to give a DNA sample—no, that kind of patience he didn't have. Not when lives were at stake. He had enough frequent-flyer miles for a free flight to Atlanta. He knew what he would do come Saturday.

⁓

When Dani arrived home, two letters were waiting for her. She opened the one from Stanford University first.

Dear Ms. Trumball,

We are very pleased that your husband has accepted the position of dean at our law school. When he was here last, he discussed with me the possibility of starting a new clinic at the school for students to gain experience working on overturning wrongful convictions. I wanted to reach out to you directly to let you know how much I would welcome doing so and having you head it up. In addition to the students, you would be provided with a budget to hire any additional personnel you needed to run the clinic effectively. I sincerely hope you consider this offer, as I know it would enhance the law-school experience for many of our students.

Yours, Jacob Harris, President, Stanford University

My own staff, Dani thought. *I wonder if Tommy would come with me?* As soon as she thought it, she knew it was impossible. He still had three children at home, all of them teenagers. They'd fight hard not to leave their friends. Still, Tommy was always complaining about the New York winters, and the weather was certainly nicer in Palo Alto.

She put the letter down and picked up the next one, with a return address from the Santa Clara District Attorney's office.

Dear Ms. Trumball,

My brother, Jacob Harris, has let me know that your husband has accepted the position of dean of Stanford Law School and will be relocating here over the summer. He's also informed me that he's hoping you will accept a position at the law school to create a new innocence clinic for the students at the school and head it up.

As you are no doubt aware, integrity-conviction units are starting to take root in prosecutorial offices throughout the country, and I have been thinking of starting one here at the Santa Clara District Attorney's office for some time. I've taken the liberty of looking into your background. With your experience as a federal prosecutor, and your record of overturning wrongful convictions, you would be the perfect person to start such a unit here in Santa Clara.

I realize that I am competing with my own brother. However, at Stanford, you would spend much of your time supervising students, which would take away from directly representing clients. The Santa Clara District Attorney's office is the largest prosecuting agency in Northern California, with a cutting-edge criminal laboratory. It represents 1.7 million people in fifteen cities. There are, at present, 190 attorneys who prosecute forty thousand cases a year.

I would be very interested in meeting with you to discuss such a position. Please let me know if this is something that would interest you.

Yours,

Rachel Harris, District Attorney, Santa Clara County

Two job offers, and she hadn't even met either of the prospective employers. She thought about both. It would be advantageous to have access to a top lab, along with the budget of a government agency. But she knew it would be unlikely that she'd get to pick her cases. Bureaucracy came with rules and restrictions. Not the freedom she was used to. She had to admit, though, that the thought of starting a law-school clinic appealed to her. She'd enjoyed training Melanie, and expected she would feel the same with students.

Everything seemed to be pushing her to leave New York, to leave HIPP, to leave Jonah's school, where each year his teachers nurtured him. To leave Katie, who'd become part of their family. Yet, did long-distance marriages really work? It wasn't just Jonah who'd miss his father. She would miss Doug terribly.

She put down the second letter and just stared at both as she chewed on her bottom lip. Maybe it wasn't outrageous to think Tommy would go with her. Maybe the California sun would entice his whole family. Maybe she could leave New York and still have the life she wanted. Maybe, maybe, maybe.

———

By 8:30 a.m. Saturday, Tommy was on a flight to Atlanta. He rented a car at the airport, and shortly before noon arrived at Jessup's home. A car was in the driveway—a good sign. He strode up to the front door, rang the bell, and a few minutes later, Jessup opened it. A scowl briefly passed over his face before turning into a smile.

"Tommy, isn't it? What are you doing here? I thought everything was finished with Jack Osgood."

"There are still a few loose ends. Mind if I come in?"

Jessup held the door open for him, and he stepped inside.

"Come on into the living room."

Tommy followed him in, then both sat down. The house was quiet. "Family here?"

"They're at the mall, shopping. So, how can I help you?"

"I guess it's no surprise to you that we're focusing on Greg Johnson."

Jessup shook his head. "You're barking up the wrong tree there. I've told you that before."

"Sometimes we don't really know our friends. They can be good at hiding things."

"I know Greg. He wouldn't kill anyone, least of all Kelly."

"Maybe so. But tell me, when you were growing up, did you ever see him do anything cruel, maybe to animals?"

"Of course not."

Tommy was prepared to continue peppering him with questions about Johnson, wearing him down until finally he'd ask to use the bathroom, but a phone call cut short the interrogation. When the phone rang, Jessup picked up the receiver, noted the number, then said to Tommy, "I've got to take this. It's work."

As Jessup pressed "Answer," Tommy asked, "Mind if I use the john?'"

Jessup nodded, then pointed down a hallway. With the phone in hand, Jessup left the living room and walked through the kitchen to his study. Tommy made for the hallway, but once Jessup was out of sight, slipped back to the foyer and quietly made his way up the carpeted stairs. He found the master bedroom. As expected, it had its own bathroom, with two sinks set in a vanity. He opened the top drawer on the right side and found a hairbrush. A smaller hairbrush was in the top drawer on the left side. He figured the larger one was Jessup's and, using a comb from the drawer, scraped off some of the strands of hair caught in the bristles, then slipped them into a plastic bag. Just to be cautious, he did the same with the smaller brush, then pocketed both bags. Hopefully, at least one strand had a root attached.

Quietly, he returned to the living room and was already seated, looking bored, when Jessup returned. He remained another twenty minutes, then left, his cache safely tucked away.

J essup didn't discover something was amiss until he readied him-self for bed that night. As he brushed his teeth, his eye caught on his hairbrush, visible in his half-open drawer. That's where he kept it, but always snugged up tight against one wall of the drawer, not cockeyed like it was now. He slid the drawer all the way open. Why did it seem so clean? There were always hairs stuck in it, enough that he worried about ending up bald. Could Rose have cleaned it? No, she would've done a better job. And Rose never went in this drawer. Why would she? It was his, just like hers was hers.

He shook his head. *I'm being paranoid.* But he couldn't shake the feeling that something was wrong. *That investigator.* He thought back to his visit, then remembered the phone call that had pulled him away. He remembered Tommy leaving the living room. And suddenly it hit him—Tommy hadn't come to talk about Greg. He'd wanted a DNA sample.

He felt his chest tighten, and sweat formed on his brow. *It's time. I've got to leave.* An overwhelming sadness descended on him. His own childhood had been darkened by his mother's disappearance. Now, he would do the same to his children. It wouldn't matter that he hadn't wanted to leave them, that he loved them beyond com-prehension. To them, it would only matter that he was gone. And Rose? He loved her, of course. She was the type he'd always been drawn to—slim, blonde, pretty. Yet, it hadn't kept him from seeking out the others, the ones who looked as he'd needed them to look— who looked like Kelly. His love for Rose hadn't kept him from killing the others.

It wasn't his fault, he told himself. It was something inside him, something beyond his control that forced him to succumb to that need. That need for control, for power. That need for Kelly, again and again.

Can I wait until the morning? He decided he could. DNA testing would take days, if not weeks. He would leave tomorrow, tell Rose that a meeting had come up at the last minute, someplace he needed to fly to. An early Monday-morning meeting that required him to leave on Sunday. But he wouldn't fly anywhere. He'd get in a car and drive. Drive to his new life as Patrick Barnes.

He'd prepared for this. First, the new identity. Then, he'd gone to his bank and withdrawn $200,000 from his savings. This would give him the cushion he'd need to start over. Rose wouldn't know until after he'd disappeared. He paid the bills; she never looked at the bank statements. He would drive to the airport, leave his car, then rent another. He'd drive the rental to some big city, then, as Patrick Barnes, purchase a new car for cash. Something nondescript.

Once he'd done that, he needed to do one more thing before he headed west, before he began living Patrick Barnes's life. Tom Noorland was responsible for wrenching him away from his children. He would make him pay for that.

As soon as Dani arrived in the office Monday morning, Tommy told her what he'd done.

Dani leaned forward on her desk and pressed her hands to her cheeks. "Oh, Tommy, you shouldn't have. I'm not even sure it would be admissible."

"Why not? I'm not working with the police, and I was invited into his house."

"True. But even so, at this point, there isn't even anything to compare it to."

"There's the DNA from the bite mark on Grant. When that comes back belonging to someone other than Osgood, we'll have the hairs to test against it."

Dani sighed. "We don't even know if that will happen—the ADA wasn't even sure the sample was enough to test."

Tommy balled his fists. "I know it's Jessup. He shouldn't be allowed to get away with it."

"One of the police departments down South will get him. Let them do their jobs."

"Sure. I'll let them be the leads. But I'm still on this. We always say it's not enough to get our client off. There's still a stench over him if we don't find the real perp. I know it's Jessup. And this DNA will prove it."

Later that afternoon, Dani was deep into writing a brief when ADA Franklin called. "You were right," he said. "The DNA didn't match Osgood."

Relief flooded through Dani. Believing he was innocent was not the same as DNA confirmation. Now, she had that. "So, you'll drop the charge against him?"

"Yes, for now."

"Did you get a match for the DNA?"

"No. It wasn't from someone in the system."

Russ Jessup wouldn't be in the system, Dani thought.

"I think I know whose it is."

"Yeah? Who?"

"Russell Jessup. He knew the first victim and lives in Atlanta."

"What makes you think it's him?"

Dani didn't want to get into all that Tommy had found—the gas credit-card receipts and the dates he traveled for business, both of which matched up with the dates the victims were murdered. Although she didn't know how Tommy had gotten his information, she was fairly certain it wasn't completely legit. "I have a sample of Jessup's DNA. Can you run it against what you found on Grant?"

"Now, how did you manage that?"

"My investigator obtained it while he was in his house, conducting an interview."

There was silence on the other end at first. Finally, Franklin said, "DNA testing is expensive. We don't usually do it without more."

Dani filled him in on everything she'd learned from Milgram about serial killers, and about Jessup's concussions, and his fractured family.

"All right. FedEx me the hairs, and I'll have them tested. In the meantime, I'll send someone to his home to question him."

She hung up, then buzzed Tommy to let him know. "Our job is finished. Osgood is cleared of Braden's murder, and now the charges are being dropped in Grant's murder."

"I'll consider the job over when Jessup is behind bars."

There were still a few things left for Dani to do. First, she called Osgood at the prison and let him know the good news. Next, she called Amy Shore. Although Osgood's placement there had been temporary, she was happy to welcome him back. "He's a sweetheart," she said. "And Doris is so fond of him." Amy agreed to pick Osgood up from the jail when the paperwork was completed.

That out of the way, Dani began to prepare a motion. Typically, after she'd proven clients' innocence and obtained their release, she'd seek compensation for their wrongful convictions. The nightmare of spending years incarcerated—in some cases on death row, for crimes they hadn't committed, deprived of their family and friends—didn't end when they were finally free. They'd lost the years they would have spent working, building careers, starting their own families. They'd enter society without money, without health insurance, many times without skills, and often with no home to return to. Recognizing that, thirty states provided compensation to help former inmates begin the healing process. Georgia was not one of the thirty. Instead, her motion was against Osgood's father, to recover the money that rightfully belonged to Jack after his mother had died. That money would pay for his stay at the group home and provide a cushion for him as he began to rebuild his life.

Dani had promised Harry Osgood that he could keep the money—all he needed to do was make his son part of his life. But that sorry excuse for a man didn't do that. He deserved to suffer, even if only financially. And Dani was going to make sure that happened.

Detectives Kyle Simpson and Alicia Herzog pulled up to Jessup's home just before 7:00 p.m. When Rose Jessup opened the door to them, Simpson first reacted to the redness around her eyes and the paleness of her cheeks.

"Thank goodness you're here," Rose said.

Simpson glanced at his partner. "We're looking for Russell Jessup, ma'am," he said.

"Isn't that why you're here? I called the police to report him missing this morning." She began crying, something Simpson suspected she'd been doing for a while.

"We're not from your local precinct. We came here to speak to your husband."

"But that's just it. He's gone."

"Gone where?"

"I don't know. He told me he was leaving on a business trip, but he never returned. I spoke to his boss this morning, and he said there wasn't any trip." Now, her sobs became louder.

"When was this, ma'am?"

"Sunday. Sunday afternoon. But he always calls me when he gets where he's going. And I keep calling his cell phone, and it goes straight to voice mail. I'm afraid something's happened to him."

Simpson had suspected they'd be wasting their time speaking to Jessup. Now, he wasn't so sure. Two days was a long enough lead time to disappear. "I can assure you, we're going to do everything we can to find your husband. Can we come in and talk?"

"Oh, yes, of course."

He and Herzog spent the next half hour gathering facts about Jessup—the car he drove, his cell-phone number, what he was wearing when he left, the company he worked for, how he liked to spend his spare time, names of his close friends. Some of it they could have gotten on their own, but it saved time coming from Jessup's wife. When they finished, they asked her to contact them immediately if she heard from him.

As they walked back to their car, Simpson said, "I think we may have found our serial killer."

J essup dropped the rental car at the Washington Dulles airport, then taxied to a Chevy dealership in Arlington. Patrick Barnes plunked down $23,350 for a black Malibu and drove it off the lot the same day. He'd driven straight through to DC and was beat. He looked for a cheap motel, then settled into his room for the night. Tomorrow, he'd head for New York, for Riverdale, where Tom Noorland lived with his family.

It had been easy getting Noorland's home address. One could find almost anything on the Internet. His search not only told him where the investigator lived, but the names of his wife and children. Social media gave him their ages. He'd picked out his target. Sixteen-year-old Tricia Noorland. It didn't matter that her hair wasn't blonde. It didn't matter if she wasn't as pretty as Kelly. He would abduct her and kill her so that her father understood the depth of loss that came with losing a child. His own children were still alive, but he could never see them again, and he felt the loss already, as though they'd been killed.

When he'd killed those other girls, he'd never thought about their parents, their siblings. He never considered the pain they would feel. Now, he knew. He hoped that knowledge would keep him from killing again. He didn't want to be a monster. They had meetings for alcoholics, for gamblers, even for sex addicts. But there weren't meetings for people addicted to the rush from killing. And it *was* an addiction. He knew it was. That exquisite feeling that filled his whole body when he watched the struggle, and then nothing. No more breath, no more life.

He didn't expect that satisfaction when he killed Tricia Noorland. This time, it was just a job, just something he needed to do to set the balance right.

He drove past their house, to become familiar with their street, at 2:00 a.m. A six-story apartment building with a doorman planted out front was across the street from their attached home. No chance of taking her from her bedroom. Instead, he would arrive at daybreak the next morning, follow her to school, follow her home. He'd do that for a few days. No one would expect him to be in New York. When he saw his chance, he'd grab her. And then he would strangle her, just like the others.

Tommy stepped into Dani's office and plopped down in the chair opposite her desk, a scowl on his face.

"What's wrong?" she asked.

"I just got off the phone with a Detective Simpson from Fulton County. They went to Jessup's home, but he'd disappeared two days earlier. The day after I was there."

Dani's brows drew together. "We were afraid this could happen."

"It's my fault. I spooked him. Dammit. I should have waited for the force to get a sample." He slumped down in the chair and squeezed his eyes shut.

"Tommy," Dani said softly, "I'll always trust your instincts. You couldn't have predicted this."

"Sure, I could have. Hammond warned me against it."

"So, what now?"

"They found his car at the airport. They checked the car-rental counter there, but none had a record of him renting a car. Now, they're checking with the taxis that service the airport. They'll keep looking for him. In the meantime, they're waiting to get back the DNA results."

Dani rested her arms on the desk and leaned forward. "Go back to work. Jessup isn't our problem. He's not your problem. The police will pick him up eventually. Now . . ." She handed him a piece of paper. "I'm taking on this new client. He had an alibi, but the jurors didn't believe him. I'd like you to try and track down the alibi, question him yourself."

Tommy nodded, then stood up to leave. At the doorway, he turned back and pinned Dani with his eyes. He held the paper up in his hand. "I'll find this guy for you. But I'm not going to stop looking for Jessup."

Dani tucked a lock of her dark-brown hair behind her ear, then gave Tommy a half smile. "I didn't expect otherwise."

———

One day later, Dani got the call from Franklin she'd been expecting.

"It's a match," he said. "It's Russell Jessup's DNA in the bite mark on Alison Grant's arm. There's no question he's our man."

"Any luck finding him?"

"Not yet. But now we have the DNA results, we're putting out an APB on him. Every law-enforcement agency in the country will have his picture. We'll get him."

Dani thanked him, and as soon as she hung up, she walked over to Tommy's desk and told him the news.

"Of course, it came back him," Tommy said. "We make a crack team."

Dani looked around. Tommy's desk was one of several in an open area. No one was nearby. She leaned into him and spoke softly. "Remember I told you about Doug's job offer at Stanford?"

Tommy screwed up his face. "Don't tell me he's taking it?"

"He's already accepted."

"What are you going to do?"

"I don't know yet. Doug said he could come back weekends for the first year while he decides if it's the right fit for him. But the kids would really miss him, and I know I'd be lonely without him."

"So, you're going to leave, too?"

"I'm thinking about it. I've been solicited for two job offers. One is at the law school, starting an innocence clinic for the students. The other is the Santa Clara District Attorney's office, heading up a conviction-integrity unit."

Tommy turned up his nose. "With the DA, you won't be able to avoid the internal politics when it comes to choosing your clients."

"That's what I was thinking, but—I was wondering—"

Tommy waited silently.

"Would you ever consider moving your family out to California, too? Work with me at the law-school clinic? We *do* make a great team. I hate the thought of breaking us up."

Tommy looked away, then back. "I wish I could say yes. I'd love to get out of New York. These damn winters are killing me. But I couldn't pull the kids away from their friends. Not at their ages. And I don't think Patty would want to leave."

Dani nodded. "It's what I figured, but I had to give it a shot."

Tommy reached across his desk and took Dani's hands in his. "I know how hard this is for you. But you belong with Doug. You'll find someone out there just as good as me to work with." He stopped, then smiled. "Well, almost as good."

~

As soon as Tommy arrived home that night, Patty met him with a worried look on her face.

"What's wrong?"

She pulled him into the kitchen, away from the living room where Brandon and Lizzie were huddled around the TV. "I think someone has been watching us—or maybe not us, but someone on the street."

"What do you mean?"

"There's a black car out there. I've seen it every day, with a man inside. He parks in different spots but always within sight of our front door."

"Is he there now?"

Patty shook her head. "He left a few hours ago."

"I'm sure it's nothing. Probably some PI who's spying on a cheating spouse in the apartments across the street."

"Still, it makes me nervous."

"Then, next time you see him, ask the doorman there"—he pointed across the street—"to tell him to leave, or he'll call the police."

"I shouldn't call the police myself?"

"Nah. Just let the doorman scare him off. Trust me, it's nothing."

CHAPTER 50

Jessup had watched the Noorland house for five days. Every school day, the two girls walked to the Riverdale/Kingsbridge Academy middle school and high school. Along the way, they'd stop and pick up a friend four blocks away; then they'd continue on together. Every afternoon, except one, at 3:10 p.m., they did the walk in reverse. The difference was on Thursday, when Lizzie and Tricia's friend left the school alone, and Tricia stayed behind until 4:30 p.m. Then, she emerged from the school and made the trek home by herself.

After the third day, a doorman had come over to him and asked what his business was there. He smiled and said he was checking out a cheating wife. "Well, find someplace else to do it," the doorman had said, and so he had. He didn't need to watch the home anymore. The rest of the week, he parked near the school. Not so near as to worry any teachers. Just close enough so that he could see when the girl arrived and when she left.

Now, he waited in his car one block from the school, under a tree, in an area without any streetlights. It was Thursday, and this time of year, it was almost dark, which worked in his favor. There were plenty of lights by the school, and he picked her out immediately when she left the building. There were three other girls with her, but as soon as they reached the sidewalk, the other girls headed in the opposite direction.

He waited until she passed his car; then, with enough distance between them, he started up the engine. He didn't need to follow her. He knew exactly what route she'd follow. He knew where he would snatch her. As she got closer to her house, she'd take a shortcut through the yard of an abandoned warehouse. He suspected her parents had warned her and Lizzie against it, especially when it was dark. But it saved three blocks of walking. He drove past her, then into the parking lot of the warehouse, then turned off the car, got out, and waited.

He stood in the shadow of the building, his body pressed against the brick wall, until she passed him. Then he took two swift steps after her and grabbed her around her neck, lifted her, and squeezed until her limp body dropped into his arms. Looking both ways around the yard to confirm they were alone, he carried her to his car. He popped the trunk, dropped her inside, then tied her hands and legs and duct-taped her mouth.

Jessup drove away with a smile. His revenge had begun.

By the time Tommy walked into his house, Patty was frantic. "Tricia's not home," she said. "I've called all her friends, and she's not with any of them."

"Did you call her friend in the band?"

Patty nodded. "She said Tricia left with her and was walking home. I think we should call the police."

"Let me drive around first, look for her." Tommy started toward the door when the phone rang. Patty ran to the kitchen to answer it, and he waited to see if it was Tricia.

A moment later, she came back into the foyer and handed over the phone to Tommy. "It's for you. He won't say his name."

Tommy took the phone. "Hello?"

"You shouldn't have stuck your nose in my life. Now you're going to know what it's like to lose part of your family."

Tommy took in a sharp breath. "Jessup?"

"That's right. And I've got your daughter."

Silently, Tommy mouthed for Patty to call the police.

"Why are you doing this?"

"Because of you, I've got to run away. Leave my family. Everything was fine until you started poking around."

"It wasn't fine. You're still killing. You must understand that people needed to stop you."

"I wasn't killing!" he shouted. "I'd stopped. I had it under control. Then you came around, reminded me of how it felt. I had to try it one more time. But that was the last." He chuckled. "Until now. Tricia will be the last."

Tommy saw Patty was on her cell phone. He knew he needed to keep Jessup talking, give the police a chance to set up a tap, try to locate him.

"You don't need to do this. Turn yourself in. A smart lawyer can probably plead insanity, get you a few years in a hospital, and then you're home free, back with your family."

"You think I'm an idiot? Five girls. No one's letting me off. If they don't execute me, I'll rot in prison."

Every muscle in Tommy's body was tensed, but he willed his voice to remain calm. "Then run away. You don't need to hurt Tricia. She hasn't done anything to you. If you want to hurt me, that's fine. I'll go wherever you want. Me for my daughter. I won't put up a fight."

"It's too late."

"It's not. Tell me what you want. I'll give you anything."

Tommy heard a hoarse laugh. "It's not too late for me. I'm going to start a new life. If I'm lucky, a new family. It's too late for you."

"No—"

"Bye-bye, Daddy."

And then there was nothing. Tommy looked over at Patty. Her face was drained of color. "Did they get a location?"

She shook her head. "They're headed over to our house now."

Tommy walked over to his wife and wrapped his arms around her shaking body. "I'm going to find the SOB. I promise you."

Once he'd made the phone call, Jessup drove to the spot he'd picked out, and then waited. It was too early to kill the girl. It wasn't as though he had to follow his prior pattern to a tee. He didn't expect to get the thrill that always accompanied a kill. No, it could draw attention if he didn't wait until later, much later, when darkness was absolute and stragglers were unlikely to wander his way. He'd scouted out this location earlier in the week. A pond, surrounded by a forest. Yes, there was a path that skirted it, no doubt serving as a spot for joggers, maybe even bicyclists, to get their daily exercise. But, if he waited, it would be too dark, too cold, for any use but his own.

He'd parked in the dirt cutout at the beginning of the path. After less than two hours, he heard feet pounding against the trunk. She was awake, but it was still too early. He wanted her awake when he killed her. He wanted her to know she was going to die. Afterward, he would report that to her father, tell him about the fear in her eyes. It would be something that would haunt that investigator the rest of his life, knowing her death was his fault. Knowing that she'd suffered.

He listened carefully to ensure no car was approaching, then opened the trunk. She stared up at him, wriggling her body as though she could get free. But she couldn't. He put his hands around her neck and squeezed once more. Just until she lost consciousness. Not more. Not yet.

—

By the time Dani arrived at Tommy's house, the police were already there. He'd called her as soon as he'd hung up from Jessup, and she'd jumped in her car and driven the fifteen minutes between their homes. Patty was on the couch, wiping a continual stream of tears from her face, as Tommy paced back and forth. A uniformed cop sat on a chair opposite the couch, gathering information. Another stood by the window. Dani sat down next to Patty and wrapped her arm around her shoulders.

"This is Officer Clayton," Patty said between sobs.

Dani nodded to him.

"Just one last thing," Clayton said. "Do you remember anything about the car parked across the way a few days ago?"

"It was black, not too big. It looked like every other sedan," Patty answered. "Maybe the doorman can tell you more."

"Okay. If you get me that picture of Tricia now, we'll get it out on an APB right away."

Dani broke in. "This man has a pattern. Every victim was killed between one and four a.m., and each was found near some body of water in an isolated place."

Tommy stopped his pacing and turned to Dani. "His pattern was to take girls from their homes. After the first, it was girls who were strangers to him. He's not following his pattern now. This is to hurt me."

"Still, he's used to doing things in a certain way. I don't think he'd stray far from that. Do you know any locations that fit his pattern?"

"Wait." Tommy left the room and came back with a street atlas of the Bronx. He placed it on the cocktail table and crouched down. Clayton joined him, and the other uniformed cop walked over. Tommy flipped to the pages for Riverdale, then pointed out four possible locations, marking each with a pen.

"We'll go right now and check them out," Clayton said.

"I'm coming with you," Tommy said.

"Not a good idea."

"I know what he looks like."

"The squad room is already getting a picture from the DMV. I'll have it in a few minutes."

Dani stood up and approached Tommy. "Let them take two locations, and you and I will go to the other two. That'll save time."

Clayton scrunched up his face. "I can't let you do that. From what you've told me, he's a serial killer. It's too dangerous for civilians."

"He's never killed with a gun," Tommy said. "And we could be running out of time."

Clayton looked over at the other cop, Officer Pincus. "They're right," Pincus said.

"I'll tell you what. I'll radio for another car so we can divide them up. If, on your own, you decided to follow us, I can't stop you. But officially, you're on your own."

Five minutes later, another squad car pulled up. Clayton showed the officers the street atlas, and each car took two locations to check out. Right before Dani and Tommy got into their own cars, ready to follow them, Clayton said, "I don't want you to get your hopes up, Mr. Noorland. This guy could be in another state by now. The chance that he's at one of these spots is remote."

Tommy just nodded, then got in his car.

⁓

As soon as Tricia woke, she knew she was still in the trunk of the car. The first time she'd come to, she'd been confused, disoriented. Then, in a rush, it had come back to her—the man waiting by the side of the building, his hands on her neck, squeezing and squeezing, and then nothing. Now, when she woke up, she remembered instantly. Her heart pounded in her chest, and fear clawed through her. *Calm down. Think.* She took one deep breath, then another, then again, and slowly, so slowly, her heart stopped racing. *Think, think,* she repeated to herself, over and over. It had been a mistake to bang her feet against the trunk door. Now, she had to be smarter.

Tricia had complained endlessly when her father insisted she and Lizzie take a self-defense class. It had been given on Saturday mornings. Lizzie thought it was fun, but Tricia hated waking up early on a weekend.

"Why are you making me do this?" she'd moaned. "None of my friends have to take it."

"None of your friends' fathers work with criminals," he'd answered.

And so, every Saturday morning for eight weeks, she and her little sister had trudged into Manhattan and learned how to defend themselves. "I hope you'll never have to use it," her father had told them. "But if something happens, you'll be prepared."

Now, she struggled to remember what she'd been taught. Her hands and feet were bound with rope. "Try to keep some space in your hands, if you're being tied up," the instructor had said. But she'd been unconscious when he'd tied her. "If you've been bound too tightly, try your teeth," she remembered him saying.

Her eyes had adjusted to the dark. She brought her hands up to her mouth, then with her fingers stripped off the duct tape. Luckily, her hands had been tied in front of her. Next, she pulled her hands as far apart as she could, stretching the rope slightly, and then began gnawing at the rope with her teeth. It had a bitter taste, as though coated with some chemical. She tried not to move, not to make any noise, not to do anything that would bring the man back to the trunk before she was ready. Her winter jacket was still on, and the trunk was warm and stuffy. Perspiration dripped down her arms as tears flowed from her eyes. She gnawed on.

She didn't know how long it took, but she began to make progress, to feel the rope loosen. Suddenly, she heard the car door open and slam shut, then footsteps walking toward her. *Does he know I'm awake? Is he coming to get me?* Once again, her heart was racing. She squeezed her eyes shut and willed herself to remain as still as possible. A minute passed, and then she smelled the smoke from a cigarette wafting into the trunk. Five minutes later, she heard his foot stamp it out on the ground. Once again, the car door opened, then closed. She let out a breath, then brought her hands up to her mouth and started once more pulling at the rope with her teeth.

Tommy followed the police car into Grant Park, then pulled into a parking spot alongside them. When they'd all exited their vehicles, he pointed to a gravel carriageway. "The lake's down this path."

"It's not likely he's here," Clayton said. "There are no other cars."

"There's another entrance, on the other side of the lake. He could have come in that way," Tommy said.

Clayton nodded; and he, Pincus, and Tommy set off in that direction. It was dark, and the quarter moon did little to illuminate the walkway. They couldn't use flashlights, as the light might alert Jessup of their approach. If he was there. They made their way slowly, and ten minutes later, they reached the lake. Nothing. Not Jessup. Not Tricia. Now, they turned on the flashlights and swept the woods, looking for any sign that they'd been there. Again, nothing.

"Damn, damn, damn," Tommy kept muttering to himself.

"Let's split up and walk around the lake," Clayton said.

Tommy shook his head. "It'll take too long. She's not here."

"We've got to be thorough."

Tommy was adamant. Every minute wasted was a minute that Tricia came closer to that monster's hands around her neck, squeezing the life out of her. "We can come back if needed. Let's go to the next one."

Clayton acquiesced, and now they used the flashlights to guide their way. Within five minutes, they were on the road again. As they drove to the next stop, Tommy took out his cell phone and called Dani.

"Anything?" he asked her.

"No. Place was empty. We're on our way to River View Park."

Two down. Two more to check. Two more to give Tommy hope. Two more to stave off the fear that had taken control of him. *Be there. Please, be there. Don't let it be too late.* Those were the words he kept repeating to himself as he sped to the next park.

———

It took almost an hour, but finally, she was able to slip her hands free. Next, she lay on her side and brought her knees close to her chest. She reached down to her feet and worked to untie the rope. When she'd managed it, she lay back, trembling from the effort. She was free. Free of the rope, not yet the man. What was he waiting for? A ransom payment, maybe? Of one thing she was certain—he intended to harm her.

When she felt ready, she slid her body around so that her feet faced the opening of the trunk, and then began kicking. She knew he'd come back, only this time she'd be ready.

As soon as the trunk opened, she kicked him in the crotch, as hard as she could. He screamed, doubling over and falling back, and as he did so, she scrambled out and began sprinting away. She was young and fast, and she thought she could outrun him.

Almost immediately, she recognized where he'd taken her. She knew this pond; she knew these woods. She'd stay on the road at first, but if he gained on her, she'd slip into the trees.

She could hear him behind her, but she kept her lead. Suddenly, she heard tires on the gravel road, and then the bright headlights of a car coming toward her. *Was he waiting for someone else? Is that why he hadn't hurt me yet?*

The car stopped ahead of her, and she heard a door open. Quickly, she veered off the road, into the darkness of the forest, continuing her running, until she stopped cold at the sound of a voice, calling, "Tricia!"

———

Tricia turned and ran back into the arms of her father, sobbing as he held her tight. Only after she pulled away from him did she notice the police car, both its front doors open. She looked down the road she'd run on and saw two cops wrestle her abductor to the ground.

"How did you find me?" she asked, her voice hoarse.

"Thank Dani for that. I was too worried about you to think straight. Are you okay? Did he hurt you?"

Tricia rubbed her neck. "He choked me until I blacked out. It still hurts. Why did he take me, Daddy? Do you know?"

"He's a bad man, honey. He wanted to get back at me for putting the police onto him." Tommy put his hand in his pocket and pulled out his cell phone. He handed it to Tricia. "Call Mom. Let her know you're okay."

As Tricia made the call, Tommy watched Clayton and Pincus pull a handcuffed Jessup to his feet and march him back to the police car. After they placed him in the backseat, Tommy leaned in. "I don't get it. You have a family, a good job, a nice house. Why? Why did you do it?"

Jessup just shrugged, then smiled. "Because it felt so damn good."

EPILOGUE

Two months later, Dani was back in Atlanta, at the sleek glass-and-concrete Fulton County Probate Court. Jack Osgood was by her side at the petitioner's table. Both Doris and Amy were seated in the gallery. Harry and Maria Osgood sat at the respondents' table, along with their attorney, Simon Greeley. They had spent the two months trying to negotiate a settlement. Dani wanted the $1.27 million that should have gone to Jack returned to him. His father began by offering the $100,000 put up as bail. Eventually, he'd offered to pay the $3,000-a-month cost for Jack to stay at Kenny's Place. That wasn't nearly enough for Dani. Jack had spent almost his entire adult life incarcerated. He deserved to have money to spend on anything that caught his fancy. Within reason, of course. Finally, having reached an impasse, they were now in court, presenting their arguments to Judge Rosenthal.

It was Dani's motion, and so she began. "Your Honor, my client, Jack Osgood, spent twenty-two years on death row for a crime he didn't commit. He has now been exonerated and lives in a group home for adults with intellectual disabilities. While he was on death row, his mother passed away. Upon her death, his father, who had abandoned the family when Jack was ten years old, swooped in and collected all her assets, despite not being the beneficiary. He justified doing so because he'd never been legally divorced from Jack's mother. However, the house, which sold for four hundred seventy thousand dollars, was Jack's mother's family home and in her name only, and both her IRA and pension named Jack as the sole beneficiary, as did her will. In total, Harry Osgood collected almost one point three million dollars that belonged to his son. We ask the court to order the respondent to return that money to its rightful owner—Jack Osgood. Thank you."

Greeley stood. "At the time my client settled the estate, his son was expected to be put to death. With no other relatives, his father then would have collected his wife's assets. His son would not be able to use those assets while in prison and wasn't expected to ever leave. My client made sure his son was able to buy what he wanted from the prison commissary—he deposited five thousand dollars in that account for Jack to use. He invested the remaining money in the startup of a business and the purchase of a home for his new family. His liquid assets total less than two hundred thousand dollars. At all times, he acted in good faith, and he should not now be punished by being forced to sell his business and home. Thank you."

Dani shot up from her seat. "Nor should Jack be punished because his father greedily took money that belonged to his son. A father, by the way, who never visited his son in prison, who never even told his son that his mother had died, and who has still not visited his son, even though he's no longer in prison. Mrs. Osgood made it very clear, in every document, that she wanted her son to inherit her assets, not her absent husband."

"All right," Judge Rosenthal said. "I understand the positions. Come back after lunch, and I'll have my decision for you."

Dani left the courthouse with Jack, Doris, and Amy and found a luncheonette a block away. The sun shone brightly overhead, and a hint of spring was in the air. After they finished ordering, she said, "I have some news. Russ Jessup entered into a plea agreement yesterday for Alison Grant's murder. He's going to spend the rest of his life in jail instead of facing the death penalty, like you did. His sister is going to jail, too, for helping him try to escape. When she gets out, she won't be able work for the courts again, and she won't get her pension."

Osgood clasped his hands together on the table, a solemn look on his face. "What about for Kelly?"

"Alison's case was the strongest because they had DNA from his bite on her arm. But as part of the plea agreement, he had to confess to Kelly's murder as well."

Osgood's shoulders relaxed, and he smiled. "That's good. I'm glad he's being punished."

"Not just him. Jessup's sister, too."

"What about the other girls?" Amy asked.

"Well, they're in different states. They might decide to try him there as well, but they don't have strong evidence. But don't worry. He's never leaving prison. He'll die there."

"I have some news, too," Osgood said as his smile grew bigger. He reached across the table and took Doris's hand in his. "We're getting married."

Dani blinked at him for a mute couple of seconds. This was the last thing she expected, and she wasn't sure how to react. Jack had no parent in his life. Should she step in and advise him as a mother would? Or step back? She was his attorney, and she'd done her job. In another few hours, it would be over. She glanced at Amy and saw a smile on her face, so she suspected Amy hadn't cautioned them. The mother in her won out. "Isn't this a bit fast? You haven't known each other very long."

Osgood nodded. "I know. But right away, I knew I liked Doris. And right away, she knew she liked me."

He had been alone for so very long, locked away from the world. Maybe she was being foolish, Dani thought, expecting him to go through a longer courtship. He'd waited twenty-two years to love someone. To be loved back. "I'm happy for you. Truly. I wish you both the best."

Two hours later, they were back in the courtroom, settled in their seats. After Judge Rosenthal took the bench, she announced that she would read her decision.

"I've reviewed the probate records originally filed with this court, as well as respondent's financial statements submitted by his counsel. It is the job of this court to ensure that the wishes of a decedent are carried out. In this case, Mrs. Osgood clearly intended that her son be the beneficiary of all her assets, including her home. The fact that he was unable to make use of her assets at the time of her death is irrelevant. That is especially so when she and her husband had been separated for more than twenty-five years, and he had contributed no child support or maintenance during that time. It is unfortunate that the respondent has invested that money in nonliquid assets, but that does not excuse his appropriation of monies that did not belong to him. I hereby rule that respondent is to pay petitioner the sum of one point two seven million dollars, less the five thousand dollars given to petitioner previously, plus interest at the rate of four percent from the date the probate of the estate was closed. So ordered."

Dani turned to Osgood. "You won, Jack. Your father will have to pay you back your mother's money."

"Now I can buy my own house."

"Yes, Jack. It's a new start for you. For you and for Doris."

Rather than heading straight home from LaGuardia airport, Dani stopped at HIPP's office. She knew Bruce never left the office before seven. She'd been putting off telling him her plans long enough. It was time. Now that she was committed to California, he had to know. She knocked on his door to get his attention, then stepped inside.

"Hi. What's up?" he asked.

"I need to tell you something. Doug has accepted a position as dean of Stanford Law. We're moving out there in July."

Dani saw a startled look on his face. "You're leaving us?"

"I don't want to. I'm going to miss HIPP terribly. Doug even offered a commuter marriage, with him flying home every other weekend. But my son reminded me that it's important to keep the family together."

"What will you do there?"

"Actually, I've already been offered two jobs. Starting an innocence clinic at the law school, and starting an integrity-conviction unit at the Santa Clara District Attorney's office."

Bruce leaned back in his chair and stared up at the ceiling. Finally, he said, "I have a third option. Continue working for HIPP while you live in California, but work from home. There's no reason why we can't keep in touch through teleconferencing. You're traveling for cases anyway. So, it's a little longer when you're flying from the West Coast. And Tommy could still be your investigator. What do you say?"

Dani ran over to Bruce. She bent over to hug him, tears streaming down her cheeks. "I'd say yes. A thousand times yes." The weight that she'd carried in her chest for months dissipated, replaced with a suffusion of joy. She'd struggled so long with leaving New York because she knew she had two families—her home family and her work family. Now, she would keep both.

It was after 7:00 p.m. by the time Dani arrived home. Doug and Jonah were seated at the kitchen table, midway through eating their dinner, and Ruth was in her high chair, the bottom half of her face and her hands covered in marinara sauce.

Dani placed the bag she was carrying on the counter, kissed Doug and Jonah on the cheeks, then took a napkin and wiped the sauce off Ruth. When she finished, she smothered her with kisses, as Ruth squealed with delight.

As Dani sat down, Jonah asked, "What's in the bag?"

"Dessert." Dani pulled the bowl of pasta over to her plate.

"How did it go?" Doug asked.

"The judge awarded Osgood his full inheritance."

"Wow. That's great. Congratulations."

"I'm happy for him. And guess what? He's getting married. To that resident he met in the group home."

A smile crept across Doug's face. "You're amazing at what you do. Maybe this is a good time to—"

Dani looked up at him expectantly.

"I know you wanted to wait until everything was put to bed with this case before you made your decision about the job offers—"

"Well—" Dani interrupted.

Doug held up his hand. "Let me finish. After that nightmare with Tricia, it reminded me of how important you all are to me. We're a family; we need to stay together as a family. And everyone in the family should be happy with where we live. I've given this a great deal of thought, and I've decided to decline the dean's position."

Dani's jaw dropped. "You haven't told them yet, have you?"

"No, I wanted to tell you first."

Dani stood up and wrapped her arms around Doug. "Thank you. That's one of the nicest things you've ever done. But I want you to take the job."

Dani laughed at the look of confusion on Doug's face. She walked over to the counter and brought the bag with dessert over to the table. "I stopped at the office on the way home and told Bruce about your job offer. He said I could continue working for HIPP from California."

"So—you want to move?"

"Yep." She opened the bag and pulled out a chocolate cake. On it was written, *California, here we come.*

Doug jumped up and pulled Dani into his arms. Jonah came over and joined their circle, as Ruth waved her arms and legs, saying over and over, "Me, too. Me, too." Dani took her from the high chair, then included her in the family hug.

"Yeah!" Jonah shouted. "We're going to have our exploit!"

They all laughed. Even Ruth.

Author's Note

Although the American Board of Forensic Odontology (ABFO) is a real organization, the character of Michael Forbes, as president of the ABFO, is fictional, as is his testimony in *Justice Delayed*. It is true, though, that the subject of bite-mark analysis has been studied in the past several years, and the National Academy of Science, a high-ranking officer in the White House Office of Science and Technology Policy, and the Texas Forensic Science Commission have all questioned its scientific underpinnings.

ACKNOWLEDGMENTS

Many thanks to the people who have helped make this book better, beginning with the members of my creative-writing group, especially Susan Boyd, Linda Dickson, Mike Doyle, Pat Fagan, Millard Johnson, Larry Martin, Dave Maurer, Mark Newhouse, Frank Ridge, Mary Lois Sanders, Estella Shivers, Mitch Smith, Penny Thomas, Allen Watkins, and Tom Zampano.

My agent, Adam Chromy, as always, provided excellent notes, and my wonderful developmental editor, David Downing, is nothing short of miraculous. Thanks also to my copy editor, Valerie Kalfrin, and proofreader, Jill Kramer, for cleaning up my errors. I am also grateful to Liz Pearsons, my editor, and the rest of the crew at Thomas & Mercer for their fine-tuning.

Finally, I thank my family—my husband, Lenny; my sons, Jason and Andy; their wives, Amanda and Jackie; and my amazing grandchildren, Rachel, Josh, Jacob, Sienna, and Noah—for their love and support.

About the Author

Photo ©2014 Darin Back

After receiving her master's degree and her professional certificate, both in school psychology, Marti Green realized that her true passion was the law. She went on to receive her law degree from Hofstra University and worked as in-house counsel for a major cable television operator for twenty-three years, specializing in contracts, intellectual property law, and regulatory issues. She is the author of the legal thrillers *The Price of Justice*, *Presumption of Guilt*, *Unintended Consequences*, *First Offense*, and *Justice Delayed*. A passionate traveler, mother to two adult sons, and grandmother to five grandchildren, she now lives in central Florida with her husband, Lenny, and cat, Howie.